HARRY'S RULES

HARRY'S RULES

BY

MICHAEL R. DAVIDSON

PUBLISHED BY

MRD ENTERPRISES, INC.
2012

HARRY'S RULES

MRD Enterprises, Inc.
PO BOX 1000
Mount Jackson, VA 22842-1000
mrdenter@shentel.net

Library of Congress Control Number: 2012912305
ISBN 978-0-615-66394-4

Cover illustration by M. Davidson

Printed and bound in the United States of America.

First printing 2012

Dedication:

To the brave men and women of the central intelligence agency who in anonymity fight the unsung battles

To the reader:

In the development of this novel the author was inspired in part by actual events connected with the dissolution of the Soviet Union and its aftermath that have been amply reported in the press and literature.

Having made this clarification it is important to emphasize the fact that this is a work of fiction and the situations described, as well as the characters and their actions are totally imaginary.

Having reviewed the manuscript, as required by law, the CIA required the following disclaimer:

"All statements of act, opinion, or analysis expressed are those of the author and do not reflect the official positions or views of the CIA or any other US Government agency. Nothing in the contents should be construed as asserting or implying US Government authentication of information or Agency endorsement of the author's views. This material has been reviewed by the CIA to prevent the disclosure of classified information."

TABLE OF CONTENTS

Acknowledgements:

In fictional format I attempted to transmit to the reader the authentic feelings of the men and women of the Central Intelligence Agency as they face the daily rigors of their chosen profession. The protagonist's thoughts in many ways reflect my own as derived from 28 years in the Clandestine Service. I am grateful for the opportunity to serve my country afforded by the CIA and the insights those years provided into the darker ways of the world. The Cold War has now been eclipsed by the War on Terror, and once again the clandestine warriors fill the front line trenches. They have my undying admiration, and I hope they can forgive me for some of the liberties I took in telling this story.

The idea for this story was largely inspired by Paul Klebnikov's Godfather of the Kremlin, published by Harcourt, Inc. in 2000. Mr. Klebnikov was the first editor of Forbes Russia. He was shot to death as he left his Moscow apartment on July 9, 2004. As Steve Forbes put it in his July 12, 2004 obituary of Mr. Klebnikov, "Who ordered Paul's gangland-style execution and why? We don't know the specific answers--yet. But Paul wrote extensively, incisively and all-too-knowledgeably about post-Soviet Russia's crime-ridden, oft-murderous worlds of business and politics. Criminal capitalists and their political allies literally have looted billions of dollars of assets from this impoverished nation." In fact, it was Klebnikov who reported the looting of the coffers of the Communist Party and USSR Treasury and the ridiculous valuations placed on enormous state assets during the chaos of the immediate post-Soviet period, and how unscrupulous men took advantage.

The forbearance of my family as I wrote and re-wrote the story and the kindness of friends who read the early manuscripts is highly appreciated.

This book might never have been published but for the encouragement and willing assistance provided by writer Bob Morris and his wife, Maka.

This acknowledgement would be incomplete without mention of my former literary agent, John Hawkins, of John Hawkins and Associates, Inc. who died unexpectedly on November 13, 2011. John was unselfish with his time and encouragement.

Last, but not least, thanks must go to President Vladimir Putin. His unrelenting mendacity provided one of the primary inspirations for writing this story. Some of the editors who first reviewed this manuscript did not believe a story about the continuing Russian-American confrontation would be relevant to modern readers. This illustrates how far into the background of the zeitgeist the problem of dealing with Russian intentions has receded. Any reasonable person with a grasp of current events and the troublesome role Moscow continues to play on the world stage could not fail to agree that the ancient Russian yearning for domination remains strong and problematic for the United States.

Michael R. Davidson

New Market, Virginia 2012

CHAPTER 1

I've often wondered how it must have been that last night in Moscow for poor old Stankov. After all those years of waiting his big opportunity was within his grasp, and he had gathered up his courage. He must have been certain Harry would be pleased.

January 1992, Moscow

The shabby little man shuffled up to the entrance of the imposing building, hunched against the bone-chilling wind of the Moscow winter. He was bundled in a heavy overcoat of indeterminate color that had seen better days and wore a fur *shapka* jammed onto his head with the flaps down over his ears. With a slight grunt he pushed the heavy metal and glass door inward, allowing stray flakes of snow to be pushed into the ornate, marbled interior. The guard, seated at a desk at the back of the lobby facing the entrance, had just begun to pull the greasy paper from around a sausage and mustard sandwich when he felt the chill blast and looked up, surprised by the interruption to his normally somnolent week-end routine. The man who had entered, Mikhail Sergeyevich Stankov, saw the guard quickly shove a half-empty bottle of vodka into a drawer before standing to adjust his gray uniform tunic and peer suspiciously toward him through the gloom of the dimly lit foyer.

Stamping the snow from his boots, Stankov approached the guard's desk as he unwrapped the muffler from around his face and removed his *shapka* and gloves, "Good evening, Sergeant," he muttered, as he bent to sign the leather-bound log book.

Recognizing Stankov as one of the people from the "special section" on the third floor, the guard looked on benignly. "What brings you here on a Friday night, sir? Nothing wrong, I trust."

Stankov raised his face to the guard, alert to any sign of suspicion but saw none on the man's broad, Slavic face. Satisfied, he replied, "No, Sergeant. Nothing's wrong. I'm leaving on an official trip tonight and there are a few things I need to clear up in the office before I go."

"Where are you off to?"

Stankov hesitated for a second. It was really none of the guard's business, but his destination was not a secret, and as annoying as it was the man was just making idle conversation. "Vienna, to audit the books at the embassy." He straightened to step around the desk.

"You'll have to leave your suitcase down here, sir," the guard said, pointing at the battered leather valise Stankov carried. "Regulations."

"Of course, Sergeant," he sighed. "I won't be long."

He dropped the valise at the side of the desk and plodded down a semi-darkened hallway toward the bank of elevators, the remaining ice from his boots leaving a trail of wet footprints in the carpet.

Five minutes later, he was at his desk, alone in the suite of offices on the third floor of the most infamous building in Moscow. He booted up his computer terminal and sat hunched over his desk stiff with barely controlled fear. Sweat beaded on his forehead despite the chill as he stared intently at the greenly glowing columns of numbers that marched across the screen. This was the most dangerous thing he had ever attempted, and he was all too aware that the intrusion would be traced to his computer as soon as it was discovered, perhaps within hours.

He fidgeted, struggling to master his anxiety, as he waited for the program to complete itself, shooting nervous glances into the corners of the room, dark except for the light on his desk where he had worked for the past year, his heart thudding heavily against his ribs. He sat up straight for a moment and wiped his brow with his sleeve.

Stankov was not a particularly brave man, but he was highly motivated. His entire future hinged on the action he was now taking, and the vision he had of that future had driven him to take the unimaginable risk.

He watched the crawling green line on the screen that displayed the progress of the file transfer until a soft 'ding' signaled that the operation was complete. He then rammed a large capacity floppy disk into the slot on his

CPU and copied the files from his desktop onto it. He extracted the disk and placed it in a flat envelope that he slid into his inner coat pocket next to the precious plane ticket out of Moscow. With the prudence of a careful bookkeeper he made a second copy and placed it in a separate envelope.

Stankov leaned over the keyboard and typed rapidly for a few seconds and then, gulping down a deep breath, pressed the execute key and watched intently as the long columns of numbers and addresses on the display disappeared, line by shimmering line. Finally, he inserted a specially prepared disk into his CPU and uploaded its contents, routing them to the mainframe in the building's basement. The virus would infect the mainframe, continuously looping and destroying data until it would be nearly impossible to retrieve and reconstruct the files he had just downloaded.

With luck no one would detect what he had done before opening of business on Monday, by which time he would be long gone. But he had no faith in luck, and for all he knew alarms might already be going off. He looked involuntarily over his shoulder at the window as if he feared some malevolently vigilant presence might be there observing his treason, but there was only the swirling snow outside.

He shook himself and slowly breathed in and out to calm his nerves. Satisfied that the procedure he had rehearsed so many times was complete, he rose, donned scarf, cap, and coat and forced himself to walk calmly to the bank of elevators.   In the lobby he signed the exit log, retrieved his bag and waved good night to the guard before walking out into the snow-swept expanse of Lubyanskaya Square where the imposing statue of "Iron" Felix Dzherzinski had stood until August of the previous year.   Removing the statue from its iconic location had been intended to symbolize the retreat of the long shadow of Dzherzinski's KGB from Russia.   But Stankov knew it had been only a deception.

Shivering not only from the cold, he turned his back on the large yellow brick Lubyanka office building, put his head down against the freezing wind, and headed for the warmth of the near-by subway that would take him south to the Paveletsky Station and the southbound rapid train for the 43 kilometer ride to Domodedovo Airport.   The Aeroflot flight to Vienna was scheduled to depart at 9:15 PM.

CHAPTER 2

"Otto"

Rosalind Christophersen came to Oslo in the early 60's as a Foreign Service secretary at the US Embassy, a small-town girl from Pennsylvania looking for adventure. She'd met, fallen in love with, and married a nice, middle-aged Norwegian and settled down to contented married life. Now 68-years-old and widowed, she was more at home in this sleepy European capital than she would have been in the United States. The city had changed, of course. Drugs and crime and immigration gradually had changed its character. But much of the popular television programming consisted of English-language American imports, and these days Rosalind spent much of her time at home in the comfortable detached house her husband had left her, and she chose to ignore the changes.

Over the years she kept up her acquaintances in the Embassy, and it was only a matter of time before the Agency recruited her. In 1983 she was asked if she would be willing for her address to be given to an individual who needed to maintain secret contact with the US government. Thereafter she occasionally received postcards marked in a certain way that she passed immediately to her contact. The Agency paid her a small stipend for this service in addition to an occasional gift of American products from the Embassy commissary. Abruptly in 1989 Rosalind was told that her services were no longer needed.

She found Stankov's postcard in her mailbox three years after this and was puzzled until she noticed the deliberate misspelling of her surname, a replacement of the "e" with an "o," connoting that this was one of the "special" messages.

Rosalind knew what she had to do and took a taxi to the triangular-shaped American Embassy at Ibsen's Gate. The building was now encircled by a high, wrought-iron fence, and protected by steel stanchions on its periphery. It hadn't been like this in the 60's, a more innocent time.

The arrival of a message from a clandestine asset via a local accommodation address provided an unusual and welcome break from monotony for the perpetually bored CIA Chief of Station in Oslo.

It was a cheap greeting card inside an envelope bearing a Vienna postmark. The card depicted the façade of the Viennese State Opera with a short message written in German saying the writer was having a nice time visiting Aunt Greta who would celebrate her 70th birthday on 2 February. The writer, who signed the name Otto, wrote that he had found a wonderful gift for his aunt.

A check of the Station files quickly dampened the COS's excitement. The operation was associated with a Russian agent code-named "Otto." The corresponding file entry was labeled "terminated."

*****

January 31, 1992 - Langley, Virginia

When Jake Liebowitz, Deputy Chief of CIA's Russia Section, discovered a copy of Oslo's report buried deep in his reading stack, he grabbed the handset of his Agency internal secure phone and called the Chief of the Russian Ops Desk

"We don't need old whores like this any longer," he was told. "Money piled up in his escrow account for years while our budget was getting tighter, so we shit-canned him in '89."

The same year the Berlin Wall had fallen.

Liebowitz was not surprised. In the past any credible penetration of the Soviet government would have been valuable, but times had changed. The current Administration and the CIA's Seventh Floor were distracted by a new war in the Middle East and intent on establishing amicable relations with the Russians, convinced that the end of Communism had left them docile and eager to become fat capitalists.

Liebowitz was surprised to learn that a junior officer, Jim Thackery, had been dispatched to meet "Otto" in Vienna. His mission was thoroughly bureaucratic. "Otto" had never been formally "terminated." The slime ball lawyers and the rules dictated that someone had to tell him 'officially' that his services were no longer required, hand him the money from his Agency escrow account, and demand that he sign a quit claim.

This is what lawyers like to do – tie everything up with neat bows, he thought.   Did the legal eagles really believe that an agent like Stankov might actually someday sue the Agency for non-payment?

If "Otto" had any information of value, at the very least Thackery would be smart enough to accept it. Liebowitz asked his secretary to fetch the ops file, just in case.

Ops files, known as 201's, in those days were kept in green 8 ½" X 11" cardboard binders with a big, red diagonal stripe on the cover.   Agents' communications plans were always stapled just inside the cover for quick reference, and this allowed Liebowitz to decrypt "Otto's" message.

"Aunt Greta" referred to "treffpunkt Greta," the meeting place where the agent would expect contact in Vienna. According to the established communications protocol he would appear at 7:00 PM every evening beginning on 2 February until someone met him.   Reference to a "gift" in the body of the message indicated that the agent had important information.

CHAPTER 3

Madrid, 4 February 1992

Yevgeniy Drozhdov passed through the double swinging doors from the Customs area out into the cavernous, dusty reception hall of Madrid's Barajas airport. Across the dimly lit space, he spotted his contact, Arkadiy Nikolayevich Yudin, a greasily prosperous type going to fat, waiting by the main entrance. Yudin's thinning hair, combed straight back from his forehead, was dyed jet black and heavily pomaded in a vain attempt to mask his age. He wore an expensive suit under a cashmere topcoat and was anxiously scrutinizing the arriving passengers. As soon as they made eye contact, Yudin turned on his heel and went out the doors.

Drozhdov followed into the parking lot across the narrow roadway directly in front of the main terminal. He turned up his collar against the cold and damp evening, typical of early February in Madrid. The two Russians slipped unnoticed into Yudin's rented Mercedes.

"Do you have it?" Tension squeezed Yudin's vocal chords to produce strangled diction.

Drozhdov produced the small packet from his inside pocket and extended it to Yudin. "I don't know if this is 'it,' but it's all I could find that matched what I was told to look for. I didn't have time or instructions from the

Center to check its contents."

Yudin snatched the packet from Drozhdov's fingers and ripped it open to reveal a blue plastic floppy computer disk. "What about the other business?" he asked.

"By the time I got to Vienna the meeting had already taken place and the American had left town. I followed him and retrieved this for you. The American had an unfortunate reaction to an injection. He's dead."

"But the traitor is still alive and at large?" Yudin was displeased.

It grated on Drozhdov that one of his targets still survived, but it wasn't his fault. And in any event, Yudin was not a <u>professional</u>. He had no business speaking like this to him. Drozhdov belonged to the elite Banner Unit, *Vympel* in Russian, controlled by Department "S" of the Sluzhba Vneshney Razvedki, or SVR, the Russian foreign intelligence service that had assumed the responsibilities of the now defunct KGB's renowned First Chief Directorate. Formed at the height of the KGB's anti-Reagan paranoia, Banner was dedicated to assassination, terror, and subversion on enemy territory. Drozhdov, an experienced Spetsnaz veteran, was an expert assassin.

He snarled, "Next time give me more than a couple of hours' notice to get to Vienna, and tell the Center they should contact me directly. It's ridiculous in the first place that I had to travel all the way here for instructions and then turn around and make the trip all the way back. But for that, both of the targets would be dead by now."

But the orders had been precise – Yudin would be the exclusive conduit for all communications on this case. In a calmer voice, Drozhdov continued, "What do they want me to do now?" He referred to Moscow Center.

Yudin bit his lip, inadvertently confirming to Drozhdov that he was out of his depth – he was a financier, not an operative, and the feral Drozhdov made him uncomfortable. "I don't know. I'll have to contact the Center, but I can't do that until I get back to my house in Marbella."

Drozhdov shrugged. He would not be punished for missing the traitor. The Center was well aware that he had been given the assignment at the eleventh hour. He had been fortunate to find the American at all after his pell-mell drive to Sankt Johann. "The traitor could already be in the States, for all we know," he said, "but he wasn't with the American."

CHAPTER 4

Ennui

Under its lofty hangarlike ceiling the "food court" aka cafeteria at the CIA's Langley, Virginia, Headquarters was not crowded at 2:30 in the afternoon. I liked it that way. If anyone noticed me at all they would have seen a tall man with long, slightly graying hair swept back from his forehead. I have a lean, angular face and a slightly crooked nose, thanks to a teenage boxing match (which I actually won). Except for the nose people say I bear a passing resemblance to the actor Clint Eastwood. I don't see it, and I'm not sure I like the idea of resembling someone so recognizable. It can be a detriment in my business.

My feet were propped comfortably on a chair, and I was idly contemplating the tassels on my well-polished Gucci loafers. I'd gotten them half-price at the Gucci store on Faubourg St. Honoré during another lifetime when I was stationed in Paris and still considered a rising star. In fact the only clothing I was wearing that was not French was the powder blue Brooks Brothers permanent press shirt.

I know, I know. Sartorial vanity is a weakness, but I'm trying to get over it, I promise.

Here and there other tables were occupied by fellow slackers. I had been in the cafeteria for about an hour and was on my third cup of coffee, but I was not concerned that anyone was likely to miss Harry Connolly, Deputy Chief of Travel Assignments. Nevertheless, it was time to head back to my office. Maybe something exciting was happening. (That's a joke. Humor was an indispensable psychological crutch at that point in my life.)

I levered my feet from the chair and held my legs horizontal to the floor for a few seconds, feeling my abdominal muscles tighten. I did this to salve my conscience over my current lack of exercise. It did no good. Shrugging my blazer over my shoulders I headed down the broad corridor to the elevator bank. There was no hurry.

The elevator whisked me to the Fourth Floor where I entered an office populated by a sea of cubicles guarded by a reception desk. Behind the desk was Cheryl, a generously proportioned African-American woman incongruously dressed in a bright green spandex pantsuit she had accessorized with an orange silk scarf.

Cheryl looked up from the latest issue of *Ebony*.

"Hi, Harry. Got any big plans for the week-end?"

"Just me, the dog, the woods, and maybe a good book."

I thought I detected a hint of pity lurking in Cheryl's liquid brown eyes, but decided to ignore it.

"Anything exciting happening here this afternoon?" I asked.

Both of us knew this was a facetious question. A pizza delivery was more exciting than anything that had ever happened in this office.

Cheryl had spent almost ten years in the same position, and she had neither expectation nor desire of moving anywhere else. Excitement was the last thing she had learned to expect at the CIA.

She rolled her eyes and intoned without enthusiasm, "Oh, yes, Harry, we got loads of excitement up here."

I threaded the way to my office through the cubicles that were occupied by definitely, absolutely, undoubtedly unexcited people who spent most of their time counting down the hours to closing time. My office was tiny, but it was better than a cubicle. Perks of the job. A quick scan of my gray metal desk confirmed that the in-box held the same tall stack of travel forms waiting for my signature that had driven me to the cafeteria an hour earlier.

Discouraged, I pulled my overcoat and scarf from a hook on the wall, and headed back towards the corridor. The same stack of stuff would be waiting for me Monday morning.

I waved at Cheryl as I strode past.

"See you Monday. Don't do anything I wouldn't do over the week-end."

By 3:30 I was in my old Jeep Wagoneer heading west on I-66 toward the Shenandoah Valley.

The rolling hills and ancient mountains of the

Appalachian, the Blue Ridge and Shenandoah ranges, came into view soon after leaving behind the neo-urban sprawl of Manassas and Chantilly. The descendants of the solid German stock which originally settled the Shenandoah Valley display their heritage in their rustic stoicism and in an inordinate number of Lutheran churches that appear wherever six houses comprise a village.

Finally turning off the highway, I steered the old but robust four-wheel drive vehicle along familiar ruts in a twisting dirt road that led ever upward to a track through the heavily wooded terrain where my current home was located. It was isolated and far from Washington and I liked it that way.

Full throated barking erupted from inside the two-bedroom log cabin as I unlimbered out of the car.

"I'm coming, Angus. Hold your horses, boy!"

I opened the door, and a small black blur sped past me in frantic search of the nearest tree.

"That's a helluva way to greet your lord and master, Angus."

The Scots terrier, his business with the tree satisfactorily concluded, dashed back to offer a proper greeting, short pointy tail wagging furiously.

I traded office garb for jeans, boots, and a thick turtleneck sweater and set about building a fire in the native stone fireplace while Angus sat expectantly at the door with his tail thumping against the floor. Satisfied that the logs were burning well, I donned an old sheepskin jacket and woolen watch cap and spent the next thirty minutes walking through the dense woods while Angus executed exuberant figure eights around me, occasionally diverted when his sensitive nose caught an interesting scent. This was our daily ritual.

By the time we returned the fire had caught in earnest. After sharing a spartan meal with Angus I poured myself a generous dollop of Laphroaig 10-year-old single malt and selected a cigar from my humidor's dwindling supply of Habanos. Smoking fine cigars and drinking fine whiskey are comforting vices and well within the reach even of those modestly endowed with money. I was beginning to fear that the scotch was becoming too important but had not yet summoned the courage to cut my intake.

Angus hopped onto the leather sofa beside me and placed his big head in my lap, hoping for an ear rub. I obliged. While the dog excelled at many activities, talking was not one of them, and the void of silence was filled with entirely too much thought. No matter how far I peered into the future, all I could see was the dog and me alone in this place.

My wife, Kate, and I purchased the cabin not far from Orkney Springs several years earlier during an uncharacteristically long stay in the United States. The nearest neighbors were the inhabitants of a turkey farm some two miles away down the mountain road. The place became a refuge for us every weekend, insulated by acres of primal mountain forest from whatever silliness might be going on in the world at large or inside the Beltway a hundred miles to the east.

Here we could pretend to be "normal" people rather than what we really were. Embraced by the absolute stillness of the mountain, somehow incongruous Tanqueray Ten martinis in our hands, it was hard to believe that life's pursuits to that point had made any difference at all in the wider world.

The practitioners of espionage refer to it as a "craft" rather than an occupation, but in fact it's a lot like crack cocaine – one taste and you're hooked. Like a viral contagion or sorcerer's spell it takes hold of you and won't let go. It opens your eyes to a parallel universe that overlays the quotidian existence of most people and affects their lives in ways they never know.

The trouble with intelligence work is that the product of your labor is only of value insofar as it is believed and acted upon by those who make policy – or "interpreted" by the analysts through whose hands it must pass before it reaches the policymakers. The judgmental capacities of Washington's political morass did not inspire confidence.

I am familiar with the face of the Enemy, and I know he is still there, in a different form but still dangerous.

I became convinced that evil existed at the age of ten. If I close my eyes, the black and white television images of the brutal 1956 Soviet repression of the Hungarian Revolution are still vivid, burned indelibly into that part of my brain that closes the synapses necessary to create motivation. Something had clicked in my young mind that led me to fight an empire destined eventually to collapse of its own weight but capable in the meantime of infecting the world with incredible evil.

The enemy was clearly identified. His persistent malevolence had been clear for the world to see in the faces of the Soviet gerontocracy. The increasingly wooden countenance of Leonid Brezhnev decomposed before our eyes, his voice slurring to gibberish and his movements becoming ever more labored and jerky, a perfect metaphor for the living corpse of the Soviet Union as it lurched on unaware that it was already dead, a terrifyingly grotesque zombie grasping at us out of our worst nightmares and holding large chunks of the world and their populations in thrall.

Now, with the USSR supplanted by the Russian Federation and under new management, the faces were different and younger, but the eyes still looked the same to me. Eternal Russia had suffered through autocracy, totalitarianism, and now had been seized by a kleptocracy.

On November 9, 1989, the Berlin Wall fell, and a stake was at last driven through the heart of Soviet communism. By 1991 the Soviet Union had ceased to exist. Not long thereafter "new management" claimed control of CIA's Directorate of Operations, and I was recalled to Washington from my assignment in Paris.

CHAPTER 5

Exile

Barney Morley, the newly appointed Chief of the Russia Section, greeted me with a politeness so distant it was barely discernible. We'd gotten along reasonably well in the past, and the cool reception was a warning sign.

At six and a half feet he was a bear of a man with closely cropped red hair and a florid, acne scarred face. A Yale graduate, the scion of a prosperous New England family, he was smart, successful, and ruthlessly ambitious. Morley was not particularly happy to have been named Chief of Russia Section just when the Soviet Union was collapsing and with the importance accorded to the Russian target in free-fall.

Without preamble he declared in a flat voice, "The Cold War is over. We're entering a new era with the Russians. These guys are no longer this Agency's primary concern. We're not going to waste a lot of energy chasing them around the world anymore."

The Agency's well-known predilection for East Coast Ivy Leaguers had not waned. The new Russia Section Chief was an experienced and resourceful officer but had little experience in Russian operations. What he did have was political clout on the Seventh Floor and a driving ambition to build his reputation and power. He was aiming for the

Seventh Floor Director of Operations job. The Washington bureaucracy, including the CIA, was heavily populated with Morleys – ambitious and capable bureaucrats who sought power for its own sake – an entire city full of God's gifts to the Peter Principle.

The Seventh Floor was enamored of technology, especially surveillance satellites. The risk-averse new boys and girls up there believed that intelligence acquired through technical means was more reliable than "HUMINT," human intelligence, and they loved the big budgets that went along with the technical collection programs. The bigger your budget, the more power you have.

Spy satellites are great, especially their military applications, but I've always been fond of pointing out that satellites can take pictures of the tops of peoples' heads, but pictures couldn't tell you what was going on inside those heads.

Dealing with people close up and personal, however, is always messy. People are unpredictable, and operations can backfire or agents can turn, and public scandal and Congressional hearings are never far behind.

Satellites are far from earth, predictable, and practically risk free.

Morley didn't bother to hide his antipathy, a feeling I reciprocated because I suspected what was coming. Morley viewed me as part of the old guard of Soviet ops officers who had no place in the new Russia Section he had in mind. I have to admit he wasn't wrong.

"You're not a team player, Harry." I was famous for playing by my own rules, but success had until now kept the bureaucrats at bay ... until now.

"I think it would be a mistake to take eyes off the Russians, Barney." It took an effort to maintain an even tone, to speak softly, knowing what was coming. But I wasn't going to give Morley the satisfaction of seeing me grovel.

Morley was ready to pounce, even at this mild statement. He stared placidly at me, his eyes as merciless as a snake's, as he intoned, "Guys like you are Neanderthals, Connolly. Things have changed, and you old KGB-chasers are out of synch with what modern intelligence is all about. What have the people in this Section ever done but walk around and service dead drops – ANCIENT tradecraft!" He waved his hand dismissively. "Hell, I just visited Moscow. It's the damned Third World over there, and you still think they're some kind of threat? We're heading in a different direction in Russia Section, and I can't afford old school thinking. You need to find another home in this building."

I knew full well that Morley did not intend to stay long in Russia Section himself – just long enough to eviscerate it and then move up the ladder to a "better" job.

"You forget that agents have to be recruited and vetted first, Barney. And by the way, have you ever laid down a dead drop?"

Spies are worthless if the spymasters cannot communicate with them. During the Cold War, a misstep in Moscow meant an agent was likely to die in a dank corridor in the basement of Lubyanka with a bullet in the back of the head. That's why case officers never referred to what they did as a "game" - the stakes were too high and the emotional toll of failure too great. The few spies we were able to place in the beast's heart were too precious and their situation too precarious for all but the most circumspect and calculated risks.

Communications are simultaneously the most necessary and the most dangerous activity in which the clandestine operator engages. If an agent cannot pass his information to his handlers, he is worthless. Morley's dismissive remark about dead drops had raised my hackles.

"You should try it sometime with twenty surveillants on your tail in hostile territory, knowing that if you make a mistake someone will die." It took months to train officers for such "denied area" assignments, and there was a high wash-out rate.

Morley smiled thinly, unimpressed. "Old hat, Connolly. The Cold War is over, and so are people who think like you."

Morley would never have spoken to me this way if he did not already have the backing of the new powers that be, and those people evidently had given him *carte blanche* to re-organize the Section. Morley likely expected me to resign, was trying to goad me into it, but some perversity of spirit enticed me to stick around, if only to annoy the new management with my continued presence.

If they wanted to move me to an insignificant position, I would pretend that I didn't mind.

Harry Connolly became an official non-entity.

*****

Simultaneously I became a difficult person to be around.

Kate had grown weary of the peripatetic CIA lifestyle, hopping from country to country, often having to cope with hostile environments that made "normal" life impossible. She had yearned for a more settled existence in the States near family and friends, and she wanted children. I think she must have seen my exile as an opportunity, but then her headaches began. The doctors diagnosed them as migraines.

Not long after my conversation with Barney Morley, a neighbor discovered Kate unconscious and barely breathing on the kitchen floor of our Annandale, Virginia, home. When I arrived at the hospital a doctor with weary eyes and a kind voice informed me she had suffered a severe cerebral aneurysm.

She did not survive.

The doctors assured me that aneurysms are congenital time bombs that are difficult to diagnose, but I wondered if the anger I had brought home from Langley had been the precipitate cause.

Kate had accepted the personal sacrifices that sharing me with the Agency entailed. Now I thought myself naïve to have expected the Agency to reciprocate the devotion I had shown to it. Like all Washington bureaucracies, Langley was buffeted by the currents and counter-currents that periodically sweep through the Capital. In the wake of a long string of public flagellations, a queasy CIA was nearly always under siege, either from the press or some politician with a need to divert attention from his own corruption. It had lost its former élan and the imaginative thinking that had inspired many of its past successes. These days "successes" could become the quarry of a Justice Department lynch mob, and "imaginative" operational proposals were more than likely to be taken apart by wary senior executives looking over their shoulders to make sure the lawyers weren't getting a feral gleam in their beady little weasel eyes.

My life was shit.

CHAPTER 6

Saturday, February 8, 1992

Saturday offered up a pale dawn that dimly silhouetted the bare trees lining the Virginia mountainside. A light snow had fallen during the night, and the ground was carpeted with a thin layer of white. The view out the cabin window could have been an Ansel Adams photo.

I coaxed the fire back into crackling life and brewed my first pot of coffee. As I prepared to light a morning cigar the phone rang. It was very early for a phone call, and of late a call from anyone was unusual.

"Hello?"

The chink of coins dropping into a pay phone sounded from the other end of the line. "Harry?"

Only my name, but I instantly recognized the voice.

"Yeah. Who else? Why are you calling from a pay phone?"

"I need to see you."

"OK, why don't you drop past my office Monday and we'll go to the Ritz-Carlton at Tyson's for lunch?"

"Bad idea. Can I see you on Union Street tonight?" He meant a bar in Old Town Alexandria.

"I hate that place, and you know it. And, besides, I hadn't planned to go into town this week-end. And it's been snowing up here."

"Harry, it's not social." The voice paused for effect before continuing, "Moscow rules."

Jake Liebowitz, my oldest and spookiest pal, sounded serious. I didn't demur. "OK, nine PM"

The line went dead as Liebowitz replaced the receiver.

Angus eyed me suspiciously. The fierce-hearted little black dog looked forward to our weekends together.

"It was Jake. He wants to see me tonight."

Angus didn't reply, but I could tell he wasn't pleased.

Remembering the unlit cigar in my hand, I returned to the fireplace and struck a large wooden match against the rough stone, studiously avoiding an accusatory stare from Angus as I held the flame an inch below the tip of the Série "D" Partagas, one of the last Habanos in my humidor.

I sat down at the small round oak table I used for breakfast and thoughtfully sipped the remaining coffee.

"This may turn into an exciting weekend, after all," I said to the dog.

*****

Driving through the outskirts of Alexandria, Virginia,

the headlights of the old Jeep illuminating the sparse snowflakes still sparkling in the air, I was intensely curious about why Jake Liebowitz had summoned me. We had climbed through the ranks together, Jake the more politically astute as well as a first-class field operator. He had disproven the adage that those who stand in the middle of the road get hit by traffic and landed a plum job as Deputy Chief of the Russia Section. He now sat in the office next to Morley. It occurred to me that Jake was yet another of the friends I had pushed away.

I parked near Old Christ Church and navigated the warren of dark streets in the north end of town before turning south toward the lights of King Street. My SDR (Surveillance Detection Route) completed, I kept to the river side of Union Street, finally pausing a half block away from the meeting place to scan the exterior of the bar before going in.

The place had one thing going for it - a superb locally produced beer - and a lot of things against it, including a well-deserved reputation as a noisy yuppie meat market. I spotted Jake at a booth at the rear nursing his standard Old Fashioned and shouldered my way through the crowd that smelled of Hugo Boss and hair gel to slide into the seat opposite Jake.

I couldn't suppress a grin at the sight of my old friend and extended a hand across the table. Quirky but tough, Jake Liebowitz' appearance was immutable: saturnine, bald and corpulent, always with a harried expression. He took my hand only perfunctorily and did not return the smile. His hand was damp with perspiration. A habitual fidgeter, he was fairly vibrating now. His eyes darted constantly around the bar.

A waitress approached the booth, and I ordered a beer. "What's up, Jake? You don't look very well."

The eyes kept moving. Jake had not removed his coat as though he expected to have to leave in a hurry.

He greeted my arrival with a question. "Were you careful coming here?"

"You said 'Moscow Rules.'"

"Good," he said, still unsmiling. He wrapped pudgy fingers around his Old Fashioned and refused to meet my eyes.

"Did you ever meet Jim Thackery?" he asked the table. "Young guy, only about thirty-five. Would have been just coming into Russian operations about the time you were leaving for Europe."

I thought back and came up with a fuzzy image of a tall, earnest young man anxious to be recruited into the then prestigious Russia Section. I had seen him just a few times during quick visits to Washington.

"I vaguely recall him. Spoke decent Russian for someone named Thackery. Picked it up at Middlebury, I think. Nice kid, but no ball of fire. Why do you ask?"

"He's dead."

Jake pulled the corners of his mouth downward. He slurped his Old Fashioned, then dug one of the cherries out of the glass and popped it into his mouth, discarding the stem on the tablecloth.

"What happened?"

I wondered what this was all about. I had no special connection to Thackery.

Jake noisily gnashed the cherry before answering. "He was killed on an assignment. I want you to look into it."

Such deaths were extremely rare in those days, but I didn't see the connection, and now I felt foolish. My interest in temporary assignments was at low ebb. My interest in everything was at low ebb.

"I'm cheerfully arranging pleasure trips for my fellow bureaucrats these days, and I don't want anything to do with the bunch that's running ops now, including you, and they don't want anything to do with me. Sorry, but that's the way it is. I'm turning you down, Jake, because I no longer care and because Barney would never let me within a mile of Russia Section anyway. You're the Deputy Chief, so find someone else."

Jake regarded me wearily from beneath shaded lids, but his response, when it came, was delivered with considerable asperity.

"Oh, no, Harry. You're not 'out of it.'" He emphasized the words 'out of it,' in a particularly nasty way. "None of us is ever 'out of it,' because we can't get it out of our blood, out of our thoughts. The trade is that seductive, and I know you too well. Whether you like it or not, I'm going to tell you a story. You will listen to it because you can't help yourself. And when I am finished, you will be very much back INTO it. Have no doubt."

Jake was in a foul temper, and he was at least partially correct in his assessment. I shrugged. "OK, Jake. Tell me the damned story. The drinks are on you, by the way."

I had already lost enthusiasm for the conversation.

Jake smirked humorlessly.

"Thackery died in Austria four days ago. He was skiing in the Tyrol, near *Kitzbühel*. We put out word that it was a heart attack." He shot a crafty look across the table. "Helped along with a needle, for Christ's sake."

Jake looked even more nervous than before. He was fairly humming with anxiety now.

"A needle?"

Jake's eyes flashed a momentary gleam of triumph. He was sinking the hook.

"I think the Russians killed him. I think it was '*mokroye delo*', a 'wet affair.' Just like the goddamn Bulgarians and their umbrellas, except this time the poison was extremely fast acting. It had to be the fucking Russians."

I was disbelieving. Contrary to popular fiction, even during the darkest days of Soviet-American rivalry, the CIA and the KGB had not gone about routinely bumping off one another's officers. We roughed one another up occasionally, and the Russians definitely dusted American agents when they caught them. They sometimes used exotic assassination techniques on émigrés and those of their own that strayed from the pack.

I still didn't see what any of it had to do with me, but curiosity led where caution told me I had no business treading.

"OK. Maybe it was the fucking Russians. Why are you blessing me with the information?"

Jake stopped vibrating for a moment and looked up, the smirk returning to his face. He was manipulating the conversation, had probably rehearsed it. But to what end?

Jake stared at me for a few heartbeats before proceeding.

"Because you're the only one who can do it," he said finally.

I shook my head and tried to look surly.

"I told you I'm out of it for good. As I said, you could never convince anyone in the Russia Section, let alone Barney, to hire me for any job."

Jake snorted and hunched over the table as much as his paunch would allow. He plucked the second cherry from his drink and waved it in the air as he spoke.

"Consider what I have just told you. One of our guys is zapped by the Russians." He ticked the points off on his fingers. "A phony cause of death is spread about and everybody feels sorry for young Jim, and a collection is taken up for the widow. But we know that young Jim was really murdered. What do you think our reaction is?"

I wasn't biting. Liebowitz was going to tell me anyway.

"I talked to Morley about it. He's not happy, but he doesn't want to rock the boat. There's too much invested in liaison with the Russians, and that's too important to risk upsetting them with accusations we can't prove. He would probably even ask for their help, but there are complicating factors. He said it's best we keep it on the back burner until something crops up that might explain it. Russia's like the Wild West these days, and it could have been a rogue operation, he says. But what I can't figure out is why our man Thackery would have been targeted by anybody."

Jake snorted again. "Murdering an intelligence officer is not a random occurrence. I think Thackery was killed by a Moscow Center-trained professional, and I want to know why."

I agreed with Jake's characterization of KGB practices. They would train the Irish and the Palestinians how to make bombs. The Czechs would make money selling plastique to KGB clients like the Libyans, and people would die in places like Berlin, Beirut, and Belfast. The truly imaginative stuff, however, they kept to themselves because the CIA would recognize it if it were used, and the Russians could not afford such close identification with mayhem on foreign soil.

Against my better judgment I asked the obvious question.

"What was Thackery doing in Austria?"

Jake managed to look smug in spite of his nervousness. "That's why I'm talking to you right now."

CHAPTER 7

Intersection

Jake sucked the dregs of his Old Fashioned from around the tiny lumps of melting ice that remained in his glass.

"Do you agree with me so far?"   He challenged, pressing for a reaction.

I was tiring of his elliptical way of getting to the point.

"What did Thackery's meeting report say?"

"What meeting report?"

Jake produced a small, bitter smile still looking into his glass, probably hoping he might find another cherry. He paused reflectively for a moment and then hunched over the table to get his face closer to mine.

"This was supposed to be a no-brainer. No contact with anyone from Vienna Station and the report to be submitted by hand when Thackery returned to Washington."

"No one found any trip notes in his luggage or on his body?"

"Nope. Unless the Austrian cops found something, but we're fairly certain there was nothing. Our relations with them are excellent."

Jake slouched back into the corner of the booth watching me out of the corner of his eye to see if I was taking the bait.

"Cut the fan dance, Jake."

He launched what might have passed for a smile in my direction and reached into his coat pocket to extract a tattered envelope that he placed ceremoniously on the table between us.

"Take a look. I dug these out of the library yesterday afternoon."

I gingerly picked up the envelope and opened the flap. Nestled inside were two Xeroxed clippings from Viennese newspapers. The first, dated mid-January, reported that the Russian Embassy had contacted local authorities concerning the disappearance of visiting Gosbank official Sergey Mikhailovich Stankov. Airline records showed that he had arrived in Vienna, but he had never reported to the Embassy. The second clipping was dated 3 February and reported that the Russian official still had not been found.

I stared at the name. It all came together now – the reason for Jake's confidence that I would agree to become involved. Stankov was no stranger.

I returned my attention to Liebowitz. "What day did Thackery meet Stankov in Vienna?" He asked.

"It would have to have been February 2nd or 3rd, a little less than a week ago. Thackery arrived in Vienna on a flight from Frankfurt late in the evening on Sunday the 31st. He died February 4th on a ski slope in the South Tyrol."

If Thackery had met Stankov in Vienna the evening of 2 February and left the next day for a ski holiday on Uncle Sam's dime, his murder was even harder to explain. If he had been carrying anything of value he would surely have returned to Washington immediately. And what had happened to Stankov, to "Otto?" If the SVR were indeed behind Thackery's creative murder, they may well have been searching for Stankov and come upon Thackery by chance. They might even by now have Stankov in custody. But if that were so why would the Russian Embassy have notified the authorities that he was missing?

I suddenly realized I was taking a lot on faith and fixed Jake with a speculative stare. That worthy shook his head sadly.

"You think I'm making this crap up? Why would I?"

I shrugged. "Maybe you've finally gone all the way around the bend?"

Jake finally relaxed.

I downed the last of my beer. "I believe you, but there are a lot of holes to be filled in. You're assuming that Thackery's death and Stankov's disappearance are connected. On the surface I'll admit it's a pretty safe assumption. But why would the Russians snatch Stankov and then report him missing to the Austrian Police? As a matter of fact, we really don't know if Stankov and Thackery met at all. Any one of several sets of circumstances, no matter how improbable, could fit the facts as we know them. What if Stankov didn't show up, but Thackery decided to go on his skiing jaunt all the same?"

The answer was obvious, but I wanted to hear Jake say it just the same.

"Shit for brains!" Jake could turn a nice phrase when he wanted to, and I couldn't suppress a grin. "He would have continued going to the *treffpunkt* until the meeting did take place. The fact that he left Vienna on the 3rd means he met Stankov the day before, on the 2nd."

"Yeah, yeah, you're right, of course. Do forgive me for thinking out loud."

"You call that 'thinking?'"

"You are too kind.

"Look, no matter what Barney Morley might want to believe, this is serious stuff. I admit that my idea is nothing more than a working theory, but it's all there is, and it's a damned reasonable theory. Trouble is nobody is really doing anything to get to the bottom of it, or somebody wants to sweep it all under the rug, avoid any investigation into the Stankov case. The medics know how Thackery died. Barney Morley and the people on the Seventh Floor know too, but they can avoid taking action because the lawyers say there is no legally acceptable proof of Russian involvement." Jake snorted. "So do they think 'legal proof' will just drop into our laps WITHOUT any action? 'Things have changed,' they told me."

It was easy to imagine Morley saying this. Change

was his motto.

"Words to live by," I said.

Jake continued, "The cornerstone of this Administration's foreign policy is to support and encourage Russian democracy and economic transformation. Barney is a golden boy at Langley and at the White House, and he intends to keep it that way. He wants to be Director one day."

"Well, that will certainly be a bright and shining day for American Intelligence," I said.

CHAPTER 8

Responsibility

"To make your long story short, for a whole variety of reasons, including 'legal' and personal ambition, nobody is going to rock the boat by accusing the Russians of murdering one of our guys. Is that what you're saying?"

"You got it." Jake looked tired. "Christ, if they knew I was talking to anybody, especially you, about this they'd feed me my balls one at a time. They weren't happy when I questioned their decision, and now I've got to keep my nose clean and toe the company line. That's why I wanted to see you tonight, and I can't afford to be seen with you out at Langley, or anywhere else for that matter. I've already stepped into enough deep shit."

"What the hell, Jake?" I recognized that this was not particularly perceptive commentary.

"Listen, beyond the obvious, there is something weird about this, and I think I know what it is. Fact is I'm scared. When was the last time you heard about the KGB killing one of our guys?"

In fact Soviet State Security had spilled the blood of many Americans: World War II POW's, the crewmembers of downed B-47 reconnaissance aircraft, Korean and Vietnam War POW's. And, of course, the KGB gleefully killed its own. But KGB officers did not kill CIA officers. I shook my head. "Not gentleman spies – it would have been too disruptive to business."

"Right. So what if I'm right and the SVR, the old KGB spy shop, actually did take out Thackery? The Cold War is over. Everything is sweetness and light, right? What's wrong with this picture?"

Annoying as Liebowitz could be, I respected his judgment. But such a murder was incongruent against the backdrop of current Russian-American relations. What could a little State Bank official like Stankov know that would have justified such drastic action? Despite the messy pile of information Jake had just dumped into my lap, I suspected that my friend had not yet told me everything.

"As much as I hate to take Morley's side, there is a lot at stake in Russia. And stop for a moment to think about the question you just asked me. 'When was the last time the KGB killed one of our guys?' Answer - probably never, at least not on purpose. That fact alone is enough to shred your theory unless Stankov somehow stumbled across something of incredible value that in some way was threatening to the Russians. He never did before, you know."

Jake curled his lip. This time I couldn't tell if it was a sneer or a smile, and it was getting under my skin. Jake was reeling me in like a big fish whose resistance was growing weaker. He just stared in silence, waiting for my inevitable capitulation.

I subscribed to a code of honor peculiar to some intelligence officers but frowned upon by many: When I convinced someone to entrust their welfare, their life, to me by accepting recruitment, I believed I became personally responsible for them. Jake knew me well, and even as we spoke, my thoughts strayed back over a decade.

CHAPTER 9

Berlin

Berlin in the late 70's was a spook's paradise, a perfect microcosm of the Cold War. The city was filled with spies, and they fed off of one another - Russian, Czechoslovak, Romanian, Polish, British, French, and American. They gave parties for one another and wined and dined one another in fashionable restaurants, and they got drunk together. The spooks chased one another because they might provide highly prized information about the espionage activities of the opposing side – counter intelligence. The Russians and especially the East Germans were by far the most adept at this. The control exerted by Communist security services over their societies was very nearly absolute, especially in East Germany, and they had no compunctions about reminding the char lady who cleaned the American General's office in West Berlin that she had a sister on the other side of the Wall.

From its dingy quarters not far from ClayAllee the local CIA contingent occasionally discovered a chink in the enemy's armor.

Sergey Mikhailovich Stankov worked for SovTorg, the Soviet trading company with an office in the American

Sector. He had appeared on the screen a few times in the past in Moscow on the edges of trade negotiations as a minor official of Gosbank. A few years earlier he would not have made it onto the CIA's targeting list, but now there was growing interest in Washington in the deteriorating Soviet economy. The Americans were having the first premonitions that Lenin's edifice was crumbling.

I assigned the Station's local team to a routine surveillance of Stankov and learned that he had a penchant for drink and liked to race up and down the Kurfuerstendamm in the shiny new Lada his office provided. It was probably the first car he ever had, and he was a lousy driver. The combination of alcohol and speed already had gotten him into a few scrapes with the police. He was married and had one child, a boy four years old. They lived in a grubby apartment on the eastern edge of the American Sector, a working class district. Photographs showed him to be skinny and wan with thinning blond hair. He didn't spend a lot of time in his office.

One day Stankov received an invitation to a commercial luncheon sponsored by the Berlin Chamber of Commerce. I had arranged to be seated next to him.

The Russian was easy to spot as he entered the elegant surroundings of the Hilton salon in his wrinkled, stained suit on legs already slightly unsteady in the early afternoon. I watched him from a distance as he made his way directly to the drinks table and picked up a Scotch on the rocks. Despite his chronically unkempt appearance he did not hesitate to engage prosperous looking Berlin businessmen in conversation, and he seemed able to hold his own in conversation. His German language ability was excellent, revealing the fact that his shabby exterior concealed a good mind. The majority of Americans assigned abroad seldom mastered any language other than English.

When we were called to table Stankov, stole glances at the place cards nearest him. A cloud of concern crossed his face when he spotted my designation as a representative of the US Mission in Berlin. He would be slow to warm to an official American, but the purpose of this meeting was just to make the contact.

We engaged in the inevitable desultory conversation of a first encounter between an American and a Russian official. Everyone knew the dance steps. Stankov wasn't volunteering anything, and I knew better than to probe. The fact that Stankov did not barrage me with the usual litany of questions designed to elicit biographic information, a template committed to memory by every neophyte Soviet intelligence officer, led me to conclude that Stankov was not a member of either of the Soviet services.

By the time we were halfway through the main course the Russian had begun to relax. The wine he gulped down by the glassful didn't hurt. I was impressed by the quantity and variety of alcohol the little Russian could put away. He had consumed two scotches before the meal and accounted for at least a bottle and a half of wine all by himself. He downed a large cognac afterwards. Yet he remained perfectly lucid, even if his motor control was slightly off. The luncheon over, I shook his hand and smiled warmly and thanked him for his excellent company during the meal, and watched as he staggered out the door. Pedestrians would have to be extra careful today on the Ku-damm, as everyone called the Kurfuerstendamm, Berlin's main drag.

Over the course of the next six months the CIA arranged for Stankov to be invited to several social affairs. Each time I would greet him, chat for a while in a totally non-aggressive fashion, and then leave him to his own devices. The Russian was warming up to the American who had become a familiar face in a crowd of strangers. It was like coaxing a timid wild animal out of the woods with a trail of bread crumbs.   Finally, surveillance and telephone intercepts revealed that Stankov was taking his wife to dinner at a mid-range German chop house on Fassanenstrasse, just off the Ku-damm to celebrate her birthday.

Kate and I were in the restaurant at a table near the door when the Russian couple walked in.

Stankov spotted me right away and froze for a moment. I quickly stood extended a hand, expressing pleasant surprise at this 'coincidence.' Stankov hesitantly introduced his wife and I shepherded them to our table where Kate was waiting, primed and ready to play her role as the bright, friendly all-American girl.

I asked, "What brings you out tonight, Sergey?"

The Russian managed to stutter that, in fact, it was his wife's birthday.

Beautiful Kate, well-rehearsed, piped, "Then you must join us at our table, and the evening will be on Harry."

Stankov, who was chronically short of money, hesitated only a moment before accepting the invitation. Our "unofficial" relationship was established.

Recruiting him was only a matter of time.

I ran him for a year, during which time he provided low-level business-related information and gossip that revealed more about West Germans dealing with the Soviets than about internal Soviet affairs. The payoff would come when Stankov returned to Moscow. I steered him toward seeking a position in Gosbank's central offices where he could work his way up the ladder.

I left West Berlin shortly after Stankov returned to Moscow. I had become rather fond of the little Russian who had been distraught at the idea of going back home.

I had met with him a couple of times since then when he had traveled to the West on official business. We always concluded these meetings by sharing a bottle of good vodka in the expensive hotel rooms rented for these occasions. After a few years, Stankov ceased to appear, but no one at Langley cared anymore.

Now death had found Thackery in the snow, and Stankov had disappeared. And it had all begun in Berlin when I had first laid eyes on a shabby little Russian clerk that I was to turn into a traitor.

CHAPTER 10

Stankov

It was a momentous step for Stankov, a step he dared not discuss even with his wife. He had cautioned her not to mention to any of their Soviet colleagues the evening they had spent with the attractive American couple. It would cost him endless hours writing up the contact and being grilled by security, he had told her. Did she want them to be sent back to Moscow to live in the dingy Stalin-era flat they had there and to stand in endless lines just for the necessities of life?

Berlin was a city unlike any he had ever experienced. Born in a small village in the Urals, he had displayed above average mathematical skills at an early age, and the efficient Soviet educational system had earmarked him for training to hone those skills. A shy, introverted boy, he had progressed quietly but steadily through the system, finally graduating from the prestigious Belarus State Economics University in Minsk.

The university curriculum was rigorous. Sergey was required to be fluent in not less than two foreign languages (he had chosen German and English). Shy and nearly friendless in a part of the Soviet Union he did not know, he turned to drink to escape the pressures of university life. Despite this shortcoming (not uncommon in the USSR), his superior skills had landed him a job at the State Bank in Moscow in the early 1970's. He spent nine years there eking out a less than affluent existence living in a sixth-floor apartment in a Stalin era building without elevators. Miraculously, he found a woman who had agreed to marry him. They had one child, a boy named Stefan Sergeyevich.

His assignment to the SovTorg office in West Berlin had been unexpected, and he did not intend to risk his first and only chance to get ahead in life by telling the KGB that he was consorting with an American. Besides, he liked Connolly. And the more he saw of the West, the more he admired it. He knew economics, and he recognized a superior system when he saw it. The comparison was inevitable every time he crossed the border between West and East Berlin.

Sergey did not relish returning to Moscow when his tour was over. When the American, Connolly, had finally suggested he might find happiness working for the CIA, Sergey had not refused.

"Will you take me to America?" he asked.

"That's something you'll have to earn. You see, your position here in Berlin doesn't give you access to the kind of information we're looking for. We want you to work for us in Moscow, at Gosbank's central office."

"But I don't want to go back to Moscow. I want to go to America."

"Sergey, my friend," the American put his arm around Stankov's narrow shoulders. "You must understand. If you were to defect now, you and your family would end up at a refugee processing center in Munich. I'm sure you could find a job eventually in West Germany, maybe as a street sweeper."

This stark image did not coincide with Stankov's vision of his future life in the West. As these words sank in, the American continued, "Your best chance to guarantee a more comfortable future for yourself and your family is to work for us in Moscow. We'll pay you well, and you'll build up a nice nest egg for when you finally come over. You'll have something to live on, enough money to start a really nice new life. If you work hard to develop access to truly important information, you'll earn even more."

"But how would we do this? It's much too dangerous for me to meet you in Moscow. Security is everywhere. I would be caught. It's impossible."

"Sergey, listen to me. I've already established a secret account for you and deposited twenty-five thousand dollars."

Sergey's jaw dropped. It was a pretty persuasive argument.

"You see? You're already on the way to your nest egg. And you needn't worry about meetings in Moscow. I won't ask you to do that, at least not for a long time. I'll give you a way to communicate with me and for me to communicate with you. To begin, I'll train you here in Berlin where it's safe. We have plenty of time before

you'll be going home. By the time your tour here is over, you'll have all the confidence in the world. If you don't, then the decision is yours whether to continue with me or not. I couldn't and I wouldn't force you to do anything against your own best interests. That's not the way my organization works."

Sergey, still slightly dazed by the idea of owning twenty-five thousand American dollars, mulled this over before asking, *"And what happens to the money if I don't want to continue?"*

"Then you don't get anything. I told you. It's already in a secret account I established for you. Once you agree to work with me and have provided good information, you can have it any time you want. Just give me a chance to show you what we can do."

"I want the money now."

"What would you do with all that money? Could you spend it and risk bringing attention to yourself? Your colleagues and friends would see that you suddenly have money. They would be jealous, and they would be suspicious. The KGB would have you in handcuffs immediately. And your family would suffer, too.

"You might think you can hide it somewhere. But how long would it be before your wife finds your stash or for someone else to stumble across it by accident? How would you explain it?"

Sergey could not dispute the accuracy of the argument. He did not plan to tell his wife anything *about this conversation. This would be best for her. The temptation, the glimmer of a new and affluent life far away from the drab, gray reality of the Soviet Union was irresistible.*

Over the months to come he met with the CIA man many times for training in clandestine communications and briefings on intelligence requirements. These meetings always took place at a safehouse in the American Sector, and Sergey came to look forward to the sessions. There was the unpleasant business of the polygraph examination, a measure that bemused Sergey. Russians were adept liars. They lived lies every day in order to survive.

But there were good times, too. Sometimes, Connolly would surprise him with a "night off" and upon entering the safehouse he would find a table laden with delicacies and liquor and he and the American would get merrily tipsy together.

When the time came to return to Moscow he was near panic. Connolly had become his lifeline, and he felt like he was being tossed back into a black and bottomless sea.

It was customary for Soviets assigned to the evil West to return to the Workers' Paradise carrying numerous gifts for their superiors, items impossible to find in the East: good fountain pens, watches, luxury foods, and above all djinsi, blue jeans. The favored brand was Levi Strauss. No recipient would question how Sergey had acquired the gifts. The CIA supplied him with a suitcase of goods.

This was the way to advancement and better access

to valuable information, and he knew precisely how to play the bribery game. He returned to Gosbank more determined than ever to carry out his instructions. He wanted to catch the brass ring of a good life in the West. Despite his less than salubrious appearance and continued drinking he continued to advance within the bank. On rare trips to the West, he triggered his communications plan, and enjoyed happy, liquid reunions with Connolly. Each time he was assured that the information he was providing was improving, and his secret account continued to grow.

*****

Given his access to Soviet economic information, Sergey was perhaps less surprised than most when the Soviet Union finally imploded. His position at the bank insulated him from the wave of unemployment that hit a huge number of less fortunate fellow Russians, and his knowledge of the West even eventually helped him advance further amidst the chaos.

In 1991, he was called to his boss's office and told he was being transferred to a new unit where he would be working closely with one of the intelligence services. A week later he found himself installed in an office in Lubyanka where he was assigned to keep the books for certain secret accounts, among them accounts set up by the KGB in the West.

Sergey could not believe his luck. Here, after a decade of conniving and moving slowly through the ranks and from department to department, was his golden *opportunity.*

His friend Connolly would be proud.

CHAPTER 11

Decision

Jake Liebowitz' voice broke through my reverie, "Harry, I'm asking you to take this on for a couple of reasons. There's one important point I've left for last."

He turned his eyes downward again as he proceeded, like a bashful suitor about to pop the question.

"You know that we still had several in-place agents in Russia when Morley took over. What you probably don't know is that we suspect there's a mole in Russian operations. And again, this is tightly held, and I should not be sharing it with you. We've lost an alarming number of agents - good ones, including several you yourself recruited - and a mole is the only possible explanation. Now we've lost an officer, and I'm convinced that the mole is behind that, as well. Remember what I said about someone preferring to stymie any investigation into Thackery's murder? There has to be something important enough to risk such drastic action, and I suspect it could be something that would help us identify the mole. What else would motivate the Russians to murder a CIA officer if not to protect such an important in-place asset?"

I felt queasy. The scuttlebutt was true. A mole could destroy an intelligence service, at the very least set back its operations for years. Trust and loyalty were the bedrock of agent handling, but they were fragile commodities. In a single stroke a mole could undermine everything and wipe out decades of work at the cost of many lives.

Across the table Jake still watched me, gauging my reaction.

"As a Deputy Section Chief, I have the authority to launch operations on my own, and if something goes wrong I can show your operation was sanctioned. But for now, I don't want anyone besides you and me to know what we are doing, and that means no official funds, no official travel orders. You'll be under my authority alone. I'll write an Eyes Only memo and lock it in my safe. Other than that, there is no way I can actively support you. You'll be entirely on your own. Without these precautions we risk the mole blowing the op. And by now you must realize why I came to you and why you are the only person for this job."

Jake was asking me to shoulder all of the risk, counting on my personal connection with Stankov for motivation. He knew me too well.

"A rat in our basement explains a lot. The Russians would resort to extreme measures to protect his identity. If this goes south I'll try to protect your fat ass."

*****

A week's personal leave was easy to arrange, and Monday afternoon I left a disgruntled Angus with a former neighbor in Northern Virginia before heading to Dulles to catch the United Airlines flight to Paris.

The cattle car seat was woefully inadequate for my height. The thoughtless toad in the seat ahead reclined into my knees, and I finally stood to look for a place that did not require acrobatic contortions. There was an empty seat at the rear of the cabin, but even so it was impossible to switch off the unbidden thoughts that refused to permit sleep.

There is a tragically wistful belief that if only we knew our antagonists as individuals, war would be impossible, but this theory is pathetically flawed. Hatreds run more deeply than acquaintanceships, deriving sustenance from past cataclysms and tragedies that cannot be changed and strength from the brute force of the masses. Occasional understanding does flicker across the chasm of historical accident that separates human beings. Hands do reach across the divide, and there are always spymasters waiting to grasp them -- ready to equip and train the owners of those beseeching hands for their own inevitable destruction.

Spymasters try to expunge their consciences with the rationalization that spies and defectors are by nature "defective" people who set themselves consciously or subconsciously on a path to be used up and discarded like so many empty cans.

At 35,000 feet I recalled a CIA seminar from years ago

that new officers were required to attend. A particularly obnoxious staff psychologist named Gary explained that his research revealed that amoral manipulators made the best case officers. "We don't want any true believers in the CIA," the shrink concluded.

What the hell did he mean by that? It seemed to me that he had somehow skipped over the concept of right and wrong, of virtue versus evil, or perhaps morality was something they didn't teach in shrink school. We were, after all, on the "right" side, weren't we? Otherwise, there could be no justification for the "amoral" acts we sometimes had to perform: deception, the manipulation of people, theft of secrets, maybe even assassination. So, if we were "good" were we just faking the amoral part? Could amorality mask virtue? Or was it the other way around? Nothing the shrink said was clarifying, but that's what shrinks are paid to do: demolish the barriers between good and evil because everything is relative, isn't it?

I believed the Agency was fighting the good fight and that there were a lot more people like me than the technocrats might suspect, so I did not torment myself with psychoanalytical angst. But you can play by your own rules only for so long before it catches up with you, and it had finally caught up with me in the person of Barney Morley. Only Frank Sinatra could do it his way all the time.

One thing was certain: Jake's mission was my last hurrah. I'd always told myself I'd stay with the Agency as long as I was doing what I wanted to do, but I'd never considered what might come after. Now here I was at the last stop on the line with no idea of where I would be when I stepped off the train. I was still in my forties, and that meant there would be no generous retirement annuity from a grateful government. What could a dinosaur with an outmoded skill set hope to do?

I'd been in a daze since Kate's death and my internal exile. My refusal to accept Langley's banishment was a sham. No matter how long my corpse haunted the hallways, nothing would change. Nobody cared in the least.

CHAPTER 12

Volodya

The next day I sat across from a fat old man in the comfortably bohemian living room of an apartment at 17, Rue de Tournon in Paris' picturesque Sixth Arrondissement. The apartment had a very "old world" feel to it, as well it should – the building in which it was located had been constructed in the 18th century. The overstuffed furniture was just a bit too large, but perhaps just right for the old man's ever increasing rotundity. Once an actively athletic young man, Volodya Smetanin at an advanced age increased in girth every year like some ancient redwood.

Only a small portion of the plaster walls was visible behind the assortment of faded photographs, memorabilia, and paintings. I had walked there from the Metro station at St. Germain de Pres.   We used to meet regularly at the Deux Magots to sip *café crème* and philosophize, a hallowed tradition of the famed cafe. I had always liked the church of St. Germain just across the street, the oldest in Paris and the burial place of the Merovingian kings.

The city of light was a Mecca for exiles, and my friend Volodya was a remarkable man and also an exile, an active participant in history to be viewed with wonder and respect because he had led such an exceptional life compared to most of the rest of humanity.

He spent his youth in Egypt, displaced by the 1917 Bolshevik coup in his native Russia. The very young Volodya became an eager and enthusiastic member of Baden Powell's Scout program in Egypt's British Colony, and to this day remained active in Scouting and spoke of it with the fondness one usually reserves for a beloved child. The tracking, camping, and survival skills he acquired were put to unexpected and rough use in the North African desert campaign of the Second World War. Volodya's area knowledge made him invaluable for behind the lines reconnaissance as a commando in the British Expeditionary Forces.

I was contemplating the dagger that hung in an honored spot above the entrance to the alcove used for dining when Volodya returned from the kitchen, bearing a tray laden with a steaming pot of tea, cups, bisquettes, two small glasses, and a frosty bottle of Stolichnaya. He caught the direction of my gaze.

"So you remember, my friend, the story of the dagger?"

"No one who has heard you tell it could forget it."

The young Volodya had used the knife to slit the throats of Rommel's sentries as he made his way in the Egyptian night through the German lines to gather tactical intelligence for the British forces. Volodya was not one to forget his obligations, and the knife now served as an icon in honor of the dead.

I had always found it difficult to rectify the cold,

stealthy killer of the North African desert nights with the figure Volodya now presented to the world. In his mid-seventies, he was very large, very rotund and jolly, an animated and highly entertaining conversationalist. He cherished life and wore gentleness like a warm cloak over a cold past. He had seen more in a lifetime that had marched through the cataclysms of the twentieth century than I ever wanted to see and had learned to accept fate with equanimity, with the stoicism of his Russian heritage.

Yet beneath his tranquil exterior Volodya was still a fighter and very much engaged in certain affairs of which few were aware. He had interesting acquaintances, and they were vital to my plan to find Stankov in Vienna.

*****

After tea and cookies we launched a valiant attack on the bottle of Stoli as I recited the story of Stankov's disappearance and Thackery's mysterious death. Volodya was a study in solemnity as the tale progressed. As thoroughly Russian as he was, he was still far from embracing a firm belief in the capacity of his native land to reform.

Beneath his craggy brows, deep in his grey eyes still were reflected the horrors he had witnessed as a child escaping from the Bolsheviks across the Crimea. His father had believed it better for his family to face the precarious existence of Christians in a Moslem land than to be absorbed by the Godless horror then descending on Russia. Volodya felt no atavistic urge to return to his homeland.

"*Chekisty*!" His jowls shook as he spat out the word, the old acronym for the agents of the Special Committee, the *Chrezvechayniy Komitet*, forerunner of the KGB. "They are still there brooding in their gilded nest outside Moscow where they still pull the strings, unchanged, unrepentant, waiting for their moment," he growled.

Volodya spoke as he poured us each another *stakanchik* of the iced vodka. "I continue to get reports. Most of the same people are still there, just beneath the layer of 'reformist' political appointees. Oh, they were hurt even before the old KGB was broken up last year. They lost absolute domestic control, but it didn't slip far from their grasp, and they are regaining ground these days. They re-organized, you know. The Federalnaya Sluzhba Bezopasnosti, the Federal Security Service, is now responsible for internal security, just like the old KGB's Second Chief Directorate, and the so-called SVR still has a lot of juice. There are old KGB types salted throughout the new government. No matter what happens in Russia, they will remain a force to be reckoned with."

In a world so addicted to change that continuities were easily overlooked, Volodya remained anchored firmly by the steadfastness of his convictions and the hard lessons of his past.

He ran an informal network of aging Russians and others with an axe to grind with the Soviet Union, an ephemeral group with no formal organization. It was an exclusive collection of men and women who knew and trusted one another – and still knew how to recognize an enemy.

"I thought you were no longer involved in this business." The chair creaked as Volodya leaned forward and stretched his arm to pour another shot of the cold spirit into my glass. His voice was a soft rumble, and there was a hint of amusement in his eyes. "I knew you'd be back."

I winced as yet another "I told you so" came my way. Within the space of a few days Jake and Volodya both had done it to me.

"This has nothing to do with anything but Stankov." I told Volodya the same thing I told myself.

"Why do you have to do this at all? I don't understand why your organization has not already brought Stankov in."

Volodya liked euphemisms such as "organization."

I sighed, "Times change, organizations change. It's a brave new world, Volodya. You and I are dinosaurs. We're members of an endangered species."

"Dinosaurs are extinct. Stankov is endangered. But this situation is absurd. What you have just described to me is a ceremony of confusion."

He leaned toward me for emphasis and then shifted back into the depths of his divan. He was still for a moment, hunkered down, his eyes half closed as he organized his thoughts. The old man became very grave as he straightened back up, fixed solemn eyes on me and announced, "I am indignant."

He sagged back again, his eyes still on me. Volodya's attitude was expectant, anticipating my next words.

"I need your help."

"Ah."

*****

The old man brooded for a long time after the American left. He had, of course, promised to help his friend, but he faced a dilemma. There was vital information he was not free to share with Connolly, information that had come to him through a ratline stretching back to Moscow itself. Unfortunately, he already had shared that information with someone else.

Connolly's description of the matter at hand had raised a flag. The death of an American, presumably at the hands of the Chekisty, troubled him greatly, but it was demonstrable proof that something precious to the Russians was at risk. As much as he respected his friend, he feared that he might have underestimated the danger.

Sighing heavily, Volodya finally picked up the phone and rang a number known to few people in Paris. Two hours later there was a knock at the door, and he opened it to a man well-muffled against the cold.

The man left the apartment thirty minutes later, and as Volodya let him out the door he prayed that he had made the correct decision.

CHAPTER 13

Communications

Descending from the apartment, I felt a pang of sympathy for Volodya and speculated how often the aging warrior was able to manage the steep, winding stairs these days. How much longer would I have this rare friend to rely upon?

A brisk walk took me to the Boulevard Saint Michel, sparsely populated on this chilly February evening with scruffy students and a few wide eyed off-season tourists looking for cheap Left Bank meals that they would find farther east on the other side of the Boulevard St. Michel in the narrow streets that ranged back from the Seine opposite Notre Dame.

Satisfied I had attracted no attention, I found a taxi queue and ten minutes later was deposited before the brightly lit facade of the Gare du Nord on the other side of the river. There were public phones on the second level, ones that still accepted coins rather than the new plastic phone credit cards that were coming into vogue all over Europe.

The receiver at the other end of the line was picked up before the first ring was completed. Jake's voice was edged with worry, and I could picture the corpulent spook at the other end of the line. "Harry?"

"Who else would be calling you like this? You got a girlfriend?" Liebowitz was at a public phone in a strip mall off of Route 7 in Falls Church, Virginia.

"I wish." His tone could be termed lugubrious.

I would not reveal Volodya, even to Jake. No one knew about my longstanding friendship with the ancient Russian or how much he had helped me in the past. I told Jake only that I was laying the groundwork that would get me to Vienna.

Jake grunted, "Are you sure no one at Headquarters knows what you are doing?"

"No one knows."

"If anything blows people will remember that you are my best friend..."

Jake was still worried about his career.

"They're too busy re-inventing the wheel at Langley to remember anything." I checked my watch. We had been talking for about forty-five seconds.

For once, no sarcastic rejoinder was forthcoming from Jake, so I continued, "I'll need to talk to you the night after next at the same time, especially if 'Otto' shows. Call the Paris number I gave you the other night and leave a new contact number. I'll call you there at the time you designate."

"I'll do it." Then, quietly, "Harry, be careful." Maybe he wasn't just worried about his career, after all.

The receiver clicked in my ear.

I couldn't shake the notion that I was setting off for the far, spindly end of a long branch listening all the while for the sound of someone sawing it off behind me.   I wondered what that poor little spy Stankov was seeing over his shoulder right now.

I walked toward the Boulevard Malsherbes past Le Cercle Militaire to a tiny mom and pop restaurant tucked into a small side street named Rue Roquepine. This had been a regular stop for Kate and me during our Paris years. We had been in the habit of taking an evening meal there at least once a week, sometimes twice.

The restaurant was an element in the communications plan I had in mind, a cut-out actually. Besides, I needed to relax, and I didn't want to do it in the impersonal surroundings of my hotel.

Maurice, the proprietor, greeted me warmly. Most of the red and white checkered oil cloth covered tables in the narrow dining room were occupied, but that made no difference. Inevitably I was invited back to the kitchen where I sat with Hélène, Maurice's wife, who happily placed morsel after morsel on my plate across a rough wooden table while we shared a bottle of the good, inexpensive house Bordeaux. The meal was completed with a large crockery bowl of the best chocolate mousse to be found in the city. I spent ninety minutes listening to prideful tales concerning the feats of the new grandson, complaints about the government and taxes, and constant exhortations to eat more.

Maurice and Hélène easily agreed to act as mail drop and take phone messages for me for the next few weeks. (It was the restaurant's phone number that I had given to Jake.) It was nearing ten PM when I finally headed back to my small hotel in one of the dark side streets behind the Place de la Madeleine. The room was small but clean and away from the street which meant it was quiet.

CHAPTER 14

On the Move

Wednesday dawned with a lowering sky that promised to dampen the *joie de vivre* of the City of Light, and a gray afternoon found me once again with a clearly preoccupied Volodya, although nothing he said betrayed a reason. I ascribed his mood to avuncular concern.

Volodya waved a careless hand toward a manila envelope on the table between us. "These are the instructions for the contact in Vienna. They are fairly straightforward, and you should have no trouble."

"Who is my contact?"

A twinkle appeared in his eye as Volodya's dark mood lifted momentarily. "Don't worry. You won't have any trouble recognizing Sasha. Just be at the meeting site on time and remember the parole."

Solemnity settled over him again.

"Are you certain you want to go through with this, Harry? It's been a long time since you last saw Stankov. A lot could have changed, and now there has been a death."

"It's too late now. I'll do this, and then I'm through

with it all. I've had it with the bastards in Washington."

"I'm not worried as much about the bastards in Washington as I am about the bastards you may find in Vienna. Promise me that you will be very careful." He clamped both hands around the arms of his chair and heaved himself with a grunt to his feet.

I embraced him and said, "Don't worry, old friend. I'll be passing back this way in a few days. Keep another bottle of Stoli on ice."

*****

Volodya ushered the American to the door, where he embraced him and planted a kiss on each cheek. His eyes as he watched his friend descend the stairs were crinkled with worry. He prayed he had made the right decision.

*****

The next day I caught the mid-morning TGV fast train out of the Gare de Lyon for the three hour ride to Geneva. I would not go directly to Vienna, and in any event did not plan to travel by air. Flight manifests are too readily available, too easy to check, and thanks to the lack of official support, I carried no alias documents. I would stick to ground transportation across porous European borders. It would take more time, but it guaranteed a lower profile.

Unable to resist the temptation, given the fact that my humidor was practically empty, I took advantage of the stopover in Geneva to renew my acquaintance with *Gerard et Fils*, my favorite cigar shop, located on the spacious lobby floor of the Noga Hilton Hotel beside *Lac Genève*. As usual, I was offered a cigar of my choice and a small glass of fine single malt scotch, in this case peaty Lagavulin. I spent a comfortable hour chatting with the proprietor before returning to the *Gare* where I purchased a First Class ticket for the overnight train to Vienna.

*****

Early the next morning I walked out of the Peterhoff Train Station into the inevitable freezing winter drizzle of the Austrian capital, a city with a reputation for music, pastry, coffee, and nosy little old ladies with umbrellas. I tried to remember a single sunny day I'd spent in Vienna but failed. If it wasn't raining or snowing, minute particles of water hung suspended in the air creating a mist that hangs over the city like a threadbare eiderdown quilt. Vienna was my least favorite European capital. It probably didn't deserve my opprobrium, but I simply did not like the joyless Austrians who wished they were German but couldn't quite measure up.

I turned up my collar against the cold and headed for the taxi queue. A short ride took me to the Opern Ring.

My destination was a small pension on Walfischgasse that lay a few blocks away.

I slung the strap of my single bag over my shoulder and trudged through the gray morning past the ornate opera house where I'd once treated myself to a presentation of Tchaikovsky's "Sleeping Beauty" that provided my only pleasant memory of the city. Across the street the elegant facade of the Sacher Hotel, still monochrome in the tenacious gloom, beckoned temptingly, and I promised myself a slice of *Sachertorte* before I left.

The pension was considerably beneath the exalted level of Vienna's best known hotel. Walfischgasse is a dark, narrow street, not much more than an alley that connects the popular Kaerntner Strasse pedestrian shopping street with Schwarzenberg Strasse to the East.

The weathered door with its peeling green paint opened onto a steep wooden stairway leading up to the reception desk on the second floor. The place did not fit into such a posh section of the city, and I wondered how it had survived.

A man of indeterminate age, as drab as the decor, sat behind the desk behind the morning paper. I addressed the paper in German. "I'd like a room, please, with a bath, if possible."

The desk clerk lowered the paper and appraised my expensive Burberry trenchcoat. His eyes widened slightly though the rest of his face retained its bored expression. "We have a room with a shower, but the toilet is down the hall." His voice was cracked, like the plaster on the walls.

"That'll be satisfactory."

"How long will you be staying, *mein Herr*?"

"I'm not sure."

The clerk shrugged indifferently and thrust a bony hand across the counter palm up.

"Documents, *bitte*."

I made no move to comply. In popular spy fiction the hero always has a ready supply of nifty alias documents, but I was on my own. After the trouble I had taken to cover my tracks, I had no intention of advertising my presence either to the local police or to the local Russian Intelligence *rezidentura* that undoubtedly was supplementing some cop's salary in exchange for a copy of the official list of guests that every hotel was obliged to maintain. There were always cops who would do this, sometimes for several different intelligence services at once. Intelligence analysts then check the register against their own watch lists. Dinosaur stuff.

I spread several high denomination bills across the counter.

"Why don't I just pay you a week in advance to guarantee the room? If I leave sooner, I won't expect anything back, and I do expect to leave sooner."

The clerk was clearly no stranger to such an arrangement.

"No problem," he said, and the money disappeared into his pocket. "Just sign the register, please."

I signed a fictitious name and in exchange was handed an old fashion room key attached to a large wooden ball the size of a tennis ball to discourage guests from walking out of the hotel with it. The room number was painted on the wooden ball.

The room was two more floors up, small and sparsely furnished. The bath was only a metal shower stall, obviously a recent addition, which stood against one wall. The door had clanged against it when I entered. The tiny shared water closet was three doors away down a dusty corridor lined with a threadbare carpet.

The ancient radiator pumped out waves of heat, making the room unbearably stuffy. With some effort I managed to open the double window a crack, after battling the layers of paint that sealed it to the sill. The sharp winter air felt good in these close quarters.

It was 13 February – nine days since Thackery's death just a few hundred miles west of where I now stood.

I tossed my coat onto the bed and settled into the room's single, worn upholstered chair to light a cigar. The smoke rose in an undulating white ribbon from the luxurious Habano and snaked through the open window to dissipate into the damp atmosphere, a perfect metaphor for Stankov. Luck would have to play a big role in finding the Russian. Luck is a precious commodity in the espionage trade, but sometimes it's all there is.

I had met Stankov in Vienna years ago and had given him the coordinates for *treffpunkt Greta*, the meeting site he had used with Thackery just a few weeks ago. There was just a chance that the Russian would remember the accompanying emergency contact instructions that called for a meeting in front of the American Express office on Kaerntner Strasse, a popular pedestrian shopping street a few blocks around the corner from the *pension*. His cue to appear at the site was two vertical chalk marks on the mailbox in front of the *postamt*, the post office, at the corner of Krugerstrasse and Akademiestrasse.

Stankov had always been excellent at his communications tradecraft. I had made sure of that. If he were still in Vienna, there was a good chance he would be checking for the signal every day. I would emplace the signal and hope for the best. If he saw it, he would come to the Kaerntner Strasse site the following night.

CHAPTER 15

"The Forest," February 12

Vitaliy Mikhailovich Shurgin settled his wiry frame comfortably into the soft leather of the rear seat of his chauffeur-driven ZIL 41041 sedan, a tight smile on his foxlike face. Shurgin loved this status symbol of the old Soviet nomenklatura. This was the latest model, a 300 HP 7700 cc. monster V-8, capable of tremendous acceleration even in this armored version. If he were honest with himself, Shurgin's affection for the vaguely sinister appearing automobile was largely based on the power and authority it symbolized.

The former KGB officer missed the "good old days." The privileges extended to those of his elite status had made them the envy and a source of fear for the regular citizenry of the old Soviet Union.

Nevertheless he had to admit that things had not turned out so badly, certainly not for him personally. He recalled that day just a few years ago when he was called to the office of the Chief of the service. Shurgin was widely respected for his abilities, a rising star. Already a General and in charge of the powerful Group Nord, he was well known in the service for his hatred of the Americans and his advocacy of stronger tactics, including assassination, against CIA operatives. He had been but one of many in the Soviet hierarchy convinced that the Americans were preparing a nuclear first strike against the Soviet Union during the Reagan Administration. It was his undoubted patriotism and determination to prevail against the State's enemies that had made him the ideal choice to carry out the highly confidential task that was entrusted to him on that day.

The driver slowed and turned off of Moscow's Ring Road, heading southward into a tree lined avenue and eventually making a sharp right turn toward a formidable guarded gateway.   But Shurgin's car did not continue through the gates that guarded the main entrance to the "Forest," as the SVR Headquarters compound is known, but rather continued past them towards the residential zone.

The heavy black automobile glided between the imposing multi-towered Headquarters complex on the right and the single story administrative and support structures on the left, finally rounding a hairpin curve before entering the exclusive residential development set aside for Russia's highest ranking intelligence officials. The driver finally turned into a wide street that dead-ended at an open field and stopped before a narrow drive leading to a large, two-story mansion that was reserved for the SVR's most important visitors. Behind the house, Shurgin knew, was a huge kidney-shaped swimming pool. Another car, a silver Mercedes, stood in the drive. His special guest was waiting for him.

Alighting from the car, Shurgin buttoned his stylish Italian suit and pulled his camelhair overcoat around his shoulders. He was bare headed, and the light winter wind ruffled his thinning reddish hair. The main door of the house opened quietly inward as he approached, and he was met on the threshold by the imposing bulk of General Yuriy Ivanovich Morozov, the Russian bear to Shurgin's fox. He was in full uniform today rather than his usual mufti in order to impress their visitor. General Morozov had been put in charge of the KGB's Directorate "S," in charge of Soviet Illegals operations all around the world shortly before the Berlin Wall fell. Despite the changes that still were taking place in Russian society, Morozov had clung to his position through it all. He was Shurgin's most intimate ally.

"How is our guest," Shurgin asked, handing his overcoat to an orderly who had rushed to attend him.

"Nervous, but interested. He did make the trip, after all, but I don't think he likes being here." Morozov glanced over his shoulder toward the double doors at the end of the entrance hall. "He was miffed that you weren't here waiting when he arrived."

Shurgin's lips compressed into a tight smile that betrayed no mirth. "We still have to show these *chyornozhobtsi*, these black asses, who's who, don't we?"

Morozov grinned and nodded his assent. "I hate these self-righteous bastards," he said between his teeth.

Both men kept their voices low as they approached the double doors on the other side of the entrance foyer.

"This is going to work, Yuriy. They may be bastards, but at least they'll be our bastards."

A uniformed enlisted man stood to attention at the double doors and opened them at a nod from Morozov. The two entered a large, brightly lit room decorated in opulent classic Soviet style with overstuffed sofas, large chairs, and heroic sculpture. Enormous windows overlooked the snow-covered garden and the empty swimming pool at the back of the house. Dark clouds scudded across the winter sky.

Seated on the edge of one of the sofas near the windows was a tall, spare man in a sober black suit over a collarless shirt. His aquiline face was adorned with a short heavy beard. His brown eyes were dark under heavy brows.

The dark man stood as Shurgin and Morozov entered the room. Shurgin extended his hand, "Welcome back to Moscow, General Hatimi." They spoke in English.

Adel Hatimi, with the rank of General, was second in command of VEVAK, *Vezarat-e Ettela'at va Amniat-e Keshvar*, the intelligence service of the Islamic Republic of Iran.

The Iranian took Shurgin's hand with just a hint of reticence, so it seemed to Shurgin, as though touching an infidel (and worse, an atheist) might somehow contaminate him.

"I hope your trip was comfortable," Shurgin said smoothly, gesturing to the sofa. "Please, sit down."

The Iranian looked fatigued from the 1,600-mile trip from Teheran. "Thank you. Quite comfortable, Mr. Shurgin, or do you prefer 'General?'" he replied, resuming his seat.

Shurgin took the chair opposite. "I'm a civilian now, my friend. May I offer you refreshment? We can offer the finest fruit and vegetable juices from Bulgaria. A light luncheon can be arranged, if you like."

"Thank you, but my time in your country is limited. Your hospitality is impeccable, as always, but I would greatly appreciate getting to the point of our meeting."

Shurgin knew that Hatimi did not relish these visits. As a graduate of Qom's Haqqani School, well known for radical Islamist extremism, he was one of a coterie of alumni that had the trust of the Mullahs. Nevertheless, only a few years ago Hatimi's former boss, General Fardust had been arrested in Tehran and charged with working for Soviet intelligence. It was a sign of the trust he enjoyed at home that Hatimi could make such a visit alone.

"Very well, General Hatimi. I can confirm to you that the first shipments are being prepared as we speak. All that we require is your signature on the agreement on behalf of your government."

Hatimi glanced at the document Shurgin had thrust in front of him. "And do you sign on behalf of your government? To my knowledge the only post you hold is with the Moscow City Government as Deputy Mayor."

"I sign on behalf of my organization, General," replied

Shurgin smoothly with a smile punctuated by sharp teeth. "Things are not always what they appear on the surface in Russia, and we discussed this matter when we first met months ago, did we not? This is a unique opportunity, and we must not let it pass. You'll be taken to the warehouses after our meeting to inspect the initial shipment. If you prefer, we can wait until afterwards to sign the agreement."

Hatimi knitted his brows for a moment, and then reached for the pen Shurgin extended to him across the table and signed the document.

Shurgin sat back with a satisfied grunt as he observed the culmination of months of work. He thought back to his first encounter with Hatimi almost a year earlier. Shurgin had opened the meeting by pointing out that Russia and Iran shared a common enemy: the United States of America. He had baldly proposed an alliance of convenience that "will paralyze the Americans and drive them from the world stage."

*****

The Iranian had been dismissive: "Your own country is in disarray and rife with corruption and violence. To our people, the Soviet Union was a 'great Satan' second only to America. By the grace of Allah, blessed be His name, Russia was defeated on the Afghan battlefield and finally defeated by the greater Satan, the Americans. Islam will defeat you again in Chechnya. Russia is weak, and I cannot imagine what you could possibly have to offer." In reality, Hatimi knew exactly what the Russians had to offer. If these negotiations were successful, the benefit to the Islamic Republic of Iran would be enormous. But one does not always share one's thoughts with infidel interlocutors. He was more interested in eliciting what the Russians were thinking.

Shurgin restrained his temper and leaned forward, smiling. "You are wrong on several counts," he began in a conciliatory but firm tone, "The Fatherland was not defeated and will never be defeated, not by you and certainly not by the Americans. A political system finally crumbled because of the rot within it. In the case of your own country, do you consider the fall of the Shah a 'defeat' for Iran?"

The Iranian did not answer.

Shurgin continued, "I care nothing for Communism and never did. My first concern has always been for the Fatherland, and the same goes for my KGB brethren. And as for the Americans, you misapprehend history, my friend." Shurgin rose suddenly, warming to his theme, and began to pace the floor. At five feet nine inches tall and 165 lbs. he was not a physically imposing figure, but when he became animated, when his ice blue eyes lit with the inner fires of his convictions, he could be incredibly charismatic and persuasive. He turned to face to the Iranian, his voice gaining strength and passion.

"We held the Americans at bay in Korea in the 50's, and

in the 60's and 70's we defeated them in Southeast Asia. The Americans are strong technologically and militarily. They are a clever people and strong as individuals. But collectively they lack the cohesiveness, the will and the attention span for a long conflict. Our agents in America and Europe supported the anti-Vietnam War movement, and the 'useful idiots' in America swallowed everything we fed them and begged for more. We turned the world against them and broke the will of America, and they cravenly abandoned their allies on the battlefield. Vietnam left a festering wound on the American psyche and provides us with a template for defeating them in any future conflict. All we have to do is to pick at the scab.

"No, my friend," continued Shurgin, becoming even more animated, "America was defeated in 1974 and will never recover from that calamity. Down deep they know they have lost their honor and their soul forever. For them, patriotism is today a dirty word. The Americans revile and distrust their own government. Yes, they remain a superpower, but their power is useless because they lack the will to employ it to their advantage, and they will always betray their allies, just as they did at the Bay of Pigs and just as they did in Vietnam."

Shurgin ceased his pacing directly in front of Hatimi. "How old is Persian civilization? How many conflicts have your people seen? How many centuries have you survived with your culture intact? The Americans have no such background. They are a mongrel nation of degraded races that becomes more divided every day, and they celebrate the centrifugal forces tearing them apart as 'diversity.' Their national passion is self-indulgence and immediate gratification, and their politicians pander to these weaknesses. They have no patience and no strategic vision. Most of their schoolchildren cannot even find their own country on a map.

"We both know history, and we know the value of patience. The Persians invented chess, and the Russians mastered it. I think the time has come for us to play on the same side of the board."

Shurgin sat down again across the table from the Iranian and leaned forward. His voice resonated with conviction. "We will regain our power and influence. We will regain our hegemony over Eastern Europe, and eventually Western Europe, as well. It will take years, but we have a plan, and we have the means. The machinery is already in motion. Your people and ours may not be fond of one another, but we can at least work together against a common enemy." Shurgin paused for effect, and then continued, "I have something to offer to you of great value to your country."

CHAPTER 16

"Magic"

Two days after signing Shurgin's document, a nearly exhausted General Hatimi, gratefully debarked from the Qatar Airways jumbo jet after over 13 hours of flying. It was nearly four o'clock in the morning in Tehran. Carrying only a single small bag Hatimi wended his way through the terminal and found his car and driver waiting in the gloom outside. He flopped heavily into the rear seat and ordered the driver to take him home. He had just enough time for a shower and a change from the dark suit he now wore to his uniform. This would be a busy day. He rested his head against the seatback and closed his eyes.

Shurgin's offer to provide clandestine assistance to the Islamic Republic's nuclear program was a welcome event, as was his parallel offer of advanced weapons systems, including anti-aircraft missile technology. Later in the year the Russian Minister of Atomic Energy would visit Tehran to formalize the agreement Hatimi had signed the day before yesterday with Shurgin. The overt portion of the agreement would engage the Russians to rebuild the Bushehr reactors. This was something Hatimi had been struggling to set up for some time. A year previously Shurgin had informed Hatimi that the Americans had agreed to an arrangement whereby the Russians would assist in rebuilding the Bushehr reactors. They did this in the vain hope of shoring up the flailing, increasingly erratic Yeltsin government. But the Americans would never know of the secret codicil of that same agreement that Hatimi carried now in his bag. Under cover of the overt Bushehr project, the Russians would provide Iran with much needed heavy water technology, including reactors. Eventually an entire heavy water facility would be set up where no one would ever find it. God is great, thought the General, the infidels will supply us the very means by which we will destroy them. Under *Velayat-é Faqih*, Islamic Rule, Persia would regain its ancient strength, and no enemy, not even the Great Satan, would dare smite her once she possessed nuclear weapons.

Three hours later, somewhat refreshed and feeling better in his starched uniform, Hatimi again boarded his car for the drive across town to the modern low rise office building that housed the offices of the Tiara Electric Company. The Islamic Republic's nuclear development program was still in its initial stages, but planning had begun not long after the Revolution of 1979 until put on hold after the Iraqis destroyed the Bushehr facility. The innocuously named Tiara Electric Company was the cover organization for the acquisition of nuclear technology and materials.

Hatimi strode into the office building heading straight for the Director's office. Bursting through the door he greeted the diminutive man behind the desk. "*Salaam Aleikom*, Peace be with you, Mansoor. Good morning."

"And with you. Welcome." replied Doctor Mansoor Davedeh, surprised by Hatimi's unexpected appearance. For the past seven years, under the cover of the small "electric company" Davedeh had headed Project Magush, the Islamic Republic's nuclear weapons development program. "Magush" means "magic" in Old Persian, and Davedeh's hard won successes thus far displayed the touch of a sorcerer.

Davedeh turned to the black clad woman who had just finished pouring him a cup of hot, sweet, tea. "Giti, will you please bring a cup for the General?" The woman scurried out of the office.

Davedeh turned back to Hatimi. "Back already, I see, from your foray into infidel territory. Do I detect excitement in your eyes?"

"Are you still in the market for plutonium enrichment technology?" Hatimi sat in a chair opposite Davedeh.

Davedeh sipped his hot sweet tea. "That's the main idea," he replied insouciantly. "Are you telling me The Russians would expand the Bushehr protocol?"

There was a soft knock at the door and Giti scuttled back in with a cup of tea for Hatimi.

"*Mamoon*, Giti, thank you," said the General to her retreating back. The two men remained silent until she had closed the door.

"The Bushehr protocol is only a façade," replied Hatimi, "My visit to 'infidel territory,' as you put it, has yielded some sweet fruit. The Russians signed a secret protocol with me. They agreed to supply two heavy water reactors, and much more."

"*Na bãbã*, you must be kidding!" exclaimed Davedeh. "Do you realize what this means for Magush? If the Russians come through, we'll be able to pursue plutonium enrichment along two parallel lines. The Indians used heavy water reactors for their first weapons-grade plutonium, you know." He rubbed his hands together. "We'll have to initiate another project. That will require another site, and lots of money," Davedeh was excited. "Will we be able to come up with the funding?"

"The Russian price is not cheap," sighed Hatimi, "But that's my job. We'll find the money somewhere. God will provide."

"*Enshã'allãh*. The Pakistanis weren't cheap either. We'll have to find someone qualified to head up the project," said Davedeh. "I'm fully occupied with acquiring the centrifuges. I think I can make some suggestions."

"Very well, Mansoor. Please draw up a list of prospects so I can begin the background checks." He stood, preparing to leave. "They must be godly men, Mansoor."

Davedeh assumed a serious mien. "But of course, General. You can rest assured." He stood to escort Hatimi out of his office.

At the door, the two men embraced before Hatimi trotted down the steps toward his waiting Mercedes. The conversation with Davideh had renewed his energy. He looked back at Davedeh before entering the car and waved at the nuclear scientist.

Hatimi instructed his driver to head for VEVAK headquarters. He had to brief his boss on developments and devise a presentation for the mullahs that would convince them to fund the new project. Hatimi harbored no doubts that he would be successful. He instructed the driver to take a route that would take them past the old American Embassy, now the headquarters for the Revolutionary Guard's Quds Force. Hatimi's heart swelled with pride every time he beheld the sight.

CHAPTER 17

Sasha, February 13

I awoke from a sound sleep to the beep-beep of my wristwatch alarm. It was eight-thirty PM - time to go. I shrugged into my Burberry and creaked down the steps past the dozing desk clerk and back out onto Walfischgasse and navigated a winding path through the maze of small streets east of Kaernter Strasse. A half-hour's walk brought me to one of the telephone booths lining the front wall of a post office. Using a plastic pre-paid phone card bought upon arrival at the train station, I rang the Paris number.

Hélène answered and when she recognized my voice, she handed the receiver to Maurice. Yes, there was a message. He recited a telephone number with the 703 area code for Northern Virginia and a time to call. The contact with Jake Liebowitz was set for Saturday afternoon – two days from now.

I would have preferred not to take the next step before talking to Jake again, but there was no remedy. The first contact with Volodya's collaborator was set for an hour from now in a coffeehouse on the other side of town.

*****

Coffee is a Viennese institution handed down since the brown beans were discovered in the deserted tents of the defeated Turks after the Battle of Vienna in 1683. The Viennese have since invented a unique terminology to describe every shade and combination of the liquid combined with milk or *schlag*, cream. Italian nomenclature pales in comparison to such Teutonic precision.

My destination was a *kaffeehaus* typical of the genre, cozy, with dark paneled walls, wooden booths, and impossibly small tables. I found a place at the bar and nursed a *kaffee mit schlag* with an eye on the entrance. The room was cast in an amber glow from glass-chimneyed lamps affixed at intervals along the wood-paneled walls. There was a rack of the day's newspapers, each one fit onto a long, slotted wooden spindle that hung horizontally on the rack. Every morning the place would be packed with the eternally self-satisfied Viennese sipping their preferred varieties of coffee, savoring sweet rolls, and reading the papers.

The door opened, and the woman who entered was tall and slender with an understated athleticism accentuated by an assured, erect carriage and confident stride, like an Olympic skier. She wore a long green Loden coat open to reveal a form-fitting charcoal gray knit wool dress with a modest Austrian hemline beneath which flashed a pair of stylish black boots. Her ash blonde hair was severely pulled back in a bun, and a small green Tyrolean-style hat complete with pheasant plume perched at a rakish angle on her head. She appeared to be in her mid to late twenties, and her ensemble was completed by a pink copy of the "Financial Times" tucked under her left arm.

I watched as she selected a table. She had arrived at precisely 9:45 PM. The newspaper was the recognition signal. I alternately cursed and praised Volodya for his taste in operational support personnel as I approached her.

"Excuse me, but didn't we meet at the home of a mutual friend in Paris."

She raked me from head to toe with clear, hazel eyes that I judged capable of destroying male egos.

"Indeed?" she responded coolly, "and who is this friend of yours?"

"His name is Volodya."

The parole complete, *bona fides* established, she motioned for me to sit beside her on the banquette against the wall. A white aproned waiter approached and I ordered a brandy. I couldn't conceal the involuntary smile that tugged at the corner of my mouth.

"Do you find something amusing?"

Switching from German, she spoke in cultured, but accented, English. Her "th's" came out as "z's" and her "g's" were brittle.

"I wasn't expecting a woman. Volodya only gave me the recognition signal and said to wait for 'Sasha.' Your name is Aleksandra?"

"Volodya loves his little jokes." The eyes softened at the corners for just a second. "Yes, my name is Aleksandra Sergeyevna Turmarkina."

I fought an atavistic urge to bend at the waist and brush my lips across the back of her extended hand.

Her appraising gaze continued steadily, and I began to feel a bit foolish because I found myself hoping that I was making as favorable a first impression as she. This was entirely irrational. I wasn't asking her to the prom.

"Harry Connolly." A decidedly inadequate effort, like a short man trying to dunk a basket.

"Volodya says I am to assist you in any way I can. He speaks highly of you. I will, of course, do whatever you and he wish of me. Please give me the details."

She was young to be one of Volodya's contacts. I trusted the old man's judgment, but death had touched this operation. I had conducted many missions solo, sometimes out of choice, sometimes because there was no other way. It was like walking a tightrope with no safety net - thrilling in execution but a great relief when finished. But I needed back-up now. I didn't want to conduct a clandestine meeting of this sort without counter-surveillance. Thackery's murder demanded such precautions.

Aleksandra compressed her lips into a tight smile. "Come, come, Connolly, do get on with it."

I decided to give her something she could reasonably be expected to do with a minimum of danger to herself.

I told her about the American Express office *treffpunkt* and asked her to position herself so she could observe the area beginning thirty minutes before the hoped for rendezvous with Stankov the following evening at 11:30 PM. She was to walk past American Express at 11:20 PM if she had detected nothing untoward and then leave the area. If she spotted anything potentially hostile, she was to leave the area immediately without walking past American Express.

She had no questions. When I was finished, she stood, made certain her tiny hat was firmly in place, and made a regal exit.

I didn't think there was a snowball's chance in hell that this half-assed operation would flush out Stankov. I was bumping up against reality, and reality told me I was flying on a wing and a prayer and was about to crash.

I ordered another brandy, lit a cigar, and sat there for another half-hour before heading back to my ratty hotel.

*****

The heavyset man who had been waiting in the shadows across the street observed Sasha's departure from the coffee house and followed her for several blocks, keeping his distance. Finally, on a narrow side street, she stopped and waited for him to catch up to her. They walked on together, deep in conversation.

*****

When I awoke next morning I caught the fading image of ash blond hair and hazel eyes on the backs of my eyelids but couldn't hold onto the rest of the dream.

CHAPTER 18

Drozhdov, February 13 - 14

While I was tossing in my sleep an assassin named Yevgeniy Drozhdov was hurtling toward Vienna in a rented BMW. Within a few hours he would try to kill me.

*****

Drozhdov had been very busy. A little over a week earlier he had tracked the American intelligence officer to a ski resort in the Süd Tyrol. Yesterday he had been summoned to another meeting with Yudin.

"The CIA believes the traitor is still in Vienna and is sending another officer to meet him." Yudin passed him an envelope. "Your instructions are inside. They include the details of the meeting site they will use. It's the best information the Center can provide for now."

Drozhdov opened the envelope and studied the document inside.

"The site is a very public place. I could wait there for days and never catch them, and if I did, what could I do with a hundred witnesses standing around?"

"The Center has a great deal of confidence in you.

General Morozov said to be certain to tell you that. Read on. You've only looked at the first page. The Center also knows the signal site they will use to trigger a meeting and the prescribed times. All you have to do is check it until you see the signal. Then you set your trap."

Drozhdov checked the meeting times.

"Yes, it can be done. At that time of night I should get them both at the same time with no witnesses."

"My instructions for you are very clear. The Center wants both the traitor and the CIA officer killed. No matter the consequences, neither of them is to leave that meeting alive."

Easy for you to say, you fat civilian pig, thought Drozhdov. You've never so much as strangled a chicken with your own hands.

"I know what is to be done, and I will complete the mission," he growled.

"The CIA officer could arrive in Vienna any time," said Yudin, "Unfortunately, we don't know where he will be staying. So you need to get there quickly. We can't afford to miss this time."

Drozhdov snorted. "Hurry up, hurry up. *Bystro, bystro*. And so here I am in Madrid again when I should already be in Vienna!"

"That's not my fault," said Yudin petulantly. "You know the communications protocols as well as I."

"*Da, konechno*, yes, of course, and the Center thinks

I'm some sort of superman who can be in two places at the same time. OK, let's finish up here so I can see if there's a flight back to Munich tonight."

And now he was burning rubber. After Linz, his destination would lie just a few hours ahead. He again cursed the circuitous communications the Center had mandated.

Drozhdov pressed harder on the accelerator. He could not afford to arrive late and disappoint General Morozov again. His first task would be to check the signal site the American case officer would be using.

*****

The following night, February 14, the SVR assassin stood well back in the shadows of a darkened alcove on Kaerntner Strasse. He had waited there, motionless, for well over an hour, his soldier's training rendering him indifferent to the damp cold that seeped through his coat. He was positioned across the street within easy pistol shot of the American Express office.

The street was all but deserted at this hour and a wet mist hung in the air. It slightly obscured his view but enhanced his invisibility, and he was pleased with his vantage point. With luck, he would be able to kill both of his targets quickly and cleanly with no witnesses.

It was nearing 11:30 PM and a lone pedestrian,

a woman, hurried down the street.   She passed his concealment without noticing him and disappeared around a corner.

Finally, precisely at 11:30 Drozhdov's patience was rewarded. A short man, heavily muffled against the cold and wearing a Russian shapka appeared at the American Express office and began pacing nervously in small circles. This must be the traitor, Stankov. A few moments later, a tall man wearing a trenchcoat emerged from a doorway up the street, startling Drozhdov who had not seen the man arrive. *How long have you been waiting there, my friend?*

The tall man crossed the street and walked past Stankov, who then turned and followed him at a discreet distance. Decent tradecraft. Now for the chase. Drozhdov grasped the pistol in his pocket and followed them. Ten minutes later, the tall man stopped on a deserted side street and waited for Stankov to catch up. The little Russian scuttled up to him and they began speaking. How convenient, thought Drozhdov. Now just stay together for a few more seconds, my dears. It will all be over for you in a moment.

The assassin crept silently to a corner position across the street from his targets and took careful aim, bracing his pistol against the side of the building. At this distance, even with the silencer, he knew he couldn't miss.

He squeezed the trigger.

CHAPTER 19

Bloody Valentine, February 14

The weather was perfect for a clandestine meeting. A nearly freezing light rain, little more than a mist, had been falling all evening, making the cobbled streets slippery and limiting visibility. There were few people out at this time of night, and that made counter-surveillance easier. I stood in a shadowed doorway watching as Sasha made her way slowly down Kaerntner Strasse past the American Express office. My watch read precisely 11:20 PM

I remained where I was until a man muffled in a heavy coat and wearing a Russian style fur *shapka* pulled far down over his head moved from north to south on the street and took up position in front of the American Express office where he shifted nervously from foot to foot. It was Stankov without a doubt. I said a silent prayer of thanks.

The crystallized moisture softened the outlines of the buildings in the haloed glare of the streetlamps as I crossed the street diagonally toward Stankov. He looked ready to bolt at the slightest hint of danger, but his fear dissolved when he recognized me. It was always this way: momentary fear erased by relief. How many times had I seen it happen?

I led the little Russian into a side street off of the normally busy Kaerntner Strasse and then north in the general direction of St. Stephen's Cathedral. We trudged slowly in the misty rain, one following the other, for several minutes until I stopped and waited for Stankov to catch up.

*****

In the shadows Sasha had re-joined the bulky man and together they observed the initial contact. The American walked past the Russian who followed him away from the lights of the tourist area. The dark figure of a third man clad in a heavy topcoat and fedora detached itself from the shadows on the other side of the street and hurried after, maintaining his distance and hugging the buildings that lined the sidewalk so he would not be seen should either the American or the Russian look back.

Sasha and her companion looked at one another in astonishment and quickly fell in behind the procession.

*****

Stankov rushed to catch up.

"Privyet, Sergey," I said, extending a hand. Stankov fervently grasped it.

"Harry, *ya ochen' rad tebya videt'*. I'm very happy to see you."

He was breathing heavily, and the familiar stench of cheap cognac hit me in the face as he embraced me in the Russian fashion.

"You have come to take me to the United States, yes?"

I wished I had a back-up location where we could have a long sit-down, but I was on my own with no local support, and safehouses don't grow on trees.

"You met a colleague of mine not long ago, Sergey. Tell me what happened at that meeting."

Stankov's eyes flooded with uncertainty.

"You do not know what information I provided? That is not why you are here? I was sure you would recognize the value of this information immediately."

He shuffled a step back, eyes wide.

"Let's go over it again, Sergey. What did you pass to my colleague?"

"The disk ... It contained the complete list ..." His voice faltered. "You did not receive the disk?"

"I did not."

So Stankov had passed information to Thackery on a computer disk – information worth a man's life.

"Do you have a duplicate? Are you aware that your Embassy has put out a missing persons report on you?"

"Harry, I do not understand. *Nie ponimayu.* I

expected you to be prepared to extract me when you saw the contents of the disk. I finally got the information you wanted me to get all those years ago in Berlin!"

He smiled ingratiatingly, extending a hand to grasp my elbow.

"The young man who met me before said something incomprehensible about ending our arrangement, but I told him it is too dangerous now for me ever to return to Moscow and that he must get the information to you personally. I told him you had promised that I could go to the United States.

"By now they must have discovered what I have done. They probably knew even before I arrived in Vienna. You promised you would take me to the United States. I have risked everything to get this information to you, and you tell me you do not realize the importance of what I have given you?"

Was this just a pretext for Stankov to defect to the good life in the US he had always desired? If so, he had certainly waited a long time to make his move, and he had developed impressive acting skills. Or had he waited until he actually possessed information he thought would justify the action?

Stankov's voice squeaked as tension constricted his throat, "I have to disappear. They must be after me. You must help!"

"Sergey, as I said: I don't have the foggiest idea what you are talking about."

"But what about *Voskreseniye*? I told your courier to hand the disk personally only to you."

Stankov had a loftier vision of my position and influence than was justified by reality.

"Sergey, the 'courier' was killed before he could get your information to me."

This was brutal, but I needed to stop Stankov's babbling and get him to the point. "Do you have another copy?"

The Russian started violently, and he swiveled his head peering into the misty shadows that surrounded us.

"Of course, I have a copy. I've not been without a copy since I left Moscow. But you've got to get me out of here. How was your courier compromised? If *Voskreseniye* knew of him they knew of me! They will try to kill me now!"

I couldn't argue with the logic, especially in light of what Jake had told me about a mole. But I had seen this sort of panic in agents before. The accepted practice is to stall for time while reassuring them of their security and the case officer's ability to protect them no matter what. On most occasions such reassurances are nothing but bullshit.

*****

Sasha and her companion had taken opposite sides of

the street, always keeping Connolly's furtive pursuer in sight. Forced to hold back or risk discovery, they watched as the man moved stealthily towards the corner where the American and the Russian had turned into a side street a few moments earlier. The man leaned forward to see around the corner and then reached beneath his coat and withdrew something that glinted in the gauzy light as he braced his arm against the side of the building.

Sasha's companion charged forward at a dead run, no doubt in his mind as to what was about to happen. As he neared the corner he heard a sound with which he was familiar – the soft plopping report of a silenced pistol.

CHAPTER 20

Wet Night

Stankov's panicked calf's eyes glinted in the half-light, his fingers still clutching my arm. I was considering how best to put him at ease when his face disintegrated showering me with bloody fragments of bone and brain.

Startled and half blinded by the blood, I froze for a split second as Stankov's hand fell from my arm and his body crumpled in slow motion to the wet pavement.

*****

As he surged from the shadows to charge across the narrow street Yevgeniy Drozhdov noted with satisfaction the results of his perfectly placed shot. The 147 grain sub-sonic round had performed exactly as expected on the Russian traitor, and Drozhdov now brought the silenced 9-mm Walther P99QA to bear on the American intelligence officer whom he expected to be paralyzed by shock and surprise. He would be an easy target.

*****

When confronted by a life or death situation the flight or fight reflex usually has a happier result when flight takes precedence, but having the time to make such a decision is a rare luxury. Pilots are trained to ignore their natural reactions when confronted by an emergency in the cockpit just as soldiers are conditioned to ignore the instinct for self-preservation in battle. At times like these the mind locks fear away and pre-conditioning takes over. Thought is not involved because by the time you think about it, you're dead.

I heard the "crick" of a slug chipping concrete from the building behind me as I hit the pavement, and my peripheral vision caught the glint of a pistol barrel, elongated by a silencer, being lowered in my direction. I cocked my leg and launched a vicious straight legged kick at the assailant's knee, striking it with my heel and was rewarded by the satisfying crunch of foot connecting with bone. There was a sharp grunt of pain and the pistol clattered to the sidewalk as the owner of the cracked knee went down hard. I rolled in the direction the pistol had fallen stretching out a hand to grasp it.

A heavy weight landed on top of me, driving the breath from my lungs. There was a knee in the small of my back, and my head was jerked sharply backward by a strong arm curled around my neck. I strained against the agonizing pressure. No fragmentary scenes from my life flashed before my eyes – only a tiny, whiny voice somewhere in the back of my mind whimpering that I was about to die.

I gave up groping for the fallen weapon and clawed at the arm locked around my neck, but the guy was too strong. I noticed with peculiar detachment that I was beginning to experience tunnel vision as my brain was deprived of oxygen-giving blood. The whiny voice went silent as my vision shrank to a point of light.

CRACK!

It should have been the sound of my own neck snapping, but my vision inexplicably began to clear, and I could breathe again. The weight on my back now felt more dead than alive.

I looked up to see Sasha looking on anxiously while someone else hauled the inert killer off my back.

Rising unsteadily to my knees on the wet sidewalk I looked to the side and saw the attacker stretched full length with blood spilling from the side of his head. A very large man wearing a satisfied expression stood over the unconscious form. The street remained otherwise silent and deserted in the chill rain.

I heaved myself to my feet with Sasha's help and staggered over to Stankov's body. In the movies when someone is shot in the head a neat red hole appears in the forehead. That's not what a bullet really does. One side of Stankov's head had been all but obliterated.

"Shit," I thought.

CHAPTER 21

New Friends

The assailant groaned and began to push himself up from the pavement, but Sasha's large and as yet mute companion calmly bent down and whacked him with the barrel of an automatic pistol.

While the big man was thus occupied, I knelt and rolled Stankov over onto his back, causing more brain matter and blood to spill onto the wet sidewalk. Stifling a gag, I methodically searched the corpse's pockets. I retrieved every item I found, including a small, flat packet from the inside pocket of the Russian's suit jacket.   There was something tiny and hard inside, and I pocketed it before Sasha or her friend could see it.

Over my shoulder I saw Sasha remove what looked like a Smith & Wesson Model 642, a compact but deadly weapon, from the pocket of her long Loden coat. She made a visual sweep of the area to make sure no one was in sight. She was no innocent amateur.

 Her companion barked something at her in whatever language they shared, and she replaced the gun in her pocket. The assailant's pistol still lay where it had fallen, and since everyone in my immediate vicinity was armed to the teeth, I picked it up. Sasha's companion observed me balefully but made no move to stop me as I dropped the pistol into my coat pocket.

As more cylinders began to fire in my brain, an idea eddied to the surface. Sasha had turned to leave on whatever errand her companion had given her, and I grabbed her by the elbow.

"Wait. Help me with this first."

I began removing the clothing from the corpse as she approached.

She asked with a hint of distaste, "What are you doing?"

"I'm buying us some time," I croaked. My throat hurt, and my voice was barely audible over the rain. "His clothes are Russian. Without them and without a head, it'll be hard to identify the body, at least for a while. The authorities won't turn to the Russians for a fingerprint trace if they have no reason to think that he was Russian. This will confuse the trail and hold up the investigation. With luck, we may be able to hold the bad guys at bay, as well, at least until they miss our new buddy here."

Sasha knelt to help, and soon we had all of poor Stankov's sweaty and gory clothes rolled into a bundle that she carried as she rushed away to be swallowed by the mist.

She returned in a relatively new Skoda automobile that she left with its motor running near the Capuchin Church. Her large friend effortlessly wrestled the limp assailant from the sidewalk and dragged him to the waiting car. He and Sasha bound him and staunched the flow of blood from his head. The guy had likely been concussed, possibly seriously.

I hoped so.

Before I got into the car I took one last look back toward Stankov's pitiful, naked corpse, now only dimly visible through the mist and rain, a pasty white splotch on the sidewalk leaking crimson streaks into the gutter.

I had put him there as surely as I if I had put the bullet in his brain. He would no longer drink too much nor drive too recklessly, and he would never reach the golden shores of the United States. I wondered where his wife was and whether his son had been proud of him. Had he planned to take them with him, or had he dreamt of a fresh start, to re-make himself into a new Stankov?

"We need to talk to this guy," I rasped, nodding toward the prisoner. "Is there somewhere safe we can take him?"

Control of the situation was quickly slipping away. Volodya's contact in Vienna was proving to be unexpectedly resourceful.

I sat in the front passenger seat with Sasha behind the wheel and my mysterious savior in the back with the unconscious assassin. The large man spoke rapidly into his cell phone in the same unknown language and then related something to Sasha. She navigated the Skoda onto the Shotten Ring and turned onto Wahringer Strasse, and finally into a quiet neighborhood in the Wahring District. After a few moments we passed through large iron gates that had swung open at our approach. A brass plaque was affixed to the wall: *Botschaft des Staates Israel.*

We were in the Israeli Embassy compound.

The wilderness of mirrors was rapidly morphing into Alice's looking glass.

CHAPTER 22

The Basement

Drozhdov was naked and bound to a sturdy wooden chair, constrained by heavy leather straps around his chest; his forearms were secured to the wide, flat arms of the chair, and his legs were similarly rendered immobile. The chair itself was bolted to a bare concrete floor.

He squeezed his eyes against the blinding light that shone directly into his face and was overcome momentarily by nausea. He suspected he was concussed as he struggled to concentrate.

There was a scrape of shoes on concrete, but he could make out no more than the outline of a man in the gloom just beyond the light's glare. The figure disappeared for a moment and then re-appeared at his the right side.

Something extended from the darkness glinting heavy and metallic as it entered the cone of bright light. It moved like some feral animal toward his right hand that lay flat, splayed against the broad wooden arm of the chair. He stared, mesmerized as his sight came into focus and he recognized the object as a large, curved pair of sharp pincers now positioned at the second knuckle of his trigger finger.

In a single, sudden movement, the pincers closed

over his finger completely severing it at the knuckle. The shock was great, and it did not take long for new pain to be added to that in already his head, and he screamed. Screaming was good. It released the pressure and emotion brought on by pain. He knew this. His training had taught him this. If he could just concentrate enough on his reaction to the torture, direct his anger, he could survive.

A voice reached him then, close to his ear, speaking in German. He could feel the breath of the speaker.

"That was just to get your attention, murderer."

Drozhdov passed out.

A bucket of ice-cold water was thrown into his face, and the voice reached him again.

"Wer bist du? Who are you?" The voice was guttural, heavy and menacing in his ear.

Drozhdov said nothing. The language was German, which meant they did not know he was Russian. His Spetsnaz training had prepared him for torture, and he could resist, he told himself, he could resist until they killed him. He clinched his teeth against the pain and remained silent.

His tormentor extended the pincers still dripping blood before his eyes.

"Pay attention now to what I say. There is one rule and one rule only in this conversation: one question, one answer. No answer or the wrong answer and you lose something else. There will be no exceptions."

The pincers were placed swiftly over the middle finger of Drozhdov's right hand next to the profusely bleeding stump of his trigger finger. Once again Drozhdov experienced the sound of metal rasping on metal as it sliced through flesh and bone. The severed finger fell to the floor beside the Russian's bound feet. He screamed again as he watched the blood spurt from the two stumps. He looked up; his face contorted, but still he could see nothing through the blinding light.

"Fuck you!"

Again the calm voice reached him from the darkness.

"Now I will give you some time to think. I'll be back in a little while."

The light was extinguished, and he was left alone in total darkness with the coppery scent of his own blood filling his nostrils. He had never felt so helpless and desperate in his life. He didn't pray because he didn't believe in God.

He was beginning, however, to believe in Hell.

CHAPTER 23

Small Talk

A man had waited at the side of the building with a gurney onto which they heaved Stankov's unconscious killer and trundled him away through large metal double doors that closed with a clang worthy of the gates of Hell.

As bollixed as this was, there was a bright side – Harry Connolly was worse for wear, but still alive.

It was important to determine the identity of the killer and who he represented. I was not a fingernail yanking kind of guy, but I needed one now. Sasha's large friend looked like he might be just what the doctor ordered, so to speak, especially if he represented Israeli intelligence.

A somberly dressed middle-aged woman, her hair pulled tightly back in a bun, led us inside and up a short flight of stairs and through a plush carpeted hallway to a small but tastefully decorated sitting room containing two sofas facing one another across a coffee table with a highly polished marble top. There was a large richly framed oil painting of Golda Meir on one wall that flattered the former Prime Minister's well-known but homely visage. Our guide indicated that we should sit, an invitation most welcome to my battered body.

We waited in silence, me, ragged and mystified,

Sasha with a Mona Lisa smile on her face, and Golda Meir regarding us like a benign grandmother. I almost expected an offer of chicken soup.

Sasha performed the formalities when her companion re-joined us. "Harry Connolly, this is Eitan Ronan."

The man possessed a broad frame atop which, mounted like a tank turret, sat a massive square head with closely cropped black hair liberally salted with gray, and bushy brows that sheltered slits that were home to vivid blue eyes.

I rose to shake his extended paw and then, again feeling the exhaustion, sank back onto the sofa. Ronan removed his jacket to reveal a tight-fitting black pullover stretched over a torso that would have been the envy of any pro football player. It didn't take a genius to guess that he belonged to the Israeli military or the Mossad.

Having insured that we were comfortably installed, Ronan excused himself and disappeared through the door.

Sasha took note of the sorry state of my hands and clothing and showed me through a short hallway off the sitting room to a white-tiled bathroom where I gratefully washed the dried gore from my hands and splashed cold water on my face. In the mirror a bleary-eyed stranger looked back at me with shocked eyes. It took a few moments to calm my breathing and I splashed more cold water on my face before returning to the sitting room. Our silent hostess was just placing a tray with a tea service on the table.

The fact that I was conscious meant that I was only just a little less confused than the guy with the bashed in head they had hauled away on the gurney. Until the Israelis had interfered, he and I had been perfectly aware of what was going on: I was meeting Stankov, and the other guy was trying to kill us. We each had a job we understood. I couldn't get Lewis Carroll out of my mind. Now we were down the rabbit hole, and I wondered how Stankov's killer was handling his encounter with the Mad Hatter.

Sasha had removed her Loden coat, and her dark gray, knit dress defined some not entirely unexpected curves. Her controlled demeanor led me to revise the estimate of her age to somewhere between late twenties and mid-thirties. She filled two cups with hot tea and sat back, crossing her long, boots-encased legs. She looked splendid.

The fact that I ached all over, was disheveled, in other words looked like crap, as I sat within three feet of this extremely attractive young woman did nothing to improve my disposition. My trousers were torn at the knee baring a shin still bleeding from the collision with the sidewalk. My neck hurt like hell from having been twisted nearly off my shoulders. This was not the most propitious moment for long dormant hormones to kick in, but the little devils had certainly been stirred to unaccustomed wakefulness.

My head hurt from more than the pounding it had taken. A discreet mission to Vienna to gather information quietly had instead produced the sudden death of

Stankov on a public street, a deadly attack on me, and the completely inexplicable involvement of the Israelis.

Sasha asked, "Would you like some milk in your tea?"

When I looked up she was leaning solicitously across the table, creamer in hand.

"No, thanks," I croaked, my voice was still raspy from the assault on my throat.

I needed to get my bearings.

"What are we doing at the Israeli Embassy, Sasha?"

Her eyes went wide and innocent. I wondered if this was learned behavior or something all women are born with so they can disarm brutish men at will. I decided they were born with it.

"You said we needed a safe place to question the attacker." She said this as if choosing the Israeli Embassy as a safe haven were the most natural thing in the world.

"Yeah, but to repeat, what are we doing at the Israeli Embassy, and where did your big buddy, Ronan, come from?"

"Eitan thought he should become directly involved after we learned of your reason for being here."

Everybody seemed to know more than I did. I silently cursed Jake Liebowitz.

"And how did you learn that?"

"From your friend Volodya, of course."

Of course -- her tone was matter of fact.

"Given what happened I should think you would be grateful that he brought us in. Had Eitan not been there ..." Her voice trailed off, but I knew what she meant – I would have died next to Stankov.

"You gave the all-clear signal when you walked down *Kaertner Strasse*. What was that all about? You didn't see that goon on Stankov's tail?"

"Oh, we saw him all right, but only after you had made contact. He wasn't following your man, at all. He knew exactly where the meeting was to take place and obviously was waiting for you. Eitan decided we should let you go ahead with the meeting and see what happened."

"It just seemed like a good idea to let me walk into a trap?"

My frustration definitely was moving in the direction of highly pissed off.

"A man was killed, for Christ's sake!"

Sasha lost a fraction of her composure and sipped her tea to avoid meeting my eyes.

"It was already too late to stop the meeting. The assassin had already found you. Eitan will explain it to you," she said and lapsed into silence.

So much for small talk. There was no way the Israeli could explain to my satisfaction playing with our lives. But I had begun to consider another problem.

No one other than Jake, Volodya Smetanin, and (thanks to Volodya) the Israelis should have known I was in Vienna. It was possible that the killer had been on Stankov's trail and had caught up with him just at the time of our meeting. I didn't automatically have to accept what the Israelis said – far from it, as a matter of fact. Such neat timing, however, would have required a lot of coincidences, and to belabor a hackneyed expression, I don't believe in coincidences.

What had the Russian possessed that Moscow Center wanted badly enough to kill for? And if they only wanted to kill Stankov, why wait until he was meeting with me? And why had my old friend Volodya invited the Israelis to the dance?

All I had was questions.

Just as my brain was beginning really to hurt, Eitan Ronan returned and dragged a chair to the table. His expression was sour, as if he had a bad taste in his mouth. He studied me solemnly for several seconds before speaking.

"Mr. Connolly," he rumbled in his Middle Eastern accent. "I must apologize for my lack of manners. I had some immediate business to attend to downstairs with our new friend."

The Israeli was well-tanned, unusual for a Vienna-based individual, especially in winter, and there was something red under his fingernails.

"You seem quite well informed about me."

"Harold Bradley Connolly, 45 years old, senior CIA field operative, multi-lingual, Vietnam combat veteran ..."

"OK, OK," I held up a hand, annoyed. "I get the point. Why don't you tell me something I don't already know? For example ..."

The Israeli interrupted. "All of that in good time, I promise. Right now, don't you think it would be a good idea for us to examine the items you removed from Stankov's body?"

CHAPTER 24

Moscow, February 15

Shurgin joined Morozov in the latter's sumptuous office on the exclusive 23rd floor of the SVR Headquarters central tower at "The Forest." He stood at the window overlooking the surrounding heavily wooded countryside in the direction of the Ring Road, his hands behind his back. Snow had fallen again, and the laden branches of the fir trees drooped under the weight.

Morozov picked up a dispatch that rested squarely in the middle of his desk and held it up to the light in his meaty hand. Shurgin turned as Morozov read the message.

"Has he been eliminated?"

"We don't know."   Morozov furrowed his brow. "Drozhdov has not reported, and we have had no contact with him since we passed him the details of the CIA contact plan. He had to move quickly and with little time to prepare."

Shurgin considered this and shrugged.

"Drozhdov is a highly capable and disciplined officer. He will report when he has news for us."

"Perhaps we should send him some help," ventured

Morozov.

"No!" Shurgin was adamant. "This activity must remain strictly compartmentalized. The Rezident in Vienna is not one of us, and I don't want our other friends involved unless absolutely necessary. This operation must remain entirely within the purview of Directorate S. This will not change." He turned back to the window. "You know better than most," he said, his eyes following the contrails of a jet high overhead in the pale winter sky, "what is at stake, Yuriy Ivanovich. As I said, Drozhdov is capable. He'll report when he can. We know about the CIA officer, Connolly, sent to find Stankov. Stankov, the little shit, will be desperate by now. He will appear at the meeting point because he has nowhere else to go. If Drozhdov hasn't eliminated him within a few days, we have your other options in reserve. For the moment a subtle approach is our best option."

Morozov was not reassured. "I'm still concerned about killing a second CIA officer. This could have consequences."

Shurgin smiled. His quick fox mind already had analyzed the situation and weighed the possible consequences.

"You know why it must be done as well as I. His death will serve a good purpose. Don't worry. Our plan will yield success. There will be no consequences. The objective circumstances have changed from the Cold War days. Mother Russia is threatened by the Americans and their allies from all sides even more than before, and I don't give a fuck how many of them we kill. They don't have the balls to retaliate in any case. They'd rather just talk."

The absence of news was nettlesome but not unusual. Officers on field assignment were expected to be self-sufficient, and Drozhdov had been handpicked by Morozov himself for this "wet work." He had been inserted into the West for just such a mission as this – to protect their most valuable secret.

CHAPTER 25

Israeli Embassy, February 15 – 1:30 AM

The contents of Stankov's pockets and the items taken from our captive lay in two neat piles on the coffee table. Not included was the small, flat packet I had surreptitiously retrieved from the deceased Russian's coat pocket. I saw no reason to reveal its existence to the Israelis.

Stankov's items included a passport, a ratty wallet containing 2,500 Austrian schillings, a surprisingly large roll of US currency that when we counted it came to nearly 5,000 U.S dollars, and a couple of old photos, one of which I recognized as Stankov's wife whose birthday dinner I had paid for so long ago in Berlin. The other showed a thin boy about 12 years old at a beach that looked like it might be Sochi. This would be Stankov's son, who had to be somewhere in his mid-teens by now.

There also was a key with a tag that identified it as belonging to a room in an obscure hostel in Leopoldstadt in the Second District near the city's center. One of us would have to pay a visit to Stankov's room.

Our basement "guest's" pocket litter revealed little. There was a key attached to a flat plastic fob that announced it belonged to a rented BMW along with a parking garage claim ticket. The wallet held documentation identifying him as Helmut Reidl of Munich, assorted credit cards in the same name, and about 500 Deutschmarks in cash. "Reidl" was probably an alias, but would be checked out nonetheless by Eitan's counterpart in Germany. There was no clue as to where the thug might have been staying in Vienna. Perhaps they would find something in the car.

"There is nothing here worth a man's life," said Eitan. "Nevertheless, two men now have been murdered, almost three." He squinted at me. "Would you care to hazard a guess as to what this is all about?"

I decided there was nothing to lose by sharing some information.

"Stankov's wad of dollars must have come from his earlier meeting with Thackery, our man who was killed before he could return to Washington. Just before he was shot, Stankov told me he had passed something to Thackery. He seemed to think it was important. What happened tonight substantiates his claim."

"Tell us about Stankov." Eitan clearly expected an answer.

If the phrase 'out in the cold' had any meaning at all, I was now on the edge of the Arctic Circle. Everything I had done in Vienna was unsanctioned, I was already a pariah at CIA Headquarters, no one besides Jake even knew where I was, and the person at the center of all this activity might already lay mutilated and unidentified on a slab in a Vienna morgue. Our prisoner was probably a Russian 'wet work' specialist, and, oh yeah, the Israelis were somehow involved.

Thanks, Jake. Did you tell me everything you know? I suspected the answer was no.

Intelligence services do nothing without a reason, and Mossad had not stepped into this fracas out of the goodness of their steely little hearts. Eitan Ronan had not brought us to the Israeli Embassy just because it was a handy hidey hole. No, this signaled 'official' and purposeful Israeli interest.

"How do the Israelis fit into this, Ronan?"

The grizzled Mossad officer's eyes bored into me, and when he responded, it was not what I wanted to hear, but it was the truth.

"Connolly, you are alone, you are clearly in danger, and you have no one but us to turn to. I would prefer that you not answer a question with another question."

Eitan clearly was an old hand at asking questions but did not excel at answering them.

"Are you threatening me, Ronan? Perhaps I should just leave now." I wondered if they would let me.

The Israeli made "tsk, tsk" sounds and shook his head from side to side.

"We will not stop you, but where will you go? Will you call it a day and return to Washington? Do you believe this is the end of the matter? They tried to kill you tonight, Mr. Connolly, and they could very well try again the second you step out onto the street."

As I considered this pleasant idea, I wondered if

Stankov's little envelope, burning a hole in the pocket of my torn pants, contained the answers to all the questions.

"I understand your hesitation." Ronan leaned toward me and rumbled in his *basso profundo,* "People like you and I do not part with information easily, but I don't think you have a choice if you want to pursue this affair to the end, whatever it might be, and remain alive."

"I'll tell you what: you show me yours, and I'll show you mine."

The Israeli smiled in what he might have imagined was a reassuring manner that actually came off as mildly threatening. I suspected that his range of facial expressions was limited.

If Ronan shared any information it would be just enough to achieve his own goal, whatever it was. As a matter of fact, that was my plan, too. Evidently Volodya had shared with the Israelis everything I had told him in Paris, and that gave Ronan an advantage.

But I still had Stankov's little packet. It might contain nothing or everything. I would keep its existence to myself until I could examine the contents – unless Ronan decided to search me.

"His name was Sergey Mikhailovich Stankov. The last I knew of him, he was working as a mid-level official at Gosbank in Moscow. I don't know what information he passed to Thackery, and nor does anyone else, except maybe that goon we brought in and whoever is pulling his strings. We had had no contact with Stankov for several years, and his file had been retired. The only reason Thackery came out to see him was to terminate him – amicably - and pay him off. As I said, that's where the roll of dollars we found came from. He told Thackery to take something personally to me, but I'm guessing that Thackery thought it was all rubbish designed to keep Stankov on the payroll or entice us to defect him. He was instructed to terminate the Russian, and he did it. He took off for a skiing holiday, and I doubt he even looked at whatever Stankov gave him."

Ronan rubbed his chin, fingers rasping against thick, black stubble.

"Your officer thought a personal ski holiday was more important than reporting to Headquarters? There was no reaction at CIA? There were no official inquiries?"

"I'm afraid not. They want to keep it quiet."

Ronan shook his head. "Perhaps some action was taken at the highest level, something you would know nothing about."

"I don't think so. You didn't see anyone besides me and our nasty assassin looking for Stankov did you? Perhaps you were looking for him too, though?"

The Israeli took a sip of tea. Ignoring the question, he asked, "What exactly did Stankov say to you before he was shot?"

"He thought I was here to extract him. He couldn't believe I had not received the package he passed to Thackery. He referred to a disk, probably a computer disk. When I informed him that the courier had been killed he said that we must have a leak somewhere, that someone was after him, and that it was vital that I take care of him. He didn't have time to say any more than that."

Eitan nodded, "I fear he may be correct about a leak. Did he say anything else, anything more specific?"

"Such as?"

Eitan slapped his knee in exasperation. "<u>Words</u>, Mr. Connolly! What were his <u>exact</u> words?"

I remembered something Stankov had said that had seemed out of place.

"He asked, 'What about *Voskreseniye?*' I don't know what he meant. The word means 'Sunday' in Russian. Maybe he was expecting something to happen on Sunday."

Ronan went very still.

Sasha spoke up for the first time, "Are you a Christian, Mr. Connolly?"

I was nonplussed by the *non-sequitur* and must have shown it. "Sort of." My mother had given me a good Methodist upbringing.

"You speak Russian very well. Tell me, what else does that Russian word mean in the context of Christianity?"

"*Voskreseniye* also means 'Resurrection.'"

Sasha nodded.

Ronan smiled broadly. "Exactly."

"I think it's time for you to show me yours, Ronan."

CHAPTER 26

Southern Spain, February 14

Fourteen hundred miles away from Vienna and many hours earlier the bullet train eased with a hiss of brakes into Seville's ultra-modern Santa Justa Station. Arkadkiy Nikolayevich Yudin awoke from his nap in his First Class compartment and stood to retrieve his expensive leather luggage from the rack above his seat. He carried his bag to the car park where he retrieved his Mercedes 600 SEL and settled into the soft leather for the 135 kilometer drive to his home near Marbella.

He was tired from the two unexpected trips to Madrid and would be happy to return to his seaside villa. His schedule called for him to meet some bankers in Cyprus the following week, providing this thing with the Center was cleared up by then, but for now he wanted to get home to Barbara, his twenty something Spanish mistress. Arkadiy stepped on the gas and the sedan leapt smoothly forward as anticipation of his homecoming elicited an urgent tumescence between his thighs.

Forty-five minutes later he pulled into his cobbled drive, the automatic iron gates clanging shut behind him. Leaving his luggage in the trunk, he almost sprinted to the front door. Once inside he strode directly to the back of the house towards the huge terrace that faced upon the Mediterranean. He could see Barbara through the sliding glass door reclined in a chaise longue by the pool taking in the last rays of the strong Andalusian sun. She wore only a thong, her ample breasts pointing majestically skyward, nipples erect in the cooling afternoon air.

The throbbing between Arkadkiy's legs became more urgent as his distended manhood stretched the fabric of his trousers. Not for the first time the Russian reflected that young girls were the best aphrodisiac. Barbara heard the door slide open and turned to see the stocky form of a rampant Arkadkiy pitching toward her, his arms outstretched. She did not love the burly 50-year-old Russian, but she did greatly appreciate the fact that he was fabulously wealthy, showered her with expensive gifts, and provided her with a luxurious house that was the envy of her friends. Barbara was a "modern" uninhibited Spanish girl of the 90's to whom sex was a pleasant uncomplicated activity and, often as not, a means to an end.

She stood and met Arkadkiy's onrush accepting his fierce kiss. While his hand fondled and squeezed her breasts, Barbara deftly unzipped Arkadkiy's trousers and freed his heavy member. Arkadkiy groaned as she fell to her knees and took him into her mouth. "Not so fast, *krasavitsa*," he panted. He picked her up bodily and carried her back to the chaise where, pulling the thong aside, he went to his knees and entered her. After only a few lusty thrusts, he ejaculated and collapsed heavily upon her.

"I missed you," he said.

Laughing, Barbara stood and stripped the thong down her leg, turned and dove into the pool. Rising to the surface and floating on her back she said, "Obviously you did, *mi oso grande*. You know I hate it when you are away on these silly business trips. Where do you go all the time? I'll bet you have some other girl somewhere."

"I would have lasted longer, *krasavitsa moya*, if I had been with another woman before coming home." Arkadkiy knew she was only teasing him.

"Will you take me to the casino tonight?" Barbara asked. "We could have dinner afterwards."

"Not tonight. I'm still tired from all this damned traveling. I got off the train less than an hour ago." He now felt truly spent and wanted nothing more than a shower and a shot of iced vodka.

"But, *osito*, I bought a new dress yesterday. I look very beautiful in it. You will be the envy of all the other men. Please take me out. I've been cooped up here in the house for nearly a week!"

"Not so cooped up that you could not get out and buy a new dress." Arkadkiy could not keep his eyes off of her naked body, still floating easily in the pool, her long jet black hair fanned in the water. "I prefer you just the way you are, my sweet, and I don't want to go out tonight. I am too tired."

He could see that the girl was disappointed. "Perhaps I have something that will make you happy to stay at home tonight," he teased. Zipping his trousers and straightening his clothes, he walked to where he had dropped his briefcase and extracted a long, elegant box. He held it up to the girl could see it from the water. "Oooh, a Valentine's present!" she squealed, paddled to the ladder and climbed out of the pool. She grabbed a large towel to wrap around herself.

"Ah, Ah," scolded Arkadkiy with a leer. "I won't give it to you as long as you are wearing that towel."

Posing prettily, Barbara allowed the towel to drop and then approached Arkadkiy. He handed the box to her and she quickly opened it. The diamonds of the bracelet sparkled in the slanting rays of the fading sun, and Barbara caught her breath. The bracelet was at least three centimeters wide, and the diamonds of best quality. This was a bauble that could support her for a long time, if ever needs be. She made all the appropriate noises and pressed her damp body against the Russian. "Very well, *mi osito*, we will stay at home tonight. Now, you go take a shower, and I will prepare a Spanish tortilla and a salad for you. I have some excellent Albariño in the fridge."

Arkadkiy squeezed one of her breasts and went back into the house. Women! He thought. They're so simple to understand. Dangle something shiny in front of them and they're sucking your cock before you know it! In this case, he had picked up the latest shiny bauble in Zurich for 125,000 Swiss francs.

CHAPTER 27

Arkadiy Nikolayevich

Just four years ago Arkadkiy Nikolayevich Yudin had been an economic advisor to the Moscow City Government. He was a highly trained graduate of the Soviet Union's Mining Institute, Gosplan's Higher Economic School. Married with two children, his annual state salary had been less than $5,000. His fat Russian wife and the two brats were still living in Moscow, and he was glad they were so far away. Fortunately, though she might imagine the debaucheries committed by her husband in Spain, Mrs. Yudin was happily ensconced in a fancy new apartment with all the conveniences and a chauffeured Volvo.

Little more than two years after the fall of the Berlin Wall, Boris Yeltsin and a group of comrades dissolved the Soviet Union -- on December 8, 1991. The action was illegal, of course, but it solidified their power and emasculated the already weakened Communist Party of the Soviet Union.

Now the Russian economy was shattered. Price reforms and the premature imposition of a "free" market had rapidly wiped out personal savings and impoverished the Russian populace. People were on the streets trying to sell their most precious possessions so they could buy *enough bread to survive.*

But tragedy for some is always opportunity for others, and another of the fledgling "democratic" government's ill-considered reforms opened the gates for an all-out pillaging of the country's most precious assets by those clever enough to seize the opportunity, and Yudin was very clever, indeed.

The very nature of the old Soviet system had been to "rationalize" the means of production through the creation of specialized manufacturing sectors, i.e. state monopolies. In the Soviet era, the Russian economy had ranked third in the world behind the US and Japan. Yeltsin's privatization of industry led to economic chaos and the devaluation of the monetary worth of all of Mother Russia's industrial and natural resource wealth to a mere five billion dollars. As a result vast, unimaginable wealth was up for grabs at lower than fire sale prices, and only a few strategically placed individuals were in a position to take advantage of the situation.

Yudin knew a gift horse when he saw one, and his Moscow city government position gave him contacts and access. His stratagem was not uncommon. As soon as it was permitted he formed a private trading company and with the connivance of friends in the vast Russian mining complex, he was soon buying Russian zinc and other ores for which he paid cheap Russian prices and exporting them to the West for sale through a broker in Switzerland at world prices. His usual profit was well over 100%. These profits were placed in a safe account in Zug, Switzerland.

Yudin calculated that his current personal net worth was in the neighborhood of $500,000,000.

Along the way he became more than proficient in the arcane financial practices of Switzerland, Liechtenstein, and the Cayman Islands. He also made some interesting friends along the way, certain of whom he could not refuse when they demanded his help. Next week he would fly to Moscow to meet them.

CHAPTER 28

Israeli Embassy, February 15 – 2:00 AM

Ronan took his time extracting a Gauloise Caporal from its distinctive blue pack and lighting it. He inhaled deeply and released a cloud of acrid smoke before asking, "What do you know about what is happening in Russia today?"

"What's happening in Russia? I thought you were going to level with me, Ronan, not continue asking questions."

"All in good time. But first, it is important that we establish a common basis for discussion. Now, I'll repeat the question: what is your understanding of the present situation in Russia?"

I inferred that the Israeli intended to determine whether he was dealing with a fool or someone who could handle the facts. I decided to play along.

"It's a mess, especially after the failed coup attempt on Gorbachev last year. Yeltsin's a drunk. He's surrounded by toadies and cronies. The economy is out of control. Peoples' savings have evaporated. The social structure is falling apart. Criminal gangs are running rampant. Moscow is worse than Chicago in the '20's and '30's. People are murdered regularly on the streets. There is nothing in stores for people to buy. Lives are being destroyed."

Ronan nodded, satisfied with the answer. "But fortunes also are being made, would you not agree?"

"Sure, but not much of it is staying in Mother Russia from what I hear."

"That is not entirely true. Generally speaking, there is a lot of criminal or at best semi-criminal activity facilitated by official venality and weak laws. But there is much more at stake than personal gain, and much that is structured and politically purposeful."

"You have my attention, Ronan."

The Israeli lowered his voice and continued, "Did you know that all the foreign reserves of Russia were depleted by the end of 1990? Nearly thirty billion dollars in gold and securities disappeared into thin air. Poof! Like that!" He snapped his fingers. "Likewise the cash and gold reserves of the Central Committee of the Communist Party mysteriously vanished, at least another twenty billion dollars. In other words, while the entire gamut of Soviet industrial and natural resources were on the auctioneer's block ridiculously under-valued at around five billion dollars, ten times that amount already had disappeared from official coffers. A lot of millionaires have been created in the new Russia, and several billionaires, but somewhere someone is controlling enough money to buy the entire country ten times over. The Russians refer to these assets as the 'Black Treasury.'"

Ronan insisted that with the handwriting on the wall

writ large, the inner circles of the Kremlin and their Praetorian Guard, the KGB, devised a plan to protect their assets and use them eventually to regain power. This was not exactly a Russian "Odessa," such as the Nazis established in the wake of World War II to fund the escapes of prominent war criminals. The Russians were not considering escape. On the contrary, the funds were intended to buy Russian assets on the cheap, to finance the establishment of banks and other funding mechanisms, both inside and outside Russia. The KGB and Communist Party leadership recognized that they could still control Russia if they took advantage of the chaotic breakdown of the economy. Not only did they fund overt financial institutions, they also provided the means by which certain individuals could acquire great wealth so long as they agreed to be controlled. And they were not so fastidious as to avoid involvement in clearly illegal activities designed to drain national resources and hard currency from the country. The KGB funded and controlled criminal gangs and used them to eliminate political and economic competitors or force them to cooperate. Sanctioned murder became a commonplace occurrence in Russia.

With just a few insiders pulling the strings, the funds were used to acquire the real prizes of Russian infrastructure, the keys to controlling the future: vast oil and mineral wealth, natural gas, electronics, automobile production facilities. And when they found that some private individual had beaten them to a prize, he was given the choice of collaboration, imprisonment or death. Greed is a powerful incentive, and many of these individuals refused to cooperate. They discovered that the criminal gangs thought nothing of staging massive shoot-outs in city centers.

"They call themselves '*Voskreseniye Rossii,*' the 'The Resurrection of Russia,' 'Russian Rebirth,' or '*Voskreseniye*' for short," Ronan concluded his dissertation. "We've been aware of them for a long time. As you might imagine many of my, ah, co-religionists were involved in the reorganization of the Russian financial landscape. *Voskreseniye* created literally hundreds of foreign bank accounts and bought controlling interests in many western financial institutions, and in many illegal enterprises. They now control banks and lending institutions and have placed their people in key positions of economic power inside Russia. They control Russia's mineral and petroleum wealth, defense industries, and soon they will have the real prize, Gazprom, within their grasp, as well. Russian gas accounts for a large percentage of Western European energy use. What do you think these fanatics will do with that power?

"There are but a handful of key individuals who know the full extent of the *Voskreseniye* organization's holdings, and even fewer know how to access the money. We know that at least one of these key people lives in Western Europe where he can travel freely to tend to the accounts and other 'business' matters. Some of *Voskreseniye*'s financial dealings are known, of course; it's impossible to keep everything secret, but the full extent of their penetration is unknown. We would like to shut them down."

"Why, Ronan," I asked. "What difference does it make to your people how much money the Russians control?"

If the CIA had downgraded interest in things Russian, it was becoming clear that the Mossad had other ideas.

"Please call me Eitan," he said. "Their money obviously gives them great power, and since when have the Russians ever been friends of the Jews, or of the West, for that matter? The Russians invented the *pogrom* and have gleefully killed Jews throughout their history. These people want to rebuild Russian national power and prestige, and I'm afraid they will turn to their old friends in doing so, and in the process seek to harm their old enemies. You know that the Soviets made huge arms sales in the Middle East, to the Syrians and Iraqis. Before 1989 they wielded enormous influence in the Middle East. About a year ago one of our people in Moscow caught wind of something perhaps even more dangerous, especially to us. That's why I'm here, and it's why you are still alive, my friend."

"Do you mind if I smoke?"

I had discovered an intact Montecristo No. 4 in my jacket pocket. Ronan lit another Caporal as I stoked the stogie. It gave me a moment to reflect on the fact that Stankov had been a banker, and whatever connection he might have had with all this was clearly where the conversation was heading. Fifty billion dollars was certainly motivation enough for the Russians to kill, but how was Stankov a threat to them? Ronan was on a roll, so I did not interrupt him with questions. I was learning a lot, and the Israelis knew nothing about the small packet I had retrieved from Stankov's pocket.

"Please, continue."

"Russian nuclear specialists began to travel back and forth between Moscow and Tehran with great regularity about a year ago, after they began discussing a commercial agreement to rebuild the Bushehr reactors. The Iraqis did serious damage to Iran's nuclear research capabilities when they bombed the Bushehr facility during the Iran-Iraq war in the 80's. They actually bombed it six times. Originally you Americans urged the Iranians to launch a nuclear power program under the Shah, of course with the proviso that American companies should make a lot of money on the deal. Eventually the Germans took over, but that ended shortly after the '79 revolution. The Argentines got involved for a while, but we put pressure on them. The Iranians worked with the Chinese and others, but their program has not noticeably progressed. It now seems that the Russians are willing to supercharge the program's development – <u>with the blessings of your government</u>, Mr. Connolly. In not too many years the Imams will be enriching plutonium and getting close to weaponization. The Iranian program is controlled by the intelligence services and the Revolutionary Guard. They are impossible to penetrate, and now we have Russian experts moving in to help them. Guess where they would target their first nuclear weapon."

I didn't doubt that Ronan's conjecture about Iranian

intentions was correct. "But, even if what you say is true, they're still decades away from achieving the ability to produce a nuke, and Bushehr is not a weapons-oriented facility."

"My friend, would you rather kill a viper when it is hatching from its egg or when it is six feet long? And don't forget that with Russian help the Iranians will make faster progress."

"What does all this have to do with how we ended up in this room this evening?"

"'Follow the money.' Isn't that what you Americans say? Stankov was a banker, but that would not normally raise a red flag. When we learned from your friend in Paris that a CIA officer had been killed after meeting him, Stankov immediately became more interesting to us. His death tonight leads me to believe that he possessed information of vital importance to someone in the *Voskreseniye* organization. But what he knew apparently died with him, isn't that so, Harry?"

Stankov's packet was burning a hole through my pocket. I had to get out of there. I didn't relish the idea of sharing a dungeon cell with the man who had attacked me. For an insane second I actually felt some nostalgia for a frothy latte in the Company cafeteria.

The next phone contact was scheduled for two o'clock Saturday afternoon which would be eight AM in Washington. It was well after midnight now in Vienna.

Ronan was staring at me across the table. It wasn't

a friendly look.

"Ronan, I'm tired and I'm still half in shock. I am truly grateful to you and Sasha for saving my life, but I need some rest and some time to think about what you've told me. I'll try to dredge up something from what I know of Stankov that will help. Nothing that happened tonight explains anything other than that someone had a strong reason to kill Stankov. I agree that he must have known something, but whatever it was probably died with him and Thackery."

Ronan was not a happy camper. He stood abruptly, gesturing to Sasha, and said, "Please excuse us for a moment. I must speak with Sasha privately."

The two left the room, closing the door behind them, but they didn't go far because I could hear their rapid conversation in their own language. They were clearly in disagreement, probably over which torture technique might work best on me. There was an ominous silence before they returned.

Ronan made no attempt to conceal his ill humor.

"I'm very disappointed, Connolly. You owe your life to us. Where I come from, that means something. Apparently you have a different view. Sasha will take you back into town now. We will meet again tomorrow. Right now I have some unfinished business downstairs."

But he didn't leave the room. He just stood there scowling in a way that made me think I was lucky I still had all my fingernails.

Sasha quickly fetched our coats and herded me to the door pursued by Ronan's glare. We traversed a short corridor to the side door into the courtyard where she rushed to the driver's side of the Skoda and was in it before I could move to open the door for her. I sat in the front seat beside her, and without a word she put the car in gear, turned around, and drove through the gates.

CHAPTER 29

Evasion

She stared straight ahead. It was still raining, and the wipers squeaked across the windshield. Before we had gone too many blocks she broke the uncomfortable silence.

"Eitan believes you know more than you are saying, and I agree with him." She shot me a sidewise glance. "He also knows that you are alone and without support from your organization. This is a dangerous position for you."

She was playing me, of course, undoubtedly following Ronan's script.

"That was quite an argument you had with him back there," I said. "What did he want to do? Make me disappear? Pull a couple of fingernails to see what he could find out?"

She shot me an exasperated glance, and I received the distinct impression that she personally had no compunctions about pulling fingernails.

Several months would pass before I would learn about her and Eitan Ronan.

*****

She had been only 12 when her parents were permitted to immigrate to Israel from the Soviet Union in 1971. Her father, an engineer, had found work at a small firm in Jerusalem. They spent two happy years integrating into Israeli society, and then on 6 October 1973, on Yom Kippur, the holiest day of the Jewish year, the armies of Egypt and Syria mounted a coordinated two-front attack on Israel. Sasha's father, in his early forties and a reservist, was immediately called to active duty and assigned to a mechanized unit under Major General Ariel Sharon to repel the Egyptian attack across the Suez Canal into the Gaza Strip, held by Israel since the 1967 war. Within days the masterful Egyptian attack pushed across the canal and, using sophisticated Soviet-supplied weapons, inflicted crippling losses on the Israelis. In short order the Egyptians had placed 90,000 soldiers and 800 tanks across the Canal, and the Israeli predicament was dire.

Within three weeks, and after a desperate struggle, the Israelis had repulsed the attack and driven the invaders back into Egypt while on the Syrian front Israeli forces advanced to within twenty miles of Damascus.

Sasha and her mother were frantic with worry. Finally, a large, rough looking man in a dusty and ragged Israeli paratrooper uniform appeared at their door. He introduced himself as Captain Eitan Ronan. He told them of how he and his men had been pinned down in the irrigation ditches and embankments of an abandoned experimental agricultural station known as the Chinese Farm by withering fire from well-entrenched Egyptian forces. Sergey Turmarkin, in one of the armored half-tracks sent to evacuate them, had purposely driven his vehicle in front of Ronan's position to protect the unit. The vehicle had been destroyed by a Soviet Sagger anti-tank rocket. Sasha would never forget watching the unashamed tears leaving white tracks down Ronan's grimy face as he recounted her father's last moments. "He ordered his men out of the APC and then drove it directly into the line of fire. He displayed more courage than I can tell you," he said. "He knew what would happen, and he sacrificed himself to save us." Ronan had made it his business to learn the identity of the heroic APC driver. He promised that Sasha and her mother would always have him to rely upon. From that moment Sasha determined that she would fight her country's foes, just as her father had done.

Ronan, with no family of his own, had watched the gangly teenager grow into a beautiful woman, determined to go to war with her adopted country's enemies. Of course, boys had been attracted to her in droves, but she took none of them seriously. She never permitted mere recreational sex to progress to anything that might lead to a permanent relationship. She completed university and excelled at every military training course, and finally, upon Ronan's strong personal recommendation, was recruited from the IDF by Mossad in the early eighties.

*****

In a tight voice she said, "Mr. Connolly, Eitan came to Mossad from the Paratrooper Brigade. Losing fingernails should be the least of your worries. But, no, he does not want to 'disappear' you. He is in fact quite concerned for your safety, and the safety of whatever you are concealing from us. He simply doesn't want to lose you."

"I don't think there was anyone else hunting Stankov besides the nut job you took prisoner. If there had been another shooter, we would have had a harder time of it. There was nobody else around."

"But someone sent the shooter, and when he doesn't report, they will send someone else to take his place."

She was right, but my immediate objective was to put some distance between myself and the Israelis. I planned to be well out of Vienna before another assassin appeared, and I hoped never to see Eitan Ronan again.

"Look, Sasha, I'm really tired. I need to get some rest so I can think this thing through rationally. If he was on his own, even if when his boss notices that he's missing a hit-man, no one will know what happened to either him or to Stankov. Stankov was missing for a long time before tonight, and it's a long-shot that anyone would connect him with a naked, mangled corpse on a slab in the Vienna morgue."

"They knew how to find you," she said flatly. "What that tells me is that WE, Eitan and I, are the only REAL security you have right now."

She took a breath, then, "Have you been completely honest with us, Harry? It's very important."

Her eyes pleaded, and I found them hard to resist – more innate feminine wile.

I replied in time-honored masculine fashion. I lied. "I have to think things out. If something occurs to me, I'll share it with you and Ronan."

Sasha didn't bother to conceal her disbelief. She expelled a weary sigh and asked, "Where are you staying, Harry?"

"Drop me at the Hilton am Stadtpark."

Of course, she wouldn't believe I was actually lodging there.

She tried again. "Please believe that at this time you have no one else you can rely upon. You will be dangerously exposed without us."

Without her Tyrolean hat her ash blond hair had fallen loose, nearly covering the side of her face nearest me.

"Don't worry. I'll be OK, and I'll be in touch."

"How do we contact you?"

"How do I contact you?"

Not bothering to hide her exasperation, she extracted a card from her coat pocket and handed it over. It was a business card from a Vienna-based export-import company.

"My personal phone number is written on the back. Call me, and I will meet wherever and whenever you say."

She didn't sound very hopeful.

CHAPTER 30

The Key

She pulled off of the Opernring and drew to the curb across the street from the brightly lit entrance to the Hilton. Turning to me she put a hand on my arm.

"Don't wait too long."

Then she turned to stare through the windshield and refused to look at me again. I stepped out of the car and stood watching as she sped away. I regretted that I would never see that perfect face again.

The Israelis would not forcibly detain a CIA officer, but they would not let me get away this easily and had probably slapped on a tail, so I headed south towards Karlsplatz away from the Hilton as soon as Sasha's car was out of sight. I was bone tired, ragged, and hurting. The Hilton was only a few blocks from the *pension* on Walfischgasse, but I wound my way through back streets heading away from the Opern Ring, and soon detected at least two shadows.

After an hour slogging through the city streets I slipped through a narrow alley, sprinted around two corners, and concealed myself in a darkened doorway. When I was sure I had eluded my pursuers, I headed for the *pension.*

It was after four AM when the night clerk answered my ring and the street door opened with an angry buzz. I climbed the poorly lit stairs and trudged wearily past the reception counter studiously ignoring the clerk's irate glare as he took in the disreputable state of my clothing. In Vienna, even slightly dishonest hotel clerks have a sense of propriety.

I took a quick shower.

Wrapped in the threadbare bathrobe provided by the management, I cast a longing look at the narrow, lumpy bed, but turned instead to the small writing table on which lay Stankov's packet.

It contained a single item – a small, flat key attached to an oblong, numbered metal tag identifying a locker at Vienna's Südbahnhof train station.

I groaned and pulled on some clean clothing. I had to get to the train station as soon as possible or risk losing whatever was in the locker. Many train station lockers were coin operated and limited to 24 hours. The meeting with Stankov had taken place hours ago, and I had no idea when he had rented the locker. It was too risky to delay retrieving whatever he had left there.

The night clerk was asleep in a stuffed chair in the lobby and grumbled to be awakened again to unlock the street door. I had changed into jeans, a thick cotton turtleneck sweater and suede half boots. The only suit I'd brought was ruined. My Burberry was the worse for wear from last evening's festivities, but it was all I had. The pistol I had recovered from the sidewalk was a reassuring weight in my coat pocket.

It had stopped raining, and some Alpine crispness could be felt in the air, even here at the center of the city. It was only a couple of kilometers to the Südbahnhof, so I could hoof it fairly quickly. In the deserted streets surveillance would be easy to spot.

I headed south along the length of Walfischgasse to Schwartzenbergerstrasse to Prinz-Eugen Strasse and within a few minutes stood before the horrible sixty-ish façade of the Südbahnhof, another monument to modern Austria's lack of taste.

The next telephone contact with Jake Liebowitz was scheduled for about nine hours from now at two PM Vienna time. Whatever I found in the locker, it was time to go home and turn this mess over the Jake. Life is short enough as it is, and mine had almost come to an abrupt end just a few short hours ago. I was surprised to discover how much I still valued it. My neck was still sore despite the hot shower, I was exhausted, and seriously out of sorts. Jake had inveigled me into this mess because he knew he could rely on my quaint belief that the Agency owed some loyalty to its agents and because he trusted me. I owed the Agency no loyalty, and I could no longer trust anybody. Stankov was the only reason I was here, and with him gone it was Jake's turn to handle the mess.

I could not suppress the vision of Stankov, dead, gruesomely killed before my eyes. The shabby little Russian would not be dead had I not preyed upon his weaknesses all those years ago in Berlin. Likewise, young Thackery, dimwit that he had been, was dead, and but for my original recruitment of Stankov would today be pursuing the next rung up the bureaucratic ladder at Langley. They were just more threads in the tapestry, broken patterns of lines that all intersected with Harry Connolly.

Tonight I would be on a train back to Paris where I would treat myself to a fine meal. I would pay Volodya a good-bye visit, and we would share a bottle of iced vodka that would soften the chastisement I intended to inflict upon his dear old person for not warning me about his Mossad connection.

Then I would figure out what do to with the rest of my life. Escaping almost certain death is cathartic and leads one to realize how precious life is, even a life that had been shattered.

*****

The station was deserted except for the usual scattering of lounging bums and skanky prostitutes that populate such venues around the clock. It did not take long to locate the baggage section and the rank of lockers nearby. I matched the number of the tag on Stankov's key to a unit, inserted it in the lock and opened it.

Inside was a battered leather valise that contained an assortment of clothing and toiletries. I lifted the bag out and walked back to the exit, the bag in one hand and my other gripping the pistol in my pocket.

Twenty minutes later I was back at the pension ringing the doorbell. The night clerk was no happier to see me return than he had been to see me leave. I resolved to give him more money.

Back in my room I spread the contents of the bag over the writing table. Stankov's clothes smelled just like the man himself and obviously had been worn often and cleaned infrequently. The toilet kit did not include deodorant. But there was a half-full bottle of Courvoisier, probably a treat purchased with the American money.

The interesting stuff was at the bottom of the bag – two envelopes, one large brown one and another small white one folded over in the middle. The large envelope contained forty-five thousand dollars. The Agency had been less generous than one might have expected with its termination package. Stankov should have had over a hundred thousand dollars in his account by now. The weasel lawyers had found a way to short him.

The smaller envelope contained a single, unlabeled floppy computer disk.

I stared at the blue plastic square for a moment and wondered if what it contained was really worth the lives of two men. Whatever it was, Jake would have the resources at Langley to find out.

At long last I fell onto the bed and sank into sleep. It was nearly seven AM. In seven hours I would call Jake and say *auf wiedersehen* to Vienna.

CHAPTER 31

Maryland, Saturday, February 15

It was six AM, and the winter sky would remain dark for another hour when Jake Liebowitz's Volvo pulled away from his house in Potomac and onto I-270 North. Two hours later, satisfied that he was not being tailed, he pulled into a strip mall just off the highway, parked and entered a restaurant that catered to the breakfast crowd. In the back, near the entrance to the lavatories, was a pay telephone. It was now eight AM in Washington on a Saturday morning – two PM in Vienna.

Jake did not expect Connolly actually to call because he expected him to be dead. The ambush he had helped arrange had been perfect, too perfect to fail. But Jake was a consummate professional, and he believed in being thorough, so now he waited beside the pay phone, just in case. Connolly might have missed the meeting with Stankov, and he would have to set up something else, but this was doubtful. Jake knew his friend too well. He was, therefore, startled when the pay phone began to ring.

Liebowitz grabbed the phone off its hook before the first ring was complete. "Harry?!"

He listened in amazement for the next sixty seconds.

His face gray with disbelief, he said, "I can't believe

Stankov is dead."

He was thinking fast.

"Shit, Harry, I agree it's time for you to come in, but not on your own. Not after what's happened. You need some local protection. Tell me where you're staying, and I'll get some muscle from Vienna Station to see you safely out of the country. I want you to fly directly back to Washington."

He listened a moment then said, "Harry, I don't give a damn what you think is best. It's a miracle your ass is still attached to your tail bone. We can't risk losing track of you and whatever the hell is on that disk. This thing, whatever it is, has long since passed the point where we can continue to play it close to the chest. I've got to bring the Seventh Floor in now. They won't be happy with me for sending you out there, but I'll get over it, and you'll be safe. Now tell me where you're staying?"

After another two minutes on the line, Liebowitz left the restaurant and sat in his car for a long time, his brow furrowed with thought, as he formulated his plan. This was not going to be easy, but it was manageable. He just wished he did not have to depend upon others to do what needed to be done now.

CHAPTER 32

Judgment

I left the rank of public phones in the WestBahnhoff and exited the building in the direction of the Opern Ring. The temperature had dropped again, and Vienna's semi-permanent drizzle had been replaced by a light snow that danced in the headlights of on-coming cars.

It was against my rules to let anyone know where I could be located, and I had at first resisted Jake's entreaties. But there was no arguing that my situation had become precarious and extraction was the smartest option. This was, after all, Jake's operation, and the decision meant that he would bring Agency resources into the operation.

I had not mentioned the Israelis to Liebowitz because I didn't want anyone to know of Volodya's involvement, not even Jake, if it could be prevented. The old Russian's life could be jeopardized were his name in any way attached to this operation, and there was no reason to break another of my personal rules, even less so given the certainty that the Russians had a mole in the Agency. Enough had gone wrong, fatally so, already without the bosses at Langley pissing themselves over an elderly Russian's and Mossad's involvement before they had any facts. As long as the Israelis did not get their hands on the disk, it made no difference anyway.

I also had omitted the part about having been assaulted and the capture of the ape that I hoped was sweating bullets in the cellar of the Israeli Embassy. If I was not going to tell Jake about the Israelis, I sure as hell couldn't explain how I had survived an attack by a professional assassin. For now, all Jake needed to know was that Stankov had been killed and that I had retrieved the disk. There was plenty of time to decide what to say and what not to say, and I was leaving the Agency anyway. Screw them.

Jake had warned that it would take a while to clear things with the Seventh Floor and set up Vienna Station contact for the extraction. The plan was for me to be escorted by air directly back to Washington. I would miss seeing Volodya again, but securing the information on Stankov's computer disk was paramount. I didn't intend to repeat Thackery's mistakes.

I slipped into the *Sacher* Hotel for a quick meal and a slice of *torte* before settling into my room with my cigars and what remained of Stankov's cognac to wait it out. The room, shabby as it was, had become a warm cocoon of safety compared to the madness that lurked on Vienna's streets.

CHAPTER 33

Breaking

Spetsnaz training is as tough as any in the world and includes incredibly cruel sessions designed to inure men to torture. But there is a limit to any man's resistance. Drozhdov was in a very dark place, and despite his determination to hold out, in the end he failed. He had lost two more fingers and had soiled and pissed himself somewhere along the way, adding to his discomfort and humiliation.

Ronan's field interrogation technique was brutal and effective. The initial questions meant nothing, but served only to demonstrate that lack of an acceptable response would ALWAYS result in punishment – in this case loss of some part of his prisoner's anatomy. It was quick and very dirty, but it almost always worked.

Drozhdov's resolve finally collapsed when the jaws of the bloody steel pincers were placed around his penis. His experience with this fiend had conditioned him to know that there were no second chances, no pity, and no hesitation to carry out threats. Drozhdov was prepared to die, but he wanted at least to die a man.

Nauseated by the stench of his own filth, demoralized by his own weakness, a thoroughly broken Drozhdov at last told Ronan that he was a Captain in the SVR's elite Directorate S. He revealed his Spetsnaz military history, his assignment to Munich as an SVR Illegal, where he lived as a German citizen and carried out assignments on behalf of Moscow Center. The more he talked, the easier it became.

*****

Ronan wearily climbed the stairs leaving behind the broken man and the noisome atmosphere of the basement interrogation cell. He desperately needed a long, hot shower to rid himself of the stench of blood, excrement, and fear that lingered in his nostrils even after he closed the basement door. He had conducted field interrogations before, and the sickness in his gut afterwards was always the same.

Finally standing naked beneath a steaming flow of hot water, he could reflect clearly on the operational situation.

The water flowed over a body that carried its share of battle scars, including not a few from bullets. At 55, Ronan was still in excellent physical condition, and he was one of the men the Mossad relied upon to get the "hard" things done as leader of the Kidon unit. This was far from the first time that circumstances had required that he view a human being as nothing more than a piece of meat that concealed information somewhere inside.

What should he do now with the captive Russian? One

option was simply to kill him and dump the mutilated body into the Danube. He decided against this, however. A field interrogation had its limits. Because of the sensitivity of the present mission and the probability that a lengthier and more sophisticated interrogation in Tel Aviv might yield more information about *Voskreseniye* activities and personnel the Russian would live a while longer. It was a rare event for a Directorate S operative to be captured, but it would be impossible and dangerous in the end to keep him alive. He would never leave Israel.

The following day Drozhdov would be drugged, strapped tight, fitted with an oxygen tank, and packed into a specially designed crate for shipment via diplomatic pouch on an El Al flight to Tel-Aviv.

The American, Connolly, was a more pressing concern. The two local surveillants Ronan had assigned to follow him lost his trail inside of thirty minutes. The man apparently had an intimate knowledge of the city, and his counter surveillance and evasion skills were superb. Ronan cursed the fact that time had been limited, and in his own arrogance he had underestimated the American.

Drozhdov's revelations made it clear not only that the SVR's interest in Stankov had been at the highest levels, but also that Connolly's contact plan had been betrayed to them. That much had been evident from Drozhdov's presence at the meeting site, but Ronan was even more disturbed by the rapidity and accuracy of Moscow Center communications with Drozhdov concerning Connolly's final rendezvous with the Russian. Ronan was convinced that Connolly was still in extreme danger, no matter how talented he might be. With no way to get in touch with the American, there was no way to warn him.   Hopefully, Connolly's skill at eluding Israeli surveillance would not lead to his ultimate destruction.

CHAPTER 34

Alarm

The object on Arkadiy Yudin's desk looked like a laptop computer and would even function as such. Concealed within, however, was complex circuitry not to be found in any normal computer. A second hard drive contained software that worked with a set of complex algorithms to encrypt messages. Other specially built solid state nodes would then compress the encrypted message and separate it into discrete bundles to be forwarded via isochronous burst transmissions.

Having typed his message, he slid open a panel in the side of the instrument to reveal a cable connector and linked the device to a plug concealed in the woodwork of his desk that led to a satellite dish on the roof of his villa. His message was transmitted to a Russian satellite in geosynchronous orbit and then downloaded to Moscow Center in less than twenty seconds.

He needed to prod Shurgin into action. The computer disk Drozhdov had handed over to him in Madrid a little over a week earlier had confirmed his worst fears. That damned little clerk had hacked into the mainframe, accessed extremely sensitive files, and copied them. Then the miserable son-of-a-bitch had erased all the data on the mainframe. The disk Drozhdov had delivered therefore was the only known copy of the files Stankov had stolen. In the wrong hands this information could be used to access *Voskreseniye* funds dispersed in various accounts around the world, something only Yudin should be able to do.

Unfortunately, the equipment Yudin had for communications with Moscow Center could only accept manual input and message length was limited. Moscow, therefore, would be unable to re-construct the mainframe files until the disk could be couriered there – a job Drozhdov was supposed to handle. But where there was one computer disk there could be another. Yudin knew that until Stankov had been found and eliminated, the secret accounts *Voskreseniye* maintained in the West would be vulnerable to exposure or worse.

*****

At the SVR's "Forest" headquarters, General Morozov was at his desk despite its being Sunday. The pleasant week-end he had planned at his dacha with his wife and son was forgotten, and his mood matched the gloomy winter weather that gusted fitfully against his window. The duty officer had notified him of the receipt of urgent communications early in the morning, and he now re-read the two yellow sheets of paper, both marked "СОВЕРШЕННО СЕКРЕТНО," top secret. The messages they contained confirmed that something had gone very wrong with the Vienna operation.   Both of the messages were from Russian agents in the West. One was from Marbella, Spain, and mounting panic could be read between the lines. The other was from Washington, D.C.

Immediate action was demanded.

He called Shurgin.

An hour later the two were shuttered in Morozov's office. Shurgin, upon reading the messages, had lost his normal glacial façade and now prowled back and forth across the room in front of Morozov's desk. "Drozhdov failed to report, and yet Stankov is dead, and the American razvedchik has a second computer disk." Shurgin's sharp mind, usually so adept at separating fact from fiction, was having trouble processing this information.

From behind his desk Morozov looked up from the documents, his thoughts tracking those of Shurgin. "If Drozhdov killed Stankov, he should have killed the American, as well. Those were his orders. It is certain that something happened to Drozhdov. We should never have sent him in solo."

"Your hindsight is excellent, Yuriy Ivanovich," snapped Shurgin. "But I'm more concerned about what we do next. Your source in Washington says the damned American has a copy of the original disk, and we don't have much time to get it back. We have heard nothing from Drozhdov and so I agree that we must assume he is out of the picture. What do you suggest?"

Morozov had no doubts about what they must do next.

"Where the scalpel failed the axe may be needed," he said. "It's time to employ a blunt instrument, and I don't think we have the luxury of waiting for the next scheduled satellite communications window."

Shurgin inclined his head in reluctant assent. He knew precisely what Morozov intended.

The General lifted the receiver of one of the four telephones arrayed across his spacious desktop. This instrument was a special untraceable encrypted line that connected him directly to its twin in an expensive villa on the outskirts of Zurich, Switzerland.

CHAPTER 35

Zhenya

The hand that lifted the receiver in Zurich was well manicured and belonged to an impeccably dressed man with longish blond hair. He was of medium height and unremarkable in appearance except for his ice blue eyes and the fact that he wore a $5,000 bespoke suit, a cream colored hand sewn shirt of Egyptian cotton, and handmade shoes. He sat behind an antique desk facing an enormous window that provided a spectacular view of the University of Zürich campus and the Zürichsee. His study was lined with books, many of them rare volumes. He had read none of them, but image was quite important to him.

The impression he contrived to impart was one of privilege and culture, but he had in fact spent years in the Soviet gulag system and his body beneath the tailored finery was covered with crude prison tattoos identifying him as a vor v zakonye, a "thief in the code." Yevgeniy Lomonosov, known as "Zhenya," led the largest and most vicious criminal gang in Russia, "The Brotherhood."

The gang had a deservedly fearsome reputation and was responsible for numerous murders, some of prominent individuals – businessmen who would not cooperate, politicians, and troublesome television and newspaper reporters. They had had Wild West shootouts in the streets of Moscow and waged bloody war against rival Chechen gangs. The Brotherhood controlled all the concessions at many major airports in Russia, as well as major railway stations. Zhenya's brother, Ruslan, remained at the gang's headquarters in Moscow's southern district while Zhenya, whose superior business acumen had long been recognized, lived in the West, where he could control the Brotherhood's far flung activities. In all, the gang counted over five thousand members in a criminal enterprise stretching from Moscow, to Miami, to Geneva, and as far distant as the Near East.

The fall of the Soviet Union made it possible for the organization to flourish in the lawless, every-man-for-himself atmosphere that had set in after 1989. Zhenya himself had travelled to Israel where he established relations with the new criminal class of that nation, composed largely of newly arrived Russian immigrants, many of whom were fugitives from the law and hardly religious. These new Russian Israeli acquaintances provided Zhenya with "clean" travel documents and put him into contact with Colombian drug cartels and Italian networks.

Finally, in 1991 he set up his headquarters in Switzerland where much of his time was taken up with laundering huge amounts of dirty money, literally billions of dollars, through far-flung semi-legitimate business enterprises and protected bank accounts.

Zhenya assiduously cultivated his image of

respectability. A family man, his wife and two children lived with him in Zürich where the children were enrolled in the best schools to which they were driven daily in a sumptuous Rolls Royce, accompanied by an armed guard. The family hobnobbed with the "best" people in a country where wealth counted for more than character.

Despite some quixotic efforts, the Swiss authorities were incapable of gathering proof of Zhenya's illegal activities or penetrating the phalanx of expensive attorneys that surrounded his operations. Zhenya and the Brotherhood were bulletproof, and their involvement in legitimate businesses and illegal operations, especially narcotics, both in the West and inside Russia prospered.

Unbeknownst to the majority of its members, the Brotherhood was largely controlled by *Voskreseniye* and liberally salted with loyal former KGB officers and Soviet era military personnel. Shurgin used the Brotherhood to keep "independent" businesses, "oligarchs," and the Chechen criminal gangs under control inside Russia and as an investment vehicle and espionage operation in the West. In exchange the Brotherhood enjoyed the privileges and advantages that only official and unquestioned government support could offer to a criminal enterprise. It was a perfect symbiosis.

"Don't worry, Yuriy Ivanovich, I understand. I'll have someone in Vienna immediately," Zhenya replied to Morozov's urgent request.

*****

In Moscow, the SVR General replaced the phone in its cradle and turned back to Shurgin. "It's done. They should be on a plane to Vienna within the hour."

Shurgin ceased his pacing. "The American will be waiting for a contact from his own people, but he won't wait more than a very few days before going to ground again. If that disk falls into the wrong hands we won't have much time to take more corrective measures, if there should be any we can take at all. Send a reply to Yudin. Tell him to be ready to travel on short notice. If Zhenya should fail, Arkadiy Nikolayevich will have to move very fast."

CHAPTER 36

A Quiet Sunday in Vienna

A quiet Sunday had slipped into a quiet night, but now there was a distant clatter.

I was working on the week-end <u>International Herald Tribune</u> crossword when the reverberation of loud voices reached me. Not long after heavy footsteps sounded on the stairs. I followed their progress and soon was in little doubt that, whoever it was, they were heading toward my door.

It was the day after my talk with Jake, and there still had been no contact from Vienna Station. It took time to set these things up, and I could only imagine the grilling my friend had been subjected to after his revelations to the Seventh Floor brass.

Stankov's computer disk was a magnet that attracted trouble and death, and I had grown weary of the dingy walls of the pension. The Courvoisier and a rapidly dwindling supply of Habanos were my only surcease. I hated going to ground, and hated waiting even more. The charm of the *pension* room had worn off quickly.

As the footsteps drew nearer, I judged there were at least two men, and they were in a hurry. This definitely sounded like cavalry, but intuition told me they were charging rather than coming to my rescue.

There were only seconds to act. The pistol was on the table next to the chair. I had removed the silencer so it would be easier to carry.

With no time to rise, I grabbed the gun and aimed, two-handed, at the door just as it was slammed back from its frame with a crack of splitting wood. A very large foot clad in steel studded boots, apparently the instrument used to break open the door, appeared and two men in dark clothing rushed inside. The first to enter waved a pistol in an outstretched arm searching for a target. My chair was at an oblique angle from the door, and that probably saved my life.

The explosion of the pistol inside the small room was deafening. The first intruder grunted and stumbled when the slug caught him mid-mass, but his momentum carried him farther into the room before he sprawled face down on the floor next to the metal shower stall. The second attacker, likewise charging pell-mell through the door, tripped over his partner and fired blindly as he went down. The table lamp shattered beside me as I hurled myself sideways out of the chair and returned fire. The first shot was high and buried itself in the doorframe, but the second found its mark, and the intruder screamed in pain. He had been hit in the left bicep, and I was at once surprised and gratified to see that his arm was all but severed. Screaming, he rolled to his right to try another shot, but collapsed before he could squeeze the trigger.

There was a lot of blood.

With adrenalin electrifying my veins I covered the half dozen steps to the two supine forms. The first lay still, but the second was moaning and trying to rise. Without thinking, I pumped a bullet into his brain. Two combat tours in Vietnam had imbedded certain reflexes to being under fire. Nothing ever made me quite so angry as having a weapon pointed in my direction.

"That was for Stankov," I snarled at the grisly mess on the floor.

My knees suddenly felt like jelly as the adrenalin ebbed and the shock began to set in. My guts clenched and I found the sink and retched.

But within seconds other sounds penetrated the fog in my brain. Beyond the wreckage of the door a woman screamed intermingled with other alarmed voices. There were several references to "*polizei.*"

More heavy footsteps sounded on the stairs. I had to get out in a hurry.

Holding the pistol at my side, I ventured a peek into the hall. A bullet instantly cracked into the wall beside me. I ducked back inside just as the hall lights, controlled by one of those curious European timers usually found in cheap hotels, clicked off, and the narrow hallway was thrown into darkness. Without hesitation I dove through the ruined doorway and rolled against the opposite wall. The light from the stairway at the end of the corridor outlined a dark figure emerging from the top of the stairs.

The fire escape was at the opposite end of the hallway.

Keeping low, I turned and ran. The fire extinguisher hanging next to the fire escape door twanged as it was punctured by a bullet, and a cloud of white vapor escaped obscuring that end of the hallway. I spun, dropped to a knee and squeezed two quick shots in the direction of the figure on the stairs.

Reaching the door, I crashed through onto a small metal landing appended to the outer wall of the hotel. I leaned back through the door, stretched an arm around the corner, fired twice more then turned and clambered down the rickety metal ladder, still slippery with snow. At the bottom I turned immediately toward Walfischgasse, sped around the corner and sprinted away.

I was yet again bespattered with gore and wished I been able to grab my beloved Burberry. My passport was in its pocket. I also regretted having left Stankov's leather valise in the room. It contained all of the CIA money.

I shoved the pistol into my belt and pulled my sweater down over the grip, still on the move and not stopping until I reached a subway station entrance. Fifteen minutes later I alighted from the train at Nestroy Platz in north-eastern Vienna.

This was crap! Less than 24 hours after Jake Liebowitz had briefed the brass at Langley three assassins had reached me before the CIA could get me to safety. There was no way they could have located me other than through a leak at the top!

I needed to warn Jake and found a pay phone and placed a quick call to Maurice who said that Jake had not called Paris to leave a new contact number and time.

I had to go black NOW and worry about reporting to Jake later. The death toll had risen to four, and I had very nearly lost my own life for the second time in as many days! My true name passport would soon be in police hands. Within days I would be wanted by the Viennese police, Interpol, and God knew who else. It would not take long for the European authorities to check with the Americans, and then all hell would break loose. There was only Jake to vouch for why I was in Vienna, and even then the CIA was likely to distance itself quickly from the potential scandal of yet another "rogue" officer.

I had ignored my own rules by revealing my location, and Jake Liebowitz's revelation that the Russia Section was penetrated had proven dramatically accurate.

There was now only one choice - the Israelis. Sasha's business card was still in my pocket.

CHAPTER 37

The Morning After

The next morning found me back in the Israeli Embassy nursing a fourth cup of strong black coffee after spending the night tossing on Sasha's couch that was a foot too short. When sleep had come it bought kaleidoscopic dreams – CIA Headquarters, the hospital where my wife had died, Volodya's apartment, Vienna and Stankov's head exploding in front of me.

I'd hidden hunkered under a blanket in the back seat of her Skoda for the ride to the Embassy. Even after a shower at her apartment, I was still in the same worse for wear clothing as the night before and felt bedraggled, a distasteful condition that seemed to coincide with Israeli company. I waited in the same sitting room as before with the portrait of Golda Meir whose gaze now seemed more reprimanding than grandmotherly. Sympathetic to my sartorial predicament, Sasha had taken my sizes and promised to find some new clothes.

She had picked me up about forty minutes after my call and driven straight to her apartment. It was small and neat, but impersonal, like a safehouse. The impression was strong that everything about this woman was operational. I was grateful for the luxury of a hot shower

I emerged from the bathroom wrapped in a thick terrycloth robe that Sasha provided. The robe was plenty large enough to fit me comfortably, and I wondered if she often entertained male visitors. She waited on the sofa in the small living/dining room. She'd changed into a nightgown and a modest flannel robe. A long, shapely leg extended through the parted front of the robe. There was a chilled bottle of vodka and two water glasses on the coffee table, and she motioned for me sit beside her before pouring two generous portions of the clear, viscous spirit and lifting her glass to me.

"Here's to seeing you again, Harry Connolly." There was a hint of triumph in her voice that put me into a peevish mood, but the vodka smoothed things out a bit.

"Rescuing me is becoming a habit for you."

When I described the hotel attack, she was astonished.

I held out my empty glass for more vodka.

She sloshed more of the nearly frozen alcohol into my glass and, as I poured it down my throat, she said, "It seems you can take care of yourself even without Mossad assistance, but I'm glad you called nonetheless. I've notified Eitan."

"I'm sure he was overjoyed."

The peevishness retreated before the alcoholic assault, and I told her about the retrieval of the disk and the plan I had hatched with Jake to escape from Vienna. It really didn't matter at this point. Langley was far away, and the Israelis were the only port in the storm. And sitting next to this woman somehow took some of the sting out of it.

She assessed me with those fathomless hazel eyes, and I couldn't decide whether they reflected compassion or whether she simply thought I was a hopeless case.

"You should have stayed with us at the Embassy. You are now completely compromised."

"Tell me something I don't already know." Peevish again.

"How did this happen? It doesn't make sense. Volodya did not explain why you are working alone."

Perhaps it was the intimate setting, the narrow escape, the alcohol, probably everything together, but mostly the vodka, heaped upon the misery of my recent existence, but I unburdened himself, and she listened intently until I lapsed into silence.

She placed a hand on my shoulder, sending an unexpected spark of electricity through me. "He'll be pleased to learn about the disk. This would all have been much better handled, and the trouble at your hotel avoided, if you had only trusted us."

What else did I expect her to say? Her voice was soft, factual, with no hint of reprimand. "We sent a team to Stankov's hotel room, by the way. It was a flophouse, and there was nothing there. He apparently did not plan to return."

"That makes sense. All his personal belongings were in the valise at the train station. The poor bastard thought I would take him straight to safety. He didn't plan to return to his room."

"Well. It's too late to worry about spilled milk."

"Cry."

"What? Why would I cry?"

"Spilled milk. The correct phrase is '<u>cry</u>' over spilled milk."

I don't know why I pointed out the malapropism. My mind was mush, and the vodka was not exactly a clarifying agent. Why had I told her all that stuff?

She considered me curiously for a second before fetching a blanket. Most unexpectedly, she leant down and kissed my cheek before retiring quietly to her bedroom.

It was the best thing that had happened to me for a long time.

I slept very little as the evening's events cycled through my thoughts. Sasha's words of warning when she had dropped me a few nights ago had been spot on. No sooner had Jake Liebowitz attempted to arrange for safe passage back to Washington than I had been compromised. The Russians had mounted their attack before even the local CIA Station could act.

As long as I had remained independent I had been invisible. But now my passport, along with two corpses would implicate me directly -- not some alias identity that

I could shed, but me personally. Communication with the Agency could no longer be trusted, and undoubtedly others would follow the thugs who had attacked me. This decision was the right one -- the Israelis offered the only safe haven.

These gloomy ruminations were interrupted when Eitan Ronan entered with an armful of the morning's newspapers.

"Now see the results of your lack of trust in us," he growled, tossing one of the papers onto the coffee table. I couldn't tell if he was gloating.

The banner headline read, "DREIFACHEN MORD IN WAHLFISCHGASSE – Amerikanisch Bürger Gesucht" (TRIPLE MURDER IN WAHLFISCHGASSE – AMERICAN CITIZEN SOUGHT). Before the end of the second paragraph my name appeared, along with a description of the bloody state of the pension room and the two bodies. Even more dismaying, my photograph, obviously copied from the passport, also appeared. The picture had been taken four years earlier, and the newspaper reproduction wasn't perfect, but it was clearly me. The front page stories in the other papers were dishearteningly similar. Having anticipated this eventuality in no way softened the pangs of desperation that lanced through my chest.

The nasty surprise was that there had been a third death - that of the *pension's* grumpy night clerk. His body had been found near the reception desk. He had been shot execution style through the forehead, another innocent caught up and murdered in the middle of this burgeoning mess. Counting Thackery that made five deaths since Stankov's arrival in Vienna.

The names of the two men whose bodies had been found in the pension room were not revealed, but the papers did report that according to the documents found on them, both were Russian citizens. The papers also reported that a large amount of American currency had been found in the room, and I again regretted not having grabbed Stankov's valise. The combination of murder and money led to much speculation in the press, and none of it was helpful to my cause.

Ronan was keen to hear my account of events, and I repeated what I had told Sasha the night before, including the fact that I had agreed to have the CIA bring me in. It no longer mattered that I had not intended to re-contact the Mossad. Circumstances had driven me back to them, and that was where I would have to stay.

CHAPTER 38

Taking Stock

Ronan listened silently, legs crossed, chain smoking his Caporals. A wry expression crawled its way slowly across his broad, sunburned visage as he said, "Sasha should be back soon with new clothing for you, and you can clean yourself up. You must be quite uncomfortable."

The Israeli might have imagined he was emanating sympathy. The dried blood on my clothing was becoming a bad habit.

Ronan glanced again at the newspapers spread across the table.

"In the meantime, there are things I need to tell you and a decision you must make."

He raised a meaty hand into the air as though he were swearing an oath. "I understand your consternation and I understand your loyalties are with your own country and your own organization."

He was only half right about that. I was as finished with the CIA as it was with me. Neither had a choice.

Ronan continued, "But for the time being you find yourself in extraordinary circumstances that require hard decisions. If, after you hear what I have to say, you wish me to do so, I can facilitate contact with the CIA, and you can let them bring you in."

He shot a doubtful glance across my bow. "Frankly, I know nothing of what is happening inside your Agency, but it is clear enough that you were betrayed and set up for a kill. Either the CIA itself betrayed you or you have a traitor in very high places with the ability to act quickly and decisively. In either case, I don't think you will want to go back to them now. It could be fatal."

I had operated solo countless times in the past, but could always count on the Agency's capabilities. Now, the Agency, or at least someone in it, had become a mortal enemy. Who had Liebowitz briefed? Certainly Barney Morley. Could the Chief of the Russia Section be a spy? I found myself half-hoping it was true because the other possibility was really ugly.

Ronan continued to lay out my predicament in dismaying detail.

"Your true identity is now a matter of public record and there is a manhunt with you as the objective ongoing at this very moment by the Austrian authorities. There can be no doubt that you will in short order become the subject of an Interpol alert, as well. If you turn to the American authorities, including the CIA, you have no guarantees. You are in the middle of an operation that has gone terribly wrong -- fatally wrong -- and your organization, unfortunately, does not have a reputation for protecting its own. They may well toss you to the wolves, as they have done with others for much less. You say that there is only one person who can vouch for your role in this affair. Should you go back to them, you should be very certain that this person has the power to shield you.

"Your involvement in a triple murder, indeed the official assumption that you are the murderer, true in the case of the two men who attacked you in your room, will be also reported to the American authorities. They will be hunting you too."

"Thanks, Ronan. That makes me feel all better."

Undaunted, he pressed on. I think he was enjoying it the way a sadist enjoys pulling the wings off a fly.

"I can offer you protection, at least temporarily. I know your situation, and I know the truth, and I may eventually be able to clear you. But in exchange you must cooperate without reservation."

Ronan's not unexpected analysis was dead-on accurate. And the implicit threat was clear. I could have expected nothing else.

I removed Stankov's computer disk from my shirt pocket and tossed it like a poker chip onto the table where it landed with a click in front of the Israeli.

"This is all I have to bargain with."

I was betting blind into a royal flush.

Ronan stared at the blue floppy disk for a moment without reaching for it, then plucked it from the table and said, his voice uncharacteristically soft, "Whatever it contains justified several deaths and very nearly your own."

The burly Israeli gingerly replaced the disk on the table.

"You will recall what I told you the other day about the billions of dollars missing from the former Soviet Government. It may interest you to know that your friend Stankov's name appears in our files in this connection. He is mentioned only a few times and always as a minor character, but we do not doubt that he was in some way involved with the missing funds. He rose in Gosbank to mid-level management and only last year was transferred to the bank's special section that handles financial administration for the Russian intelligence service. This comes directly from a trusted Mossad source in Moscow, and there is supporting information from your friend Smetanin's sources."

My face must have betrayed surprise. Ronan continued, "I cannot believe that the CIA had no knowledge of this. Was there no communications plan for this agent?"

"There was a plan, but only if he were able to travel to the West. Even so, his file had been retired. His meeting with our man here was intended to officially terminate the relationship. He had no internal commo capabilities."

What a waste it all had been. Stankov's recruitment in Berlin, the way the Agency nurtured him in the beginning, the promises made to him. And the responsibility the Agency accepted for him upon his recruitment. When Stankov didn't hand over the Crown Jewels, Headquarters lost interest and relegated him to the trash heap. And all the while the Russian had doggedly pursued the goals we had set for him, had continued to burrow his way up into the bureaucracy.

Stankov's last words had been: "You do not know what information I provided? That is not why you are here? I assumed you would recognize the value of this information immediately."

No. The CIA does not nurture its agents. There is no patience among the bureaucratic elite which runs the place. If an agent does not "produce" immediately, if his dossier gathers dust for a while, he is deemed worthless. There is no room for humanity in the modern Intelligence "business," no room for the nurturing patience the classic art of espionage demands.

I looked up to find Ronan's eyes still fixed on me.

I said, "All I can tell you is that Stankov without a doubt believed that whatever is on this disk is valuable; so valuable that he thought it would buy him a golden parachute."

"Let's hope he was right. The most logical explanation is that he was a courier for whatever information is on the disk, information too valuable to trust to electronic communications. Or, perhaps he simply stole it. In any case, he recognized its importance and tried to hand it over to the CIA.

"The man who killed Stankov and nearly killed you had some useful information that he was finally only too eager to divulge. His name is Drozhdov, and he is an SVR Illegal, based in Munich. He is the same man who murdered your colleague, by the way. Drozhdov told me he recovered a computer disk from your man and carried it personally to a Russian in Spain named Arkadkiy Nikolayevich Yudin. He passed Yudin the disk at a meeting at the airport in Madrid. Yudin actually lives in Marbella in a large villa on the coast. Drozhdov was then ordered back to Vienna to continue the search for Stankov ... and for you.

"Yudin was a mid-level functionary in the Moscow City Government with considerable experience in the Soviet mining sector. After the dissolution of the Soviet Union he made a fortune selling Russian commodities, primarily metals and minerals, through a cut-out firm in Switzerland. He controls vast funds and has interests in many enterprises, including some in the United States. He is an authentic 'oligarch,' as the genre has come to be called. Just a year ago, however, he began to live a more sedate life and settled down in Spain. His wife and children remain in Moscow. He travels frequently to places like Vaduz where we believe he manages various financial holdings. Drozhdov's confession leads me to conclude that Yudin is somehow associated with the group that controls the missing Russian funds, the group that calls itself *Voskreseniye*."

This was all fascinating stuff, but something Ronan had said had caught my attention.

"Ronan, if Drozhdov delivered a disk to Yudin, why did he return to Vienna? Wouldn't they have thought their operation had been a success?"

"That, my friend, is a good question. It's likely that they wanted to tie up a loose end. After all, Stankov was still missing, and still possessed sensitive information. You also should consider the fact that the Russians knew Stankov's contact plan, the same contact plan you used to find him. They also obviously knew he was still alive and would be meeting someone – you – who also would have to be eliminated."

Something ugly and uncomfortable squirmed at the back of my mind. There was a possible explanation, actually a very logical explanation, for how all this had come about -- one that I didn't want to believe.

CHAPTER 39

The Black Treasury

Ronan continued his narrative. "*Voskreseniye* is made up mostly of former KGB officers of all ranks who seek the re-instatement of Russia among the pre-eminent world powers. They are not communists. Few in the KGB, the 'Sword and Shield of the Revolution,' ever believed deeply in Communism. Nevertheless, they do have a profound belief in their *otechestvo,* their Fatherland, as they call it. They believe in the inevitable supremacy of Russia, especially in Europe, and they harbor a deep and abiding hatred for your country.

"As I explained earlier, it is this group that controls the so-called 'Black Treasury.' Think of it -- they have implanted their people in every institution, both legal and illegal, of post-Soviet Russian society. They control several criminal gangs, most particularly the Brotherhood, a group with strong links among recent Russian émigrés to my own country. They have taken advantage of the failure of the economic reforms and the innate corruption of the modern Russian kleptocracy to purchase or acquire by force the most prominent levers of the Russian economy. Soon they will control everything in Russia, including the government and the military. They intend to use their power to restore hegemony over the former states of the Soviet Bloc, and even further, they seek the means to exert their influence over Western Europe, as well. They will use Russia's vast oil and gas reserves without restraint to blackmail the West to achieve these goals.

"They now sit and wait as the Yeltsin Government implodes in an orgy of corruption, blackmail, drunkenness, and greed. They will be ready to take control when the current Government finally self-destructs."

Ronan's sophistication was surprising. The thuggish exterior concealed a first rate mind.

I considered the American government's futile efforts to "control" and "guide" the development of democracy in Russia. *There are none so blind as those who will not see.* The American plan had been ill-advised and disastrous.

"Anyone who ever dealt with them knows that the KGB was the most capable institution in the Soviet Union," I said. "The Russian spooks are using the same techniques they used to topple or infiltrate foreign governments to topple their own. Too bad my guys seemed to have lost interest them."

Ronan grimaced. "It's incredible, actually. The SVR must be amused by what their mole is telling them. Their disdain for the United States must be tremendous."

Sasha still had not returned from her shopping trip, and I had almost forgotten my disreputable state, so engrossing was the conversation.

The Israeli continued. "Now I come to the reason we

injected ourselves into your operation."

"No matter the reason, it was lucky for me."

"No doubt, but the reason is important, important for Israel.

"About a year ago Russia and Iran signed a nuclear cooperation agreement. Since then we have detected a pattern of Russian officials and technical personnel travelling to Tehran. There also have been some high level Iranian visits to Moscow, not all of them overt. We do not doubt that The Iranians have already signed or soon will sign agreements to purchase weapons from Russia, and we have documented information that the Russians have replaced other foreign teams working on Iran's nuclear development program at Bushehr. Needless to say, we don't trust them. Should the Iranian fanatics ever possess nuclear weapons the consequences for Israel and the world could be fatal."

I had to agree. "One of the key strategies of any group seeking to restore international clout to Russia would have to involve re-establishing and shoring up its Cold War alliances with the bad boys of the Middle East."

Ronan nodded. "They have hundreds of millions of dollars tied up in the Iraqi oil industry, for example."

"And so, when you learned that I was coming to Vienna to meet Stankov, you thought it might involve this *Voskreseniye* group, and you wanted to get your hands on the information?"

"Yes. Nothing important happens in Russia without

Voskreseniye involvement."

"And what would you have done had that meeting taken place with no problems and you knew I had the disk?"

Ronan locked eyes with me. "Whatever we had to do. Certainly Sasha was prepared to play her part if need be."

Had they planned to steal the disk while Sasha took me to her bed?

"Um hum," I said. "And if the honey pot ploy failed you would have found another way?"

Ronan's face clouded over, but before he could reply Sasha burst into the room with several shopping bags filled with clothes.

Forty-five minutes later after another shower and a shave in the Embassy's facilities I was finally dressed in clean clothes – dark brown corduroy slacks and a maroon turtleneck cashmere pullover. I had to admire Sasha's taste.

We gathered again around the table in the reception room.

A Gauloise in one hand, Ronan held a computer print-out in the other. Excitement showed through his phlegmatic veneer.

Handing the paper to me, he said, "This is a list of bank accounts, addresses of financial institutions, companies, and access codes. The balances in the accounts are staggering, but they amount to less than half of the funds we know to have been in the *Voskreseniye* treasure chest, the 'Black Treasury.' We must assume that they have expended a lot of money buying up businesses, paying bribes, etcetera, and in investments like Iraq. A lot of the original money must be tied up in equity around the world. These accounts must contain most of their remaining liquid assets. They amount to roughly twenty billion dollars."

This was a lot of pocket change. "OK," I said. "What next? Will you make the information public? Reveal the extent of their influence, their plans?"

Ronan shook his head. "I'm afraid no one would believe us, and even if they did, what could be done about it? The accounts are 'legal.' No one in Russia is going to admit that the original funds were secreted out of the country by intelligence operatives. They are not going to admit they are involved in criminal activities. The power these people seek has already been bought and paid for. Their plan is already well advanced. No, it's too late to stop them or eliminate the group. They will inevitably control the reins of power in the new Russia, and most Russians would probably applaud the *Voskreseniye* plan if it were made public.

"No, we're not going to make anything public. We're going to hurt them. <u>We're going steal as much of their money as we can before they can slam the door shut!</u>"

CHAPTER 40

Monday Morning – Langley, Virginia

Jake Liebowitz sat at his desk in the executive suite of CIA's Russia Section struggling to maintain his equilibrium. Before him lay a Flash message from Vienna Station reporting that the Austrian press was full of stories of a manhunt for Harry Connolly, who was wanted for questioning in connection with three murders at a Viennese hotel. The hotel night manager, as well as two unidentified men found in Connolly's room, had been killed by gunshot. Other hotel guests reported hearing a raging gun battle the previous night. Numerous shots had been fired in Connolly's room, as well as in the hotel corridor. The official investigation would take days, but in the meantime one Harry Connolly, a US citizen who had occupied the room for some days under an assumed name, was missing and urgently wanted for questioning. Interpol and the American authorities had been notified and their assistance requested.

Liebowitz' heart was in his throat. He could anticipate the shit hitting the fan within a very few moments because he knew Barney Morley was at that moment digesting the same news from Vienna. It was going to be a helluva start to the week.

Liebowitz managed to put in a quick call to Harry's

office in Travel before Morley's anticipated roar.

"Jake, get in here!"

Morley was a big man, and the volume of his shout was barely diminished by the thin wall between their offices.

Liebowitz took a couple of deep breaths, stood up, and walked to his boss's door.

The office was adorned liberally with photos of Morley with the famous and near-famous – a typical Washington vanity wall. He had carefully built his reputation and cultivated the "right" contacts over nearly 25 years in the CIA and was widely considered to be on the threshold of even further advancement.

As Liebowitz entered Morley stood behind his desk and waved the Vienna message in an upraised fist.

"What the hell is this about, Jake? Are they talking about OUR Harry Connolly? What's he doing in Vienna? The Seventh Floor is in an uproar."

There was a row of chairs against the wall facing Morley's oversized desk, and Liebowitz plopped himself wearily into one of them. When he spoke his voice was strained, and the words came out haltingly.

"Barney, I just called Harry's office. They say he took some vacation days and hasn't been in the office for at least a week. They don't know where he is."

"Goddamnit!" Morley exploded. He stared balefully at Liebowitz across his photo festooned desk. "I never liked that overdressed sonuvabitch! That's why I got rid of him." Through clenched teeth he asked, "What the hell's going on in Vienna? First Thackery gets himself murdered on a milk run. Stankov disappears, according to the Russians, and now it looks like Connolly is there, and three more people are dead! And what's all this money they found? If it really is him, it won't take long for someone to discover the Agency connection. I can only imagine the goat fuck that will cause. This whole building is going to get a lot of stink on it fast because we can't keep secrets anymore, and now we have another fucking rogue on our hands. Thank God I pushed him out of this Section."

Liebowitz remained silent until Morley brought his anger under control. There was a lot riding on how Jake handled this moment. Not everything had gone as he had planned it, but he thought he still could salvage his objective.

CHAPTER 41

Morley

Morley finally dropped into his chair and stared in sullen expectation across his desk at Liebowitz. His voice tired, he asked, "Well, what's your take on this? Connolly is your buddy, isn't he?"

Liebowitz pulled a long face and sighed, his eyes downcast.

"Yeah, I've known Harry for a long time, but I haven't seen him in months. After his wife died, he moved clear out of town. It was a hard blow when you fired him and kicked him out of Russia Section. This Section had been his whole career, and he was a damned good officer, even you have to admit. God alone knows what went through his mind when he was reassigned to Travel. Harry is an operations officer. It's in his blood. He must have been furious."

Liebowitz paused. Morley's face had grown ashen and now flushed red.

"What are you getting at Jake? You think I'm to blame?"

"What is the Russia Section's biggest problem right now, Barney? Why don't we have any operations left worth talking about?"

Morley's voice went flat as the realization hit him. "The mole. You think Connolly is the goddamned mole."

Liebowitz leaned forward.

"I hate to even suggest such a thing, but with everything that's happened in Vienna ..." He allowed his voice to trail off into meaningful silence. "Harry's just not the same guy anymore."

Injecting just the right amount of anguish into his voice, he continued, "God, this is awful. I don't want to believe it, but let's look at the facts. We've been turning the Section upside down looking for the leak. Harry hasn't been in the Section for some time. Nevertheless, he knows all the operations because he's been personally involved in most of them, and has read all the files at one time or another. He was being considered for your job at one time, you know, Barney."

Morley snorted. "Yeah, he certainly had the access."

Liebowitz shook his head sadly. "And Stankov? Hell, he RECRUITED Stankov."

"You think he was behind what happened to Thackery?"

"If Harry is the mole, it's a reasonable assumption, isn't it?"

"But how could he have learned that Thackery was meeting Stankov in Vienna?"

This was tricky, but Liebowitz had anticipated the question and formulated a completely plausible response.

"Who knows? Thackery's assignment was a milk run. No one was treating it as high priority or even as particularly sensitive. Harry could have heard about when he saw the travel orders. And he's still friendly with Russia Section folks. You know how it is. They admire him. But I think it's more likely that Thackery himself consulted with Harry before his trip. Jim must have known that Harry was the recruiting officer. The two did know one another, and Harry still has quite a reputation in the Section."

Morley found this reasonable.

"Yeah, I'll bet Thackery did talk to him." He shook his head. "But why kill Thackery? What the hell could have been so important about Stankov?"

"Again, we just don't know and probably never will unless Harry is captured or gives himself up. Whatever it was it was important enough to risk blowing everything up by getting involved personally. This could only have been the action of a desperate man."

Morley was still considering ways to protect himself. This couldn't be happening. "But what is this latest stuff about? What about these three killings in Vienna? Two of these dead guys are Russians, according to the press."

"Stankov is still missing in Vienna. Remember the notice the Russians put out. This has to be connected. Here is what we do know: Stankov, Harry's agent, calls for a meeting; we're pretty sure that Thackery met Stankov and then was murdered; shortly thereafter Harry Connolly takes leave and disappears and then turns up in Vienna.

Maybe Stankov somehow had discovered that Harry was the mole. Harry clearly has done something rash, to say the least. It's possible the Russians decided they would be better off if he were dead. Of what use could he be to them once he'd blown his cover? It would just be a big political problem for them. The dead Russians in his room support that theory. And now the whole world is looking for him on suspicion of murder. Even if he was not the mole, his actions will be traced back to the Agency, and there will be hell to pay, possibly even a Congressional investigation. Harry Connolly will be traced right to this office, even if you did kick him out."

Liebowitz' words were calculated to chill Morley to the bone. He was a Company man, a team player. He'd done everything right. He could envision all those years climbing the bureaucratic latter, saying the right things, and finally placing himself in line for real power now going for naught. If this should come to public attention, the onus would fall on him personally as Chief of the Russia Section. He knew how the Washington game was played, and his "friends" would turn on him in the blink of an eye. Scapegoating was a well-honed survival skill in this town. The political appointee Director of Central Intelligence sure as hell wasn't going to take the blame.

"What do you think we should do, Jake?"

"If you expect to salvage anything, you need to mop things up before anyone else can get to Harry. You're the boss, Barney. The decision is yours. If something is not done fast, he could turn up in Moscow. He may already be on his way there."

Morley was quick to grasp Liebowitz' meaning. "Go back to your office, Jake. I'll take care of it."

Liebowitz had to be sure. "What are you going to do?"

Morley glared at him. "I'm going to send a team out to rid ourselves of a problem," he snapped.

Liebowitz returned to his own office and sank heavily behind his desk, the chair creaking under his weight. He gazed out the window at the tree lined shores of the Potomac and beyond into Maryland. The pieces were now positioned on the chessboard for the end game, maybe not according to his original plan, but still good enough for a checkmate in a few more moves. He had had to move fast, but his manipulative skills were considerable. He sighed contentedly. All he had to do now was make a phone call to the 'Washington Post' and wait.

CHAPTER 42

Fallout, February 18

Gerry Hancock surveyed the carnage that had visited the small hotel room. Beside him stood Chief Inspector Hans Freibeck of the Bundespolizei, the Federal Police responsible for Vienna. Hancock knew that Freibeck actually belonged to the Stapo, or Staatespolizei, Austria's counterintelligence service.

"Any first impressions, Mr. Hancock?"

Freibeck undoubtedly had his own ideas, but he was curious to learn the thoughts of the head of the FBI investigative team that had arrived in his city the day before. Freibeck did NOT know that 'Hancock' was not the American's real name or that he and the two men with him were members of the CIA's quick reaction "mop-up and retrieval" squad, stationed at Andrews Air Force Base outside Washington. Hancock's assignment was to investigate the Vienna events involving Harry Connolly, locate Connolly, and eliminate him.

"I'm wondering why someone with Connolly's means would have been staying in a dump like this."

The crime scene was a mess. A table and chair had been knocked over, a copy of the <u>International Herald Tribune</u> open to a half-finished crossword puzzle lay on the floor, and a lamp was broken, but the most salient features were the yellow outlines of two bodies drawn on the threadbare carpet. There was a lot of blood. Hancock's nostrils filled with the coppery scent.

"That's where the guy with the head shot fell?" Hancock pointed to one of the body outlines with massive blood stains around the head.

"Yes," replied the Austrian policeman. "Most curious."

"How so?"

"You saw the two bodies last night when we visited the morgue."

Hancock recalled his revulsion at the sight of the destroyed face and head of one of the two bodies he had examined. "Yeah. It's pretty obvious which one of them left those bloodstains."

"I quite agree, but there is something you don't know."

Hancock concentrated on Freibeck's face. "Please, go on."

"Several days ago a nude male body was found not far from here. The head bore a wound remarkably similar to what we observed last night. We found several rounds drilled into the walls of neighboring buildings, very special sub-sonic bullets designed to produce maximum effect upon impact."

"An assassin's weapon." Hancock wondered where the hell Connolly could have gotten his hands on it.

"Precisely. Even more interesting, the rounds we

recovered from this crime scene are of the same type and caliber. The same gun could well have been used in both crimes."

"So Connolly has been murdering people in Vienna for several days now?"

"So it would seem, but the bullets found at the other crime scene were too distorted get a perfect match. Also, there are other curiosities associated with this matter."

Hancock was getting impatient with the way the Austrian was eking out information. If there was anything that would permit him to locate Connolly, he needed it NOW. He wished Freibeck would drop the Sherlock Holmes act and get to the point. He held his temper in check, however. It wouldn't do to antagonize the Austrian.

"Please go on, Inspector. I'm all ears."

Freibeck stepped into the room and gestured for Hancock to follow him. He pointed to some bullet holes in the far wall.

"A lot of shooting occurred in this room, Mr. Hancock – a LOT of shooting. Pistols were found near the bodies of both of the dead men. Also please take note of the fact that the door to the room is off its hinges and the frame is cracked. If I had to guess what happened here, I would deduce from the crime scene that the two dead men broke into the room and attacked Connolly, who killed them in self-defense. We also know for a fact that your man did NOT kill the desk clerk. It appears that the man with the destroyed face killed him. The bullet was a match for the pistol found near his body. And then there is the curious matter of the nationality of the two deceased gentlemen."

He shot Hancock a sly look. "What do you make of that, Mr. Hancock?"

Hancock caught the implication. It wouldn't be the first time that a US clandestine operation had spilled over into Austrian civil society.

"So far as we know, Inspector, Connolly had no official business in Austria. You mentioned another body that was found on the street. What can you tell me about it?"

"Just as I said: the body was discovered on a back street not far from this hotel, at least within reasonable walking distance. The slugs we dug out of the wall are the same type as the ones found in this room, apparently fired by your Mr. Connolly. The body we found still has not been identified."

"So you think Connolly killed at least three people, including the unidentified victim?"

"All the evidence is circumstantial, of course, but it is certainly possible."

"What can you tell me about where Connolly might have gone?"

"Nichts, nothing. We know he fought a running gun battle in the hallway out there and escaped down the fire escape into the alley that runs alongside this building. We found no traces of blood along his escape route, so I think we can safely assume that he was not wounded.

There was a reported sighting of a tall man without a coat, possibly a foreigner, on the subway that matched the description of Connolly. He was last seen at the Nestroy Platz station. After that, nichts."

This was definitely not good news for Hancock. If necessary he was prepared to seize Connolly from the Austrian authorities or kill him from a distance, but the renegade still eluded capture. Hancock wondered whether his target might have had some outside assistance, the Russians, maybe. But if that were so, how to explain the two dead Russians in Connolly's hotel room? What the hell was going on here?

"I have another question for you, Mr. Hancock." Freibeck's voice brought Hancock back to the present.

"Yes?"

"On that table over there the investigating officers found an old leather valise. It was filled mostly with dirty clothes – all Russian or Eastern European, by the way – but there was also an envelope."

"What sort of envelope?"

Freibeck smiled thinly. "An envelope of American manufacture, actually. It contained a considerable amount of American currency."

Hancock had no idea what this might mean. What he did know was that his investigation was getting nowhere fast. Langley would not be pleased.

"And what do you deduce from this, Inspector?"

"I was hoping you might be able to shed some light on it, Mr. Hancock."

*****

The retrieval team Barney Morley had sent to Vienna returned with a plethora of confusing and contradictory information about what had happened, but there was absolutely no trace of the fugitive.

Three days had passed since the news of Harry Connolly's bloody appearance in Vienna became public, and Morley was facing Armageddon with the Seventh Floor brass. He now stood sweating in the elevator as it whisked him towards a meeting he wished he did not have to attend.

Entering the suite of rooms leading to the Director's office he caught sight of his direct boss, the Director of Operations Freddy Walsop, and the Agency's General Counsel sitting side by side on a sofa awaiting their summons. The attendance of the General Counsel did not bode well.

Finally admitted into the Director's spacious office, the three sat like naughty schoolboys in chairs ranged in front of Director Russell Stanford's desk. Stanford, himself a respected, high-powered "K" Street attorney had been appointed DCI a year ago by the new President. A capable, intelligent man, he had been disappointed by what he found at Langley and even more disappointed to learn that the President of the United States had discontinued personal meetings with the Director of Central Intelligence. Stanford didn't plan to stay here much longer. He was a dollar a year man, and he certainly didn't plan to leave under a cloud. To say that he was unhappy with this Connolly situation was a vast understatement.

The DCI's prosecutorial stare drilled into Barney. "What the hell is going on, Morley? This is your bailiwick. What is all this crap in the press? Who is leaking this stuff?"

Morley tried his best tack. "But you see, sir, it's NOT really my bailiwick. I kicked Connolly out of Russia Section a long time ago."

"Yes, I know," said Stanford, his voice even. "Let me see. Connolly was a twenty-plus year veteran of Russian operations with a stellar record," the Director lifted a file folder from his desktop, and Morley saw that it was Connolly's personnel file.

"In fact," continued Stanford, "he was one of the most highly qualified Russian operations officers in the Agency." He paused to glare at Morley. "And you fired him."

The accusatory tone was unmistakable. "He wasn't part of the team, Director," persisted Morley, "he was a relic of the past, with old ideas. He just didn't fit in. At any rate, I got rid of him."

Morley glanced in the DDO's direction in search of support, but Walsop refused to meet his eyes. Morley knew at that moment that he was finished.

Stanford resumed his rant.

"And since then you've lost every Russian agent. A mole has destroyed your Section, Morley, and according to the press, THE PRESS, mind you, that mole is Harry Connolly. After the callous, idiotic way you handled this man, is there any wonder he turned against us? And now you've put us all in the soup!"

CHAPTER 43

Persona Non Grata

I spent the night in a sparsely furnished guest room at the Israeli Embassy. Sasha had made another foray through the shops of Vienna returning with a complete wardrobe for me, as well as a suitcase and toiletries. Whatever plans the Israelis had, they must include travel.

Eitan Ronan spent much of the time on the secure line to Tel-Aviv, and the contents of Stankov's computer disk were transmitted electronically to the same place.   From what I could gather from the few times I'd spoken with Ronan during the course of the day, he was conjuring a strategy with his superiors that involved the data from the disk.

It listed nearly a hundred hidey holes for the Russian funds in places like Liechtenstein and the Cayman Islands. Getting at the accounts would be a difficult and far flung affair.   And much of the money was held in trusts or invested in private companies and impossible to retrieve.

Tuesday morning the big Israeli had more depressing news.

"I've heard from our Cosmos representative in Washington."

Cosmos is the code name for Mossad liaison with the American services.

"There is a burn notice out on you, my friend. CIA liaison told our representative that you are in all likelihood a Russian mole and should be treated as a hostile. Informally, CIA told us they don't care if you are captured or killed, and frankly they would prefer the latter."

What Ronan said next was even worse.

"The 'Washington Post' somehow got hold of the story. They've taken the information provided by the Austrian press and added that they've learned from a confidential source that you are a mole and on the run. They've named you publicly as a suspected Russian spy and murderer. The 'Post' also reports turmoil at the CIA, and the Head of the Russia Section is being held accountable.

"You are *persona non grata* everywhere, my friend."

I had never thought I could feel sympathy for a preening bureaucrat like Barney Morley, but he too had been set up. And the same person had done both jobs.

No matter how many times I thought it over, I always arrived at the same dismaying conclusion. Jake Liebowitz was the only common thread that ran through all that had happened. *Jake the snake. Jake the mole!*

Concealed beneath an unprepossessing exterior Jake Liebowitz was gifted with a razor sharp intellect that was admirably attuned to the art of espionage. Somewhere along the way the art had overwhelmed the cause it was intended to serve.

I did not presume to understand Jake's motives. What it is that turns a person into a traitor? Are defectors, after all, only defective people? Or is it that, as LeCarré put it, betrayal is a form of worship? There was no Rosetta Stone to provide the answer. Most tradecraft practitioners identify the classic motivations with the acronym MICE – money, ideology, compromise, and ego.

Sometimes opportunity becomes motivation, but the motives for betraying the trust of one's country fall into six major categories: money, sex, conviction, revenge, fear or coercion, and just plain love of risk-taking. And each of these has multiple sub-categories. Motivation can be negative or positive. Probably a majority of professionals would aver that money is the primary motivator, but the mechanisms that create spies and make them tick are usually too complex to narrow down to a single type.

There are true spies -- those intrepid individuals who assume the guise of a foreign nationality or surreptitiously enter foreign territory to spy upon the enemy. Such were the men and women of the Allied intelligence services who parachuted from black planes into occupied France, for example, or Soviet "Illegals" like Rudolph Abel. These people are true patriots, not traitors or defectors, and so cannot be described as inherently "defective."

Some recognize evil in the regime under which they live and it is conscience that dictates betrayal. Such are the best human sources, though they can be notoriously difficult to handle because their righteous zeal often leads them to take risks that lead to their own destruction. Such people are seldom "recruited" in the classic sense. They volunteer themselves for the suicide mission when the opportunity arises and entrust their lives into the hands of spymasters.

Spymasters target the motivations and weaknesses that can be exploited for recruitment. Fear or money, or both are powerful incentives to commit treason. However, the quality of information from weak or blackmailed sources is notoriously unreliable.

Finally there are those amoral characters that yearn for the intellectual challenge and thrill of danger that espionage offers, people to whom betrayal offers a sense of power.

What had driven Jake to the Russians? I would probably never know, but if I had to guess I'd say it was ego, a quality he had in abundance. From the moment he had called me just a little over a week earlier, he had played the master manipulator. He had used everything he had learned throughout our long friendship, pushed every button and yanked every string to put me on the spot in Vienna, to use me to bait the trap for Stankov - and to get me killed in the process.

All my precautions, the third-party communications system via Maurice in Paris, everything I had done to stay below the radar had been for naught because from the beginning, even before I left Washington, Jake knew the precise spot, the *treffpunkt* on Kaerntner Strasse, where Stankov would be lured to his death.

The Russians had reacted fast to the unexpected

situation created by Stankov's appearance in Vienna and his call for a meeting via the accommodation address in Oslo. They had not been fast enough to get him the first time, but they had killed Thackery and retrieved one of the disks - poor clueless Thackery. If only he had returned directly to Washington to report after his meeting with Stankov, he might still be alive.

Instead the rookie had chosen to discount everything Stankov told him or was so keen to have his skiing holiday that he convinced himself that the disk was low grade ore.

There was no "Eyes Only" memo in Jake's safe that would exonerate me. Jake had designed my departure from Washington to look hasty, with no official sanction. I was on my own, and there was no one in Washington who could or would help. At this very moment Jake would be hammering away at the nails in my coffin.

My rotund friend must have been shocked when I turned up alive. Nevertheless, "Jake the Snake" had recovered quickly and set me up for the kill a second time.

It was brilliant. Not only had he arranged for my death, but he also had succeeded in casting me as the traitorous mole and hung the blame for Thackery's murder around my neck. Well done!

Had pinning the mole rap on me been foremost in Jake's mind from the start? The information Stankov carried was clearly important to the Russians, but setting up a scapegoat to divert attention from himself would have been of equal or greater importance to Jake, and he had played his hand brilliantly, manipulating the actions of both the Russians and the Americans.

Barney Morley had been blindsided and left to take the blame. He would be out within days.

A CIA team must be on its way to join the manhunt, along with the Austrians, Interpol, and assorted Russian death squads. Jake had to be feeling pretty cocky that I was alone with no place to hide and that one or the other of these pursuers in the end would bring me to ground.

But none of them knew I had linked up with the Israelis. On the negative side, the Israelis could do anything with me they liked, including shooting me and handing my still bleeding corpse over the CIA. Everything depended upon whether Eitan Ronan was a man of honor.

CHAPTER 44

"A bris is out of the question."

Ronan interpreted my thoughts correctly.

"Don't worry, my friend. I think we need to work together. Do you agree?"

"Of course."

What choice did I have? But conviction was lacking.

"You are a versatile and capable man, Connolly. And you have proven that you are a survivor. Frankly, you surprised me. Who knows? When this is all over the CIA may welcome you back as a hero!"

I was unable to discern whether this was in earnest or deadpan humor. The Israeli was unreadable.

"What was it that Spartan mothers told their sons when they went off to war? 'Return carrying your shield or carried upon it?' Believe me; the CIA would much prefer that I just disappear. Too much china has been broken already."

"Well, we'll see. You have a lot of work to do today with our technicians. We've developed an alias _persona_ for you that you should have no trouble pulling off." His shark's teeth glinted in a grin that I assumed he intended to be reassuring. "You will undoubtedly be pleased to learn that I am making you an Israeli citizen, at least temporarily. First we must do something about your appearance."

"A *bris* is out of the question," I deadpanned.

For the first time since I had met him Ronan roared with laughter.

"Oh, no, I won't make you THAT much of an Israeli."

The tension of the moment was broken.

A few hours later a Mossad technician cut my hair a lot shorter that I was used to wearing it and applied a color rinse that left it a deep brown, erasing the gray that had begun to show at the temples. Surprisingly, there was a tanning booth in the basement of the Embassy and after a liberal application of tanning lotion and a session in the booth my skin had assumed a nice shade of burnished bronze. Brown contact lenses completed the transformation. The tech took several photos and a short while later handed over two passports, one Israeli and the other Argentine. Both were in the name of Raoul Kahane, a dual national. There was also an American Express card, a Visa card, Argentine and Israeli driver's licenses, and other assorted 'pocket litter.'

I assessed "Raoul Kahane's" appearance in the mirror. The treatment had taken about ten years off my apparent age. At a little over six feet, still lean despite my recent lack of exercise, and now with a tan, short dark hair, and brown eyes, I looked like a different person. "Hello, Raoul. *Shalom.*"

Ronan and Sasha were equally impressed by the transformation.

"The tan looks good on you," she pronounced, a smile tugging at the corner of her mouth.

Ronan asked, "Are you up for some travel?"

"I can't stay here forever, although I am developing a taste for *hummus*." The dish seemed to be a part of every meal at the Embassy. "Where am I going?"

"<u>WE</u> are going to Spain.   While Tel-Aviv is working out how to drain the Russian accounts we need to ask Mr. Yudin a few questions, and in the process prevent him from taking any countermeasures to protect the accounts using the disk Drozhdov gave him. Then we're going to try to move money to accounts we have created, and then bounce the funds around the world a couple of times to confuse any attempts to trace them."

He grinned broadly, or perhaps it was a grimace - I couldn't tell. "We need to buy some time. If we are successful the money will end up funding Israeli defense projects to protect us against whatever the Russians are cooking up with the Iranians. I like the irony."

"You know, Ronan, I don't think anyone has tumbled to Mossad involvement in this. As much as I like the thought of a jaunt to Spain, are you sure it's a good idea?"

"<u>Very</u> good, Harry. That's where you come in.   It's why we need you to make this trip. We want Yudin to see <u>you</u>, not us, and report it back to Moscow Center. You will remain the constant in the entire affair, and it will confuse the hell out of the Bolshies."

The Mossad needed me to front for them, show my face, and perpetuate the fiction that I was a rogue. This would make me a permanent target for the Russians, a hunted man.

"You want to paint a big bull's eye on my back."

"Perhaps only a little bigger than the one already there."

There was not a trace of contrition or sympathy in his voice. "It may not work out that way, depending on circumstances, but we must continue the deception. You make a wonderful false flag."

"Everything that's happened here in Vienna represents a great success for you, doesn't it?"

Both Ronan and Sasha were watching closely, trying to gauge my state of mind and willingness to proceed. Ronan shrugged.

"Certainly a stroke of luck, but only a step towards success. You should start calling me Eitan, by the way."

He placed a beefy hand on my shoulder. "We know what you have been through and that you are in a terrible position. Bluntly speaking, it is horrible for you, but could be very useful to us. Our profession compels us to take advantage of any circumstance that promotes our interests. Success equals opportunity plus preparation plus execution. You understand this as well as anyone."

He was right. There was no other option but to

continue moving forward, not only to stay ahead of my pursuers, but also in the hope that we might arrive at some resolution that did not leave me face down in the street or in jail for the rest of my life. There was a wake of death and chaos spreading behind me, and for the time being I had no allies other than these two people.

"You're right, Eitan. I want to hurt these sons of bitches as much as I can. They tried to kill me twice. Hell, I WANT them to know I've hurt them!"

Ronan appeared gratified, and Sasha's expression relaxed. Ronan pointed at Sasha.

"Mr. Kahane, meet Mrs. Kahane. You two will be traveling as a couple. Even with your altered appearance, this will be safer. They're looking for a single man, not a couple."

CHAPTER 45

Morning in Moscow, February 18

Vienna should have been a simple, straightforward affair for the Russians. There had been little time in which to act, but thanks to Liebowitz they had precise details of when and where the Russian traitor would be contacted. Their assassin had been too late to kill Stankov, but performed well in tracking down Thackery and recovering his disk. It had been Shurgin's personal decision to kill the CIA officer thus breaking the "standing rules" of the old KGB-CIA dynamic. This was a new game – HIS game, and he would make the rules now. The old restraints imposed on Soviet intelligence by the defunct Communist political leadership no longer applied.

Liebowitz slyly suggested that there could be a silver lining in Stankov's initial escape. The mole hunt at Langley was drawing dangerously close to him. Why not engage in a little deception and set someone else up to take the fall?

Morozov was deeply chagrined by the recent turn of events.

Across the table, Shurgin sat chewing his lip, a sure sign that he, too, was worried. Urgency lent a sharp edge to his words.

"Drozhdov knew about Yudin. He met him in Madrid. If somehow the American captured him, the Marbella operation could be compromised. We should send some protection to Yudin and retrieve the disk before there are any more surprises."

If Yudin panicked he could do considerable harm to *Voskreseniye*. Yudin was not the "professional" that Lomonosov was, and nor was he as well protected. It had been prudent to disperse responsibilities for setting up the accounts and handling the funds, and Yudin was extremely trustworthy, but in the present situation Shurgin was unwilling to take chances. Yudin had personally set up most of the accounts not controlled by Zhenya, and he had a vital role to play in regaining control over them.

Shurgin's tame "oligarch" would need watching, as well as protection.

"An excellent and timely thought, Yuriy Ivanovich. By all means tell Zhenya to get a team to Marbella immediately. Do it now. Don't waste a moment, and don't reply to Yudin until you receive confirmation that the team has actually arrived. It should not take long. They can fly directly into the Malaga airport from Zurich."

*****

Zhenya was surprised by the second call from Moscow. Gingerly replacing the receiver, he sat thinking for a few moments, elbows on his desk, his long manicured fingers steepled before him. The sky was lowering outside, promising snow.

Even one phone call from Morozov was a rare event, and now he had received two within the course of a few days. Moscow Center was in a panic. The thought did not please him. Zhenya's international operations relied heavily on former KGB officers, communications channels, technology, and agent networks, especially in the Middle East. Just as the Brotherhood was useful to Voskreseniye, Morozov and his organization added a completely new dimension to Zhenya's criminal capabilities and accounted in large part for his ability continually to elude the legal authorities of several countries, not the least here in his adopted Switzerland.

Whatever Morozov needed, Zhenya was more than happy to provide. He depressed a button under his desk, and a few moments later his senior lieutenant appeared at the door of his study.

"There is a problem. We need to dispatch a team to look after Yudin in Marbella. Get them in the air immediately. I want them in place by this evening," he looked again out the window at the lowering sky, "if they can get out before the airport is socked in. Call my pilot and have him prepare the Gulfstream. Tell the team that if they are good boys, maybe Yudin will give them a go at that Spanish whore he has living with him."

CHAPTER 46

On the Move

Eitan Ronan ruled that even with my altered appearance it was too dangerous to try to leave Austria by air. Instead, we would drive across the border to Germany and fly out of Munich to Malaga where we would pay a call on the Russian "oligarch."

Mid-morning Wednesday, Sasha drove us to a parking garage near the WestBahnhoff where we exchanged her Skoda for a BMW 750IL.

Within minutes the powerful sedan had carried us out of the city heading west toward the autobahn to Munich. A hint of snow to come was in the air, and a strong wind occasionally buffeted the heavy car. Clouds scudded across the sky as we raced them westward toward Munich.

Sasha handled the big car with confidence and skill. I was next to her in the front seat, with Ronan in the rear, as she navigated expertly along the A-1 toward Linz. The drive would take approximately four hours. Ronan had reserved seats on a Lufthansa flight out of Franz-Josef Strauss Airport, just north of Munich, to Malaga departing the same afternoon. It would be at least 10 hours before we arrived finally in Spain far to the south - unless someone spotted me along the way.

I was not in a talkative mood, and we drove in silence for most of the way. Ronan dozed in the back seat, and Sasha concentrated on the road as a light snow began to fall.

For the thousandth time I mulled over my situation. On one level, at least, that of personal ruin, Jake had won. Ronan and the Mossad could offer no guarantees that I could clear my name, and even if that were possible, there was now too much *stúrm und drang* in the press in Washington for the Agency ever to welcome me back. Under the best of circumstances I would be tied up in legal battles for years to come, and there was a better than even chance I would spend the rest of my life in prison. The growing anger toward Jake Liebowitz was burning a hole in my gut.

Ronan had not explained what we were to do in Spain, whether because he had not fully formulated a plan or because he didn't have one. He was acting on speculation, flying by the seat of his pants, and there was no choice but to cling desperately to his wing. I didn't imagine for a moment that we would just stroll into Yudin's home and discuss what he knew about stolen Russian funds over glasses of chilled Spanish sherry. All we had was his address, his connection with *Voskreseniye*, and the fact that he had a copy of Stankov's disk that must be recovered.

Planning was already underway in Tel-Aviv to exploit the financial records, and alarm bells were surely clanging in Moscow. Yudin obviously played an important role for the

Russians or the records would never have been delivered to him. Ronan suspected that the accounts could not be fully accessed by the Russians without Yudin's assistance.

As Sasha swung the sedan from the A-1 to the A-8 and sped northwestward Ronan stirred in the back seat.

"It's time to talk about the next step."

CHAPTER 47

Marbella, Spain – Evening, February 19

Marbella, with its privileged situation on the Mediterranean coast, is a jewel filled with costly villas and condos overlooking the sea. Originally founded by the Romans some two hundred years before Christ, it had been occupied by the Moors for 700 years until the 15th century and still retained a faintly Moorish character, albeit with a glitzy, distinctly Western overlay of nightclubs and restaurants populated enthusiastically by wealthy jet setters.

We had arrived at Pablo Ruíz Picasso Airport near Malaga an hour earlier, having barely made it out of Munich ahead of a storm front. A Mossad contact met us with a briefcase containing three Glock 23 compact 40-caliber pistols, extra 17-round clips, and holsters. Thus armed, we rented a fast Alfa-Romeo and headed for Marbella.

The change from gray, wet Vienna to the colorful Spanish Mediterranean coast was striking. The fading rays of the setting sun reflected softly off orange tiled roofs and cast deep, purple shadows across the hilly landscape as we sped westward along the coast.

There was a hint of jasmine in the air as we drove through the exquisite town and continued west along the N-340 highway towards Puerto Banús and the exclusive

Puente Romano neighborhood where Yudin's villa was located. It was nearing six PM and darkness had fully embraced the town by the time we finally parked the car on a quiet street a couple of blocks from the villa.

Until recently the most visible foreigners in the high rent districts along Spain's Gold Coast had been Arabs, wealthy Saudis prominent among them, who found the fleshly pleasures available to them there a pleasing diversion from the restrictive customs of their homelands. Their wealth ensured that no debauchery was out of their reach, and local officials were easily bribed to overlook frequent excesses.

Now Russians were supplanting the Arabs -- the so-called "oligarchs" who had amassed great fortunes in the course of the few years since the fall of the Soviet Union. They bought villas, cars, hotels, indeed anything that took their fancy, and they did not mind the exorbitant prices charged by the delighted locals.

Yudin's eight-bedroom villa, large even by Marbella standards, stood on the "Golden Mile" adjacent to the famed Puente Romano hotel. The compound was totally enclosed by walls punctuated with electrically controlled gates. Servants' quarters and garages were separate from the house across the expanse of an Olympic size pool.

The February evening was cool as the two Israelis and I paused in our reconnaissance to consult on the next move. Ronan's plan was simple: go in, take control of the house, retrieve the disk and any other records, and squeeze the Russian for additional information.

Ronan made me nervous.

"I don't want any more rough stuff, Eitan, at least no more than absolutely necessary."

I had caught a glimpse of Drozhdov a few days ago as he was wheeled, tied to a gurney, out of the Embassy. The Russian's face had been ghastly, and his hands had been wrapped in bloody bandages. I had no love for Stankov's killer, but torture was abhorrent.

Evidently, as one of Mossad's "hard men" Ronan had no such compunctions.

"Neither do I, Harry. Neither do I. But if all that has happened over the past week is to have any meaning, we have to neutralize any efforts Yudin might make to protect the funds, and we have to do so without revealing Mossad involvement."

I could concede that point, and I accepted the importance the Israelis attached to remaining invisible. "We have to do so without showing the Mossad hand and you want to make certain Yudin knows who I am so he can report it to Moscow."

"That is correct. Are you ready?"

I didn't think it would be difficult to overpower Yudin, and it certainly would not be as dangerous as facing down three men in a gunfight in a hotel in Vienna. The idea here was to get in and out WITHOUT raising a ruckus.

The villa waited, silent in the deepening shadows.

Choosing a spot not illuminated by street lamps, we went over the wall aided by a conveniently placed tree. This brought us into the compound behind the house, a few yards from the servants' quarters. Ronan quickly found the phone box and disabled it, which also should disable the alarm system. His job then was to check the grounds for anyone who might be present, such as servants, and neutralize them should it be necessary. The servants' quarters looked deserted. Ronan would keep out of sight and maintain perimeter security. Sasha and I would find Yudin.

We drew our weapons, attached the suppressors, and went in.

CHAPTER 48

Yudin and the Night Visitors

Arkadiy Nikolayevich Yudin had been hard at work since receiving Morozov's orders to check the accounts listed on the disk. The lack of an immediate response from Moscow to his message about Drozhdov had left him in a nervous and uncertain state.

Seated at the desk in his study, he uttered a steady stream of choice curse words culled from several languages. He had made telephone call after telephone call beginning the day before, Monday, as soon as financial institutions were open and learned that several large accounts already had been drained electronically. There was nothing he could do to retrieve these missing funds. Once transferred, the funds could be bounced from place to place until finally they disappeared. These were mostly relatively small commercial accounts that could be accessed remotely, set up that way for convenience as they were used frequently to move funds. Anyone with the pass codes could access them.

There was still time. Yudin himself had set up many of the accounts, mostly in so-called private banks. These accounts could not easily be accessed, nor could money be transferred out of them with a simple phone call or computer link. Many banks would not accept an anonymous transfer from a numbered account. Banks had their rules, and they usually wanted to know the origin of transferred funds. Whoever was draining the accounts would require time to make arrangements with receiving banks, and such arrangements had to be made in person.

So far, approximately two billion Swiss francs were missing from five accounts. To be sure, this was an enormous sum, but it barely scratched the surface of the amounts he oversaw for Shurgin. Yudin would have to ask for the use of one of Zhenya Lomonosov's private jets, but with luck he would be able to save the remaining funds.

When he had been a small child and his mother made paskha, traditional Russian Easter bread, she would give him the mixing bowl and a very small spoon. Little Arkadiy would scrape the remaining sweet dough off the sides of the bowl and the tiny spoon insured that the gooey mixture would last a long time.

Whoever was stealing the Russian money was doing the same – scraping small amounts with a small spoon. But even so, given enough time, the thief could get all the dough. Yudin needed to get ahead of them. He did not look forward to the marathon travel that lay ahead, but he could not afford to wait. As it was, he was alone in Marbella, and his only tools were a single telephone and his computer. With funds deposited as far away as the Cayman Islands, he would be weeks at his task. He toyed with the idea of taking Barbara with him. She would find it exciting, and Arkadiy could use the company. Fucking her at 30,000 feet in Zhenya's jet would be stimulating.

Dragging his thoughts away from that lofty reverie, he forced his attention back to the task at hand. There were several accounts he had not yet been able to check. A great deal of the money in his charge was invested in private companies and international projects, such as oil exploration in Iraq. These investments, he knew, were safe because they were not liquid. Yudin put his face in his hands, rubbing his tired eyes, and remained that way for a few moments. He would send another message to Moscow Center immediately, he decided. Zhenya must send the jet to Malaga.

When he looked up again, a tall man who looked vaguely familiar stood just inside the doorway of the study pointing a gun with a silencer directly at him.

"Nye dvigaysya, don't move," the man said in excellent Russian. His voice was calm, but commanding. Once he had swallowed his surprise, Yudin's first thought was to push the alarm button on the console in front of him.

"Place your hands flat on the desk, Arkadiy Nikolayevich," the man said, advancing toward him, "and don't move them again unless I tell you."

Yudin froze. He couldn't tear his eyes away from the gun. His mind locked on an image of a bullet travelling at high velocity straight at his head. He did as he was instructed, but his thoughts were spinning out of control. Was this Morozov's man? Had the intelligence chief sent an assassin to murder him? True, the situation was bad, he thought, but it was not his fault. He had nothing to do with losing the account information. Why would Morozov do this? Regardless of the reason, Yudin knew that if Morozov wanted him dead, he soon would be.

"Where is the disk?" The tall man was now in front of the desk, directly across from Yudin, and he suddenly recalled where he had seen him before. This man was not Clint Eastwood, but bore a striking resemblance.

Yudin's eyes flicked involuntarily to the laptop computer. His mouth opened and closed repeatedly, but no sound emerged, like a fish out of water gasping for oxygen.

At that moment Barbara stumbled through the study door, shoved roughly from behind by a strikingly beautiful woman with ash blond hair. The blonde was holding Barbara's arm twisted painfully behind her back, and she held a pistol to the Spanish girl's head.

"Everything under control?" the tall man asked the blonde – in English! So he was not Russian, after all!

"Yes," replied the woman in the same language. "There is no one else in the house. I found this one upstairs in the biggest damned bathtub I've ever seen." Yudin belatedly took in the fact that Barbara was dressed only in a large terry robe.

The blonde pushed his girlfriend into a chair against the wall and secured her hands to the arms of the chair with what looked like bands of plastic. Barbara struggled against the restraints, but a threatening gesture from the blonde quieted her. The Spanish girl's eyes were wide with fright.

"W-who are you," Yudin finally managed to stammer, this time in English. This was the language he and Barbara used with one another.

The pistol remained aimed unwaveringly at Yudin. "My name is Harry, and you and your friends have given me a hell of a time over the past couple of days. But they're dead now. I've gotten pretty good at killing Russian scum. I thought I'd bring the war home to the boss. I'm tired of dealing with lackeys."

This news shocked Yudin, and he was not sure he believed it. How could the feral assassin, Drozhdov, have been defeated?

Despite her fear, Barbara had been listening intently. "Arkadiy, what is this man talking about? What do they want?"

The blonde slapped Barbara sharply across the cheek, leaving a red mark. "Keep quiet!"

The Spanish girl began sobbing quietly.

"Are you going to kill me?" Arkadiy's voice rose in pitch. The sudden violence against Barbara frightened him even further.

"Maybe," the man shrugged, "Maybe not. It depends."

"I don't know what you want," the Russian whined. "You've made a mistake!"

The man's eyes narrowed. He leant menacingly over

the desk and placed the end of the silencer directly against Yudin's forehead. It hurt.

"It's you who made the mistake," his voice still soft and menacing. "How do you think I found you? One of your friends told me who you were before I put a bullet into his ugly face. I shot him right in the eye." He moved the pistol from the middle of Yudin's forehead to his left eye. "Maybe I should do the same with you right now."

"Please, no!" Yudin shouted. "Yes, I admit it. I know the one called Drozhdov. But he does not work for me. I gave him no orders. He only delivered the disk to me."

"So, you DO have the disk."

"Th-the disk?" Yudin was stammering again. He knew how much depended on the information on that disk. Without it, without the account numbers and pass codes, the cash might never be recovered. "I gave it to someone else. I don't have it anymore."

The man stood back. "You're lying. The disk is right here in this room. As a matter of fact, I'll bet it's slotted into this computer."

The man bent down, keeping his pistol aimed at Yudin, and pressed the release button on the computer's floppy drive. A blue disk popped out, and the man retrieved it. "Several people died for this, and one of them was a friend of mine."

"I d-don't know what you're talking about."

This stranger held the key to billions of Voskreseniye

dollars in his hand. Yudin was horrified.

"OK. Let's take a look." The man turned to the blonde. "Come on over here and see what's on this."

He returned his attention to Yudin.

"Get up. Keep your hands in the air."

He gestured with the gun, and Yudin rose from his seat. The man shoved him hard across the room and pushed him down into a chair next to Barbara where he bound him with the same kind of plastic strips the blonde had used on Barbara.

The blonde took a seat behind Yudin's desk and slipped the disk back into the floppy drive, concentrating on the computer's screen. When the request for a password appeared she typed in a series of numbers without hesitation, and the screen lit up with columns of names and figures.

"This is it," she said.

The man had not moved his eyes from Yudin.

"Well, well. It looks to me as if you were lying to me, Arkadiy. What do you think I should do with you?"

Before the Russian could reply, two men burst through the door of the study, guns in hand.

CHAPTER 49

Gunfight

Ivan Dimov's Spetsnaz-trained eyes immediately assessed the situation as they rushed through the door. Nikitin had burst into the room just ahead of him. Nikitin was rash, but this suited the more circumspect Spetsnaz veteran. Just as a wary old roebuck allows a younger one into the forest clearing first, Dimov left rashness to the young. In any case, the undisciplined vor v zakonye was not good at following orders.

There was a pistol on the desk beside the blonde working with the computer and she presented no immediate threat. The tall man standing beside Yudin held a pistol, but their sudden appearance had taken him completely off guard, yielding the advantage to Dimov and Nikitin.

The latter -- always one to shoot first and ask questions later -- fired at the man who launched himself sideways onto the floor underneath the trajectory of the bullet, which lodged itself instead into the chest of a half-dressed, dark haired girl tied to a chair beside Yudin. The white terry cloth of her robe blossomed red, and her head flopped back, dead eyes frozen wide.

Yudin began to scream.

The man rolled on the floor away from the chairs and his silenced Glock coughed twice; one of the rounds caught Nikitin in the abdomen and exited his back, leaving a hole the size of a grapefruit. Nikitin doubled up and fell to the floor clasping his mid-section as the shooter swung his pistol towards Dimov.

The Russian's reflexes were very fast, and he snapped off a shot with automatic precision. His bullet found its mark and the man's gun spun from his hand and skittered across the tiled floor. Dimov had shot to kill, but his target had been moving, and he saw that the man had been hit in the side but was still alive. He could have double-tapped him then and there, but there was a second target in the room, and she was now reaching for the pistol on the desk.

Dimov swept his weapon towards the woman. Everything transpired in the course of just a few seconds, and Dimov quickly covered the space between them. He could easily kill her before she could retrieve her weapon and take aim, and the woman obviously knew it.

She hesitated for a fraction of a second, eyes blazing, and then carefully raised her arms and stepped back from the desk. She stood perfectly still and didn't say a word.

"Pick up your weapon with two fingers only, place it carefully on the floor, and kick it into the corner," Dimov ordered.

She obeyed, never removing her eyes from him.

"Now, come out from behind the desk. Keep your

hands in the air."

Yudin was hysterical, gaping at the girl's body slumped in the chair at his side. Her head lolled back and her dead eyes stared blankly at the ceiling as blood puddled beneath her.

"They were going to kill us! They know about the disk."

Dimov knew nothing of any disk. His assignment had been only to protect Yudin. He looked at the intruders. The man, in evident pain, had pulled himself to a sitting position against the wall, one arm hugging his side. There was something familiar about him.

"Who are you?" demanded Dimov.

The man hesitated for a moment, and Dimov raised his pistol to point it directly at the woman's head.

The man said, "My name is Harry Connolly, CIA. Who are you?"

Dimov immediately recognized the name. He looked more closely now at Connolly. His appearance had been altered but not enough to make him completely unrecognizable from the photograph he had been shown before being sent to Vienna.

"Yes, I can see who you are now. You got away from me in that hotel in Vienna, Connolly, but it won't happen twice. And you are in no position to ask questions. Why are you here? Who sent you?"

Yudin yelled, "He said he killed Drozhdov."

Dimov raised his eyebrows. He knew Drozhdov from

his Spetnaz days. This soft American razvedchik had managed to kill two of his colleagues in Vienna. Could he really have taken out a trained operative like Drozhdov, as well?

"Now how did you ever do that?" he asked in a soft voice.

Nikitin was in a fetal position, groaning and bleeding all over the floor, his blood running along the grouted grooves between the square Spanish tiles. The American nodded toward him.

"Just about the same way I got your buddy over there."

Dimov studied the American for a moment. "I think I'm going to enjoy interrogating you. I hope you continue trying to lie to me for a long time. It will make the questioning much more interesting, and I can think of a LOT of questions."

He kept one eye on the woman as he spoke.

CHAPTER 50

Death

I sat slumped against the wall pressing my hand tightly to my side as blood seeped through my fingers. *Where the hell is Ronan?* The Russians' pistols were not silenced, and the Israeli had to have heard the shots. Had the two toughs already killed the big Mossad officer? There had been no warning before they burst in, and I didn't think the Ronan could have been taken silently.

It felt like the slug had broken a couple of ribs, and the wound burned like hell. There was a lot of blood, but it wasn't a fatal wound. *How do we get out of this?*

The Russian with the pistol was about 5' 8", muscular, closely cropped blond hair. Unmistakable military bearing. He was dressed in jeans and a black leather jacket over a dark sweater.

Maybe I could distract him long enough for Sasha to reach her pistol. I tried to rise, keeping eyes on the man still with his weapon at Sasha's head. She had said nothing since the two Russians had burst into the room and now stood very still with her hands in the air. My pistol had come to rest against the wall at least ten feet away, too far.

The thug on the floor emitted mewling, gurgling

sounds. Blood dribbled from his mouth and his face had long since gone white. He was clearly out of commission for a while, possibly dying. Judging from the widening circle of red under him, he might well bleed out in a very few minutes. His companion showed no concern as he concentrated all his attention on Sasha and me.

I looked toward Yudin and noticed for the first time that the Spanish girl had been shot. She did not appear to be breathing. Yudin was glaring at me with a combination of terror and malevolence.

The Russian kept his pistol aimed at Sasha's face and ordered her out from behind the desk. Her expression was inscrutable. I wondered what was going on in her mind. She must be wondering about Ronan, too.

The Russian barked an order at her.

"Go and help your friend to his feet. I want you to tie him to a chair. Then you can release Mr. Yudin."

Yudin continued to glare, and his mouth now twisted into a mean triumphal grin.

"Now, you *sukin syn'*," he spat, "It's your turn to answer questions. And then you will die, slowly, I hope, and we will have a little fun with blondie over there. What do you think of that?"

"I think you're a fat asshole."

Where the hell was Ronan?

"Tie him up," the Russian again ordered Sasha.

There was nothing we could do. We were disarmed,

and I was losing hope that Ronan would appear at about the same rate I was losing blood. If the Israeli were going to do anything, surely he would have done it by now.

Sasha helped me to a chair and bound my wrists to the arms with a pair of the plastic zip cuffs we'd brought with us. A new wave of pain and nausea washed over me as I was forced to remove the pressure from my side. Finished, Sasha turned and faced the Russian with the gun. She still had not uttered a word.

"Now, untie Yudin."

As the Russian moved menacingly toward her she raised her arms above her head and spoke for the first time.

"No."

"Oho, a defiant little bitch, aren't you." The thug advanced quickly on her and thrust his pistol directly at her face, only inches away from her. "Do what you are told, *pizda*, MOVE! If you're a good little girl, maybe I won't shoot you in the face when the time comes."

Before the threat was fully out of his mouth, Sasha's left arm slashed down and she grasped the top of the Russian's pistol, simultaneously forcing the barrel away from herself inwards and down, towards the Russian's groin. Before the gun was halfway through its arc she pressed its ejector button, and the clip clattered to the floor, leaving only one round in the chamber.

With equal speed she clapped the open palm of her right hand against the Russian's left ear. As her opponent staggered back, baring his teeth in surprised pain and anger, Sasha wrenched the pistol from his grasp and smashed her opponent savagely in the face with the grip, always moving into his body, keeping him off balance, forcing him back with slashing punches and elbows to the head and kicks that followed one another like the blows of a jackhammer. She finished him off with a crushing knee to the groin and a final crack on the side of his head with the pistol. The Russian went down hard, and she stood over him, her chest heaving. It looked as if she were deciding whether to kill him or let him live.

I blinked and for an instant forgot the searing pain in my side. It had happened so fast, like a conjuring trick. One minute the Russian held all the trump cards; the next Sasha was standing over his crumpled body.

Yudin was screaming again. He could believe no more easily than I what he had just witnessed.

"You filthy *pizda*! You whore. You can't do this!"

Sasha looked over her shoulder at the hysterical oligarch and smiled wickedly. She retrieved the clip from the floor, rammed it into the Russian's pistol, turned and pointed the weapon at the fallen man's head.

"Don't shoot!" It wasn't that I felt any sympathy for the bastard, but this man knew who I was, and this was a stroke of luck that could guarantee the success of our plan to conceal the Israeli hand. The Russian would confirm that it was Harry Connolly, rogue CIA officer, who had mounted the raid.

It required a couple of deep breaths for Sasha to bring her rage under control. She was clearly in a killing mode, whether aroused by the fierce hand-to-hand combat or some atavistic inner urge, but she finally lowered her weapon and settled for a vicious kick to her helpless opponent's face that rendered him fully unconscious.

She walked over to the still groaning second intruder, knelt and examined at him. When she stood up again her face was a mask I hardly recognized as the demure girl I met only a few days ago in a Viennese coffee house.

"He won't last long," she announced impassively of the man on the floor, and then she turned her attention to Yudin, "But I might let *you* live if you're a good little Russian boy."

If I had harbored any lingering doubts about Sasha's professional capabilities they had been erased in an entirely spectacular fashion. She was a *sochen*, a highly trained Israeli field agent, as lethal and ruthless as they come. That she was a cold-blooded killer, as well, was not in doubt.

I had killed people on this hopelessly bollixed mission, but that had been in self-defense. Shooting someone point blank while they were helpless to defend themselves was another thing entirely. I flashed back to the scene in the hotel room in Vienna where, fueled by adrenalin, I had executed a wounded man. Maybe I wasn't so different, after all.

Sasha approached Yudin, still tied to his chair, and put her face very close to his.

"Listen, you fat shit. Now you are going to tell us everything we want to know. There is one dead person and one about to die in this room right now, and it would not bother me to add a third."

She straightened and brought the pistol to bear on the *oligarch*, who tried to shrink into the upholstery, his bravura now dissipated.

Sasha left him to contemplate his predicament while she released me from the zip cuffs. She knelt in front of me.

"I need to see your wound."

It was painful even to raise my left arm far enough to pull up the blood soaked sweater. She examined my side, probing none too gently, her aggressive energy still not fully used up.

"You're lucky. You might have a broken rib or two, but other than that the damage is superficial. She found some towels in the bathroom adjoining the study, poured some of Yudin's expensive whiskey onto them and dressed the wound with long strips torn from the towels.

"That should do until we can take care of it properly. How do you feel?"

"Not good, but not so bad that I can't finish this."

It cost some effort to stand up, and I stood swaying for a moment waiting for the nausea to pass, still wondering what had happened to Ronan.

When the room had stopped spinning I said, "You'd

better have a look around."

She raised a perfectly plucked eyebrow at me. "Why?"

"But what about ..." I couldn't mention Ronan's name if they were to maintain the fiction that he was operating independently, but Sasha immediately understood.

"Don't worry. Everything is under control."

She jerked her head in the direction of the doorway, and there was Ronan, standing well back out of Yudin's line of sight. The Israeli nodded and smiled grimly as he replaced his pistol in his holster. He'd held back so as not to reveal himself and risk blowing the plan -- he was that cold-blooded. My initial distrust of the man was turning to distaste. The guy was as much a thug as the Russians.

Of more immediate concern was the fact that there was no way to know whether the gunshots had been heard. It was unlikely, given the expansive grounds surrounding the villa, but prudence dictated that we complete our task quickly.

Encouraged by Sasha and the presence of two corpses and the unconscious man on the floor, the "oligarch" turned cooperative and described the *Voskreseniye* organization's off-shore financial network sufficiently to permit us to gauge the amount of damage we had done, as well as how far there still was to go.

Anxious now to please he volunteered the name of a high ranking Moscow city official, former KGB General Vitaliy Mikhailovich Shurgin, as the head of *Voskreseniye*. There was plenty of information for Mossad analysts to chew on.

Sasha tore up Yudin's study, and with some grudging directions from him discovered some interesting electronic devices and documents. All of these, plus Yudin's laptop computer were bundled into a bag made from another of the oligarch's luxurious giant bath towels.

We left him tied to the chair and joined Ronan in the foyer. My side burned like hell, and I was anxious to get out of there. The Russian that Sasha had overpowered was beginning to groan and would soon recover consciousness, but he was in no condition to come after us.

Instead of heading for the exit, Sasha helped me to a seat and moved away to confer quietly with Ronan in their own language. After a moment the big Israeli turned and went into the study.

"What the hell is he doing?" I was startled. "If Yudin sees him it'll ruin everything!"

Sasha did not reply, and then Yudin shrieked and there was the cough of a silenced pistol.

Ronan returned to the entrance foyer. "What did you do?" I was angry. "You killed him in cold blood!"

"We'll talk about it later," replied the Israeli. "We have to get out of here before we have any more unexpected visitors. There's no time to waste."

He led the way back through the house to the veranda doors we had entered originally. Ronan practically had to lift me bodily to get me back over the wall.

Sasha took the wheel again, and Ronan sat in back with me. Once we were well away from the neighborhood he made a call on his cell phone then gave Sasha directions. After a half-hour we pulled up to a doctor's office on the outskirts of Marbella where a nameless surgeon of Jewish origins gave me an injection, patched up my side and bandaged my torso tightly.

Ronan announced that we would drive through the night to Madrid, where help was waiting to get us onto an El Al flight to Tel Aviv.

If the broken ribs and the sutures were painful, the sudden disgust that had seized me when Yudin had been murdered in cold blood bothered me even more. How many more lives had to be taken? It had been bad enough before Marbella, but now the Russians would hold me responsible for three more deaths, including Yudin and his girlfriend, both bound and helpless when they were killed.

CHAPTER 51

Tel-Aviv, February 22

I woke up in a bed in a private hospital room that I would learn later was in a special wing of the Assaf Harofeh Medical Center, just outside Tel Aviv. The window permitted the bright sunlight to illuminate the fresh flowers that decorated the metal table at my bedside.

The doctor in Marbella had shot me full of antibiotics, put in temporary sutures, and tightly bandaged the broken ribs. Large and regular doses of painkiller served to make the long drive to Madrid tolerable, and I managed some fitful sleep in the rear seat.

El Al security assured a quick and discreet entry to Barajas Airport where we received the sort of VIP treatment that must be afforded routinely to celebrities to get them quietly and unobtrusively through the rigors of boarding. First class seats, more painkillers, and a really fine single malt whiskey finally combined to ensure that the long flight to Israel passed in relatively pain free sleep.

Several stern and quietly efficient men dressed in white met us at planeside at Ben Gurion Airport and bundled me into an ambulance. The indefatigable Sasha sat at my side. Her ministrations belied the ruthless operative that

I now knew lay beneath the attractive exterior. Ronan also rode with us, but I pointedly ignored him throughout the journey. Unperturbed, the Israeli sat quietly with his own thoughts, the Mossad's very own Golem.

Memories of arriving at the hospital were vague. The ambulance had pulled into a basement bay, and they had wheeled me to an elevator that carried us to an upper floor where a team of doctors and nurses waited. A quick needle in the arm, and now I awoke in this room.

My appetite returned with a vengeance and I was just finishing a lunch of fresh fruits, juice, olives, hummus, and bread when there was a soft rap at the door, and Ronan entered smiling broadly in a pretty good imitation of the shark from "Jaws." Some people look scary even when they don't intend to, but I'd given up trying to fathom the Golem's intentions.

"You look well, Harry."

He came and stood at the foot of the hospital bed where I lay propped up in a sitting position on snow white pillows.

"Are you ready to get out of here?"

The acrimony resulting from the murder of the helpless Yudin had not abated. On top of that I still didn't understand how the two intruders had gotten past Ronan. I still didn't know how much I could trust him. Was he my savior or my jailer?

"Yeah, but I'm not sure where I might go. I'm a mad dog murderer wanted on several continents, you know."

The thoughtful Israelis had made no attempt to keep the truth hidden from me. I had been the recipient of a steady stream of the international press. The story originated by the *Washington Post* about the rogue CIA officer turned killer had spawned a cottage industry dedicated to blackening the name of Harry Connolly. More than a week had passed since the Vienna incident, but the story was still going strong.

What was worse, I realized I had only myself to blame for having trusted Jake Liebowitz, and even more so for having accepted the fool's mission he had offered. My situation was acutely untenable.

Unfazed by my bitter observations, Ronan eased his large frame into the chair beside the bed and sat there staring at me, his expression inscrutable. He was wearing khakis and a leather bomber jacket over a loose fitting black silk shirt. He looked like a Russian Mafioso.

"The doctors tell me you're recovering nicely and should be none the worse for wear after a week or so of rest and recuperation. We have one of our safehouses waiting for you near the beach in Caesarea, a few kilometers north of here. You need a rest and some sea air after all you've been through."

R&R sounded good, but what then? It wasn't hard to envision the nightmare of entanglements that would be required to clear my name, if it could be cleared. All my bridges were in flames.

In the absence of a reply from me, Ronan continued, "Aren't you curious about how things are going with the money? It's the reason you're here, after all."

There was a gleam in his eyes.

"I suppose so."

"I had to get special permission from the *memuneh,* the Head of Mossad, to share this with you, Harry. But you performed an incalculable service for our country, and he is grateful. And the *memuneh's* gratitude is something special.

"Given the way the Russians reacted to their theft, we believe the disks we recovered from Stankov and Yudin might well be the only copies. The moment the disk you gave me arrived in Tel Aviv our people began setting things in motion to empty the Russian accounts. This will take time and a lot of preparation that I don't fully understand, but the idea is to grab as much of the liquid assets as possible before the Russkies take countermeasures. This is not a thing that can be accomplished overnight, and it is not a task that can be completed without a certain amount of risk. Some of the accounts in private banks require a personal appearance to initiate a funds transfer, and our people must be prepared carefully – the Russians know they have a problem. We also have to open new accounts and ensure that they will accept the transfers. But it is a delicious irony, is it not, that Israel will use Russian funds to pay some of the bills for our own defense? That could be a lot of fighter planes and tanks.

"We can't get at the investments in private companies and certain projects around the world, including many we identified that are tied to criminal activities. We will wound *Voskreseniye,* but we won't kill it. They'll still control of the majority of their activities and reap the benefits, but even so, we now have a long list of *Voskreseniye*-funded enterprises that we can monitor and perhaps even penetrate and disrupt. This information alone is invaluable. And it is information we can use as trading material with the intelligence services of several countries, including your own.

"You should be proud of what you have done," he concluded with a passion that surprised me.

My eyes strayed to the window and the cloudless blue sky beyond.

"I'd be a little careful about sharing anything with American intelligence, if you know what I mean. In a way, I can't help wishing none of it had happened. People lost their lives because a long time ago I recruited Stankov."

Ronan sat back in his chair and folded his arms.

I couldn't hold back the bitterness and no small amount of self-pity that colored my voice leaving the words bitten off, hurling staccato bullets at Ronan. "It might have been more fitting if that guy's aim had been better in Marbella. Then you wouldn't have this loose end to tie up."

I looked hard at the big Israeli. "Like a loose end named Yudin. That's no way to kill a man, Eitan. He was tied to a chair for Christ's sake!"

Ronan released an exasperated sigh, rose to his feet, and stepped over to the window. He stood there with his broad back to me for a few seconds before turning back. When he did, his face was serious and his eyes appraising.

"Your country practices capital punishment, doesn't it? Do they give condemned criminals a fair chance to get away after sentence is passed or do they strap them down and shove a needle into them before they can do more harm."

I said nothing.

"Yudin was no different. Sasha was convinced that the Russians could still use him, and this would endanger our operation and our people. He set up many of the accounts and, given more time, may well have been able to access them. In fact, he was already working on it. We were not prepared to take him prisoner, especially with you wounded and needing care. There was no other choice."

He shook his head. "I didn't enjoy it, you know. We are not wanton savages. But you must understand one basic fact about Israel and Israelis: we are in a war for survival and have been since our country was re-born. We don't have the luxury of fighting our enemies far from our own shores. They are here in our neighborhood, surrounding us and among us, and there is a fanaticism growing that promises to make the future even more dangerous. And now the fucking Russians have decided to come after us, too, by helping our enemies. We don't have time for post-traumatic stress."

It was hard to argue with him. From Ronan's perspective killing Yudin had been a justifiable battlefield decision. Ronan could square the act with his own conscience, and he didn't have to worry about a Headquarters lawyer throwing him to Justice Department wolves, either.

I pushed the lunch tray aside and swung my legs over the side of the bed. The pain in my side was not so bad now.

"What now? I can't see the future, and I sure as hell can't go back."

"I have an idea or two. Are you ready to hear them?"

I was instantly alert. "Go on."

Ronan displayed his toothy smile again.

"You know that my service has never had a non-Jewish *sochen*, officer, and it never will. But I know a good man when I see one. I'm not easily impressed, and frankly never thought I would be impressed by anyone from the CIA. But you, Harry, are an exception to the rule. I want to make you an offer you can't refuse."

CHAPTER 52

Something to Think About

No intelligence officer likes being pitched by a foreign service. It happens all the time, but it's something to be avoided because it causes a lot of problems. Standard CIA practice is immediately to report a pitch to your superiors. Then comes the polygraph accompanied by the fear that the effectiveness of its highly imperfect technology could be further eroded by an imperfect or over-zealous operator. And there is always the nagging, persistent concern amongst one's peers as to why anyone might have thought you were "vulnerable to recruitment" in the first place. That's the question you assume your superiors will worry about most, and they'll go to extreme lengths to probe for weaknesses. Careers have been cut short for less.

The Mossad was not exactly a hostile intelligence service, but I had never considered it to be a particularly friendly one either. Now I had been driven into a corner by Jake Liebowitz and the Russians, and the only escape lay with Israel – and Ronan knew it.

I was the prime suspect in at least three murders and the subject of an international manhunt by several police services. I had been declared a traitor by the American press (and so, it must be true). The Russians wanted my head and were probably looking for me under every rock. Russians believe in revenge, and they had literally billions of reasons to exact it on me now.

In light of all this, the suggestion Ronan was offering merited consideration. Things just couldn't get any worse.

"Make your pitch; broaden my outlook, if you can."

"It's really not so bad." Ronan made an effort to soften his normal gravelly rumble. "You hated what you were doing at the Agency. You are a widower and have no family ties left in the United States."

Sasha obviously had passed on to Ronan what I had told her that night in her apartment after the hotel attack. It seemed ages ago.

The Israeli continued, "I detect in you, my friend, a man who craves action, who NEEDS to be in the field. It's what you know and what you do best. I would not like to see you deprived of that life."

He rose and came to stand next to me at the window and pointed a finger toward the hills in the distance.

"Oh, we could resettle you here in Israel. You could live out the rest of your days quietly in the shadows, taking no risks. Perhaps you could take up horticulture and live on a *kibbutz* somewhere in the Golan Heights. Speaking for myself, I could not tolerate such an existence. I would wither quickly and await my own death with hearty anticipation. I suspect it would be the same for you. Am I correct?"

This struck close to home. He'd just described the way I had been living in my cabin in Virginia. "I suppose so."

"Nevertheless, I can make such an offer, and I make it freely – no strings attached, as you say. We will resettle you, and we will provide a stipend that you could live on comfortably."

"What's the alternative?"

The Israeli leaned forward. He had prepared his presentation well, as any good case officer would do, leading me logically through the steps that had brought us to this point, enumerating the difficulties I faced, and finally proposing a solution.

He launched into his peroration.

"I offer you a new life with a mission. You can never be a *Mossad sochen*, of course, but I've convinced the *memuneh* that you possess knowledge and qualities that would be of use to us in the *Kidon* unit. We are somewhat unorthodox. You are not Jewish, and you are not Israeli. I can imagine many instances in which this could be very useful, such as false flag operations."

The conversation was making me intensely uncomfortable.

"Before you go further, I have a non-negotiable condition."

"You would refuse, of course, to undertake any activity that would harm your own country."

"That's correct."

"But America is our greatest ally, perhaps the only one we have left. We wish no harm to your country."

"You're forgetting Pollard, and I'm sure there have been others."

Jonathan Pollard was a civilian US Navy intelligence analyst arrested in 1985 and sentenced to life in prison for spying for Israel.

"Personally, I think we made a terrible mistake in that matter. In any case, that's in the past, and you will recall that Pollard <u>volunteered</u> the information to our embassy in Washington. I don't see that as a problem that affects your case. Anyway, don't you have good reason to question whether you owe your country the loyalty you profess?"

"It's not my country that's screwing me." No, it was Jake Liebowitz and the CIA.

"I see your point, and we can live with your caveat. I would have been disappointed had you not mentioned it. There may be times, however, when you'll have to decide how close to the line you want to go. We will respect your decision."

"Um hum."

"It is clear to us that we need more strength against the Russians, especially *Voskreseniye.* You've worked against them and their allies for years. We can use those skills and that knowledge."

"Sure. *Voskreseniye* can just keep on blaming me for their problems and never suspect Mossad."

Handy for the Israelis, not so good for me.

Undeterred, Ronan plowed on.

"I propose the following: we'll establish a new identity for you and make enough changes to your physical appearance to escape easy recognition. We can paper your new identity very effectively. We're good at that sort of thing. We would set you up somewhere in Europe - Spain or France, for example. This is an area you know well and where you should have no trouble blending in. We believe Europe will be a major battleground in the coming years, especially given Russian recidivism. They will seek to regain hegemony over their old satellites, and they will use West European dependence on Russian natural resources – gas, oil, etcetera to bully the Europeans and enfeeble their political institutions even further, and they will continue helping the Iranians. I would like to see you working with your old friend Volodya against the Russians."

Good old Volodya. I had not thought of him for a while.

"Is Volodya working for you?"

"He is independent and runs his own organization. We've known him for years, of course, just as you have. Sometimes we use him; sometimes he uses us. It's an equitable arrangement. We need his cooperation more than ever now. When the time is right, we'll let him know you are still alive."

He paused and returned his gaze out the window. "We also anticipate growing problems associated with the ever multiplying Muslim population of Europe. Already we see the Saudis funding the construction of large mosques dedicated to Wahabism, the most virulent of the Islamic branches. There would be a lot of work for a man like you, especially against your old friends, the Russians. Thanks to you, we now have a treasure trove of new information to exploit. It could keep you busy for years. There is just one thing."

"What's that?"

"You'll have to start thinking like an Israeli. We have only one mission, one cause. As I just said, that cause is the survival of Israel. This is an ancient land. It's been fought over since the beginning of recorded history, and it remains today a focus of conflict. We are a people hardened to sacrificing our own blood and spilling that of our enemies. I promise you, if the survival of this nation is ever put at grave risk, a new holocaust will result, and the whole world will be sucked in. We have a responsibility that concerns not only our own selfish national desires, but the welfare of the entire civilized world, right here in this hard, rocky, blood-soaked land. Are you willing to accept such a burden?"

Ronan showed a surprising flair for the dramatic. What he was asking was clear enough. His country did not negotiate with terrorists. Israel could not afford to depend on weak international institutions to fight its battles in an increasingly hostile world. If I agreed to Ronan's proposal I would become another instrument of Israel's most ruthless band of guardians, the Mossad's *Kidon* unit. I would be expected to kill without remorse the enemies of this small state. This was no small request. It was not a simple matter of trading one bureaucracy for another, and there would be no going back. I could not give an immediate answer and knew that the Mossad officer would think less of me were I to do so.

"You said I'd have a couple of weeks to recuperate. Give me that time to think about this."

Ronan grunted. He had done his job. He had planted the seed. Now he would wait to see if the soil were fertile.

"Of course. I won't rush you. They'll release you from here tomorrow or the next day. I'll arrange your travel."

Two days later I was escorted back to the basement of the hospital to a waiting car. I was pleasantly surprised to see Sasha behind the wheel.

CHAPTER 53

The Russians

In response to a call for help from Dimov, Zhenya sent a team to Marbella to mop up. The young *vor v zakonye*, Nikitin, was dead by the time they arrived at the villa, with a hole through the abdomen and a large exit wound in his back. Vital organs had been destroyed, and he had bled out all over the Spanish tile floor. The team also had to dispose of the corpses of Yudin and his Spanish girlfriend.

It took some time to get a coherent story out of Dimov, who was barely conscious for an entire day before he was capable of answering questions. The mop-up team drove him to the airport and placed him aboard Zhenya's Gulfstream for the return flight to Zurich, where medical treatment could be safely administered.

After several days of intense interrogation, Zhenya passed the information to Moscow.

*****

In Moscow, Shurgin was livid.

"How much will we lose?" Shurgin and Morozov were

meeting in the latter's office.

"There is no way to know, Vitya." He used the diminutive of Shurgin's name. "It will take weeks, perhaps months, to reconstruct the files, if it is at all possible to do so. Without Yudin it certainly will be impossible to recover a large part of the funds. It was he, after all, who set up many of the secret accounts. Our people have confirmed that he was able to retrieve some of the funds before he was killed. Nevertheless, our eventual losses could be in the tens of billions of dollars."

"*Sobachoye dit'yo,* son-of-a-bitch! How is this possible? Who is responsible?"

"According to Dimov, the man he saw was definitely the American *razvedchik*, Connolly. There was a woman with him. Dimov claims he wounded Connolly."

"Yes," spat Shurgin, "and then his *suka*, Connolly's bitch, beat the living shit out of a trained Vympel operative! What are we dealing with here? What are the Americans up to? This is impossible! Are you certain your CIA penetration is not double dealing? Connolly could not have done all this by himself."

Morozov unbuttoned his uniform jacket and loosened his tie before opening a desk drawer from which he withdrew a full bottle of Moskovskaya vodka with its distinctive green label and two small glasses. It was ten in the morning.

"Let's move to the conference table and sit down. "I don't know about you, but I could use a *stakanchik* or two of this."

He heaved himself up from behind the desk and plodded wearily to the other side of his office carrying the bottle and glasses. He shot a look at his well-padded office door to make certain it was closed before continuing in a lower tone. "At least our personal accounts in Monaco were untouched. Only we have access to them."

Shurgin discontinued his pacing and sat down at the head of Morozov's conference table and drummed his well-manicured fingers on its polished wood surface. The thin sunlight of early March in Moscow filtered through the windows, casting the barred silhouettes of the blinds across the table. Morozov filled the two glasses and placed one before Shurgin.

"Our CIA source assures us that Connolly definitely was NOT acting under CIA orders. As a matter of fact, we have confirmed from several sources that Connolly truly is a fugitive from justice. He is wanted for questioning concerning the deaths of our men in Vienna, as you know, and the CIA has put out a burn notice on him, thanks to the quick action of our source."

Shurgin was a brilliant leader, but he was volatile, and Morozov, who had spent years with him as they both climbed the ranks of the old KGB, knew how to calm him down.

"This means that the American authorities, several Western police agencies, and INTERPOL, are looking for Connolly. He cannot run forever, even if he has money. Zhenya also has organized a hunt, and we can but hope that he finds the American first. It could still be possible to salvage something, perhaps retrieve the money he already has stolen. When one person accumulates so much, he cannot escape notice."

"So, has Connolly gone rogue? Is he a common criminal? Who was the woman with him? What did Dimov say about her?"

"They were speaking English before the shooting began, but he doesn't speak the language well enough to detect the subtleties of an accent. The woman did not speak after Dimov entered the room. She could be from anywhere, and it is clear that she and Connolly know one another well. But she is definitely not CIA."

"Perhaps another of the American intelligence agencies? She's clearly had advanced combat training. She could be DIA or from one of the military services."

"In which case even our source at CIA would know nothing of her. There is no coordination between the American services," Morozov finished the thought.

"It's clear that the gloves are off. They executed Yudin and the Spanish girl in cold blood."

"Yes." Morozov did not point out that it had been Shurgin's decision in the first place to discard the old rules.

Shurgin was silent for several moments, head down, putting his thoughts in order. The vodka had taken the edge off his anger, and anger would do him no good now in any event. He had learned to wait for revenge, and when the time came, his vengeance would be terrible.

"Let's think about damages. We stand to lose enormous liquid assets, to be sure, but the companies and projects we already control are safe, and we relied on Zhenya to separately control many of them because he needed them in his money laundering operations. If we had lost this much money just a few years ago Voskreseniye might have been mortally wounded. But today we are well past the point where the loss, even of the sums Yudin controlled for us, can cause much harm. We already control Russian heavy industry; we control all valuable natural resources. Gazprom will soon be ours, and the same with the oil industry. We have politicians in our pocket, and already the wheels are turning to place ultimate political power in our hands.

"The military and intelligence services are ours, as they always have been. If anyone opposes us, we have the Brotherhood to silence their voices, giving us perfect deniability.

"The Russian people have seen democracy, and it has left a bitter taste in their mouths. They yearn for a return to strong leadership, to the restoration of our country to her rightful place in the world. All of this we can give to them."

Shurgin slapped the table with the palm of his hand.

"Screw the Americans! They send their 'experts' here to 'teach' us about democracy and economics. Look at the results – breadlines, money that won't buy anything. The Americans think we can all kiss and make up and pretend we were never at odds, as if we had been playing some children's game all those years of the Cold War. They cannot even conceive of the notion that we hate them still and yearn for their destruction. They do not understand or appreciate the history and traditions of Russia. We are poised to take the reins of power and steer our Motherland to a future which we can dominate.

"We can stop the Americans in every international forum. We can frustrate and corrupt their every action. And in the meantime we will distract them with the Iranians. They will remain blissfully, even willfully, ignorant of our plans until it is too late."

Morozov nodded agreement.

"Yes, Vitya, they will be distracted. As in the game of chess, we will feint a move, and they will fall into the trap.

The General leaned across the table and grasped Shurgin's arm.

"*Shakh I Mat*, checkmate, was a brilliant idea, my friend, and you executed it to perfection. Our people have been in Iran for over a year. Already we have signed important agreements, both public and secret, with the Persians. We will now sell advanced weapons systems to them and rejuvenate our coffers. We will provide the means and the know-how, and they will be seen to be developing a nuclear weapons capability. It will take years, and we will be able to control their program at every step – to stop it, if we have to, and all the while the Americans will believe we are cooperating with them. We must move carefully, but THAT is the ultimate distraction for the Americans. With the secret investments we are making in Iraqi oil, we will gain even more influence. The Americans will whine at the United Nations, they will seek alliances with the pitifully weak Western Europeans, and in the end they will fail because there is no real will in the West anymore. The French and the rest of them are as helpless as babes. By the time they screw up the courage to take some action, it will be too late.

"The Persians will have a weapons program capable of destroying Israel once and for all, and that fact alone will strike terror into the hearts of the Americans. They can never permit this to happen because they know the zhidovtsi, the Yids, will resort to any means to protect themselves. The Middle East will be left in shambles and we will pick up the pieces. Already the Iraqis are completely dependent on us to equip, re-develop and run their oil industry. We will re-build our defense industries with Arab and Persian money. Once the shooting is over, we will step in and take over the oil fields and if the Arabs or the Persians object, they will be so weakened as to offer little resistance. We will have our revenge for the shame of Afghanistan."

Shurgin's thin lips tilted up at the corners at the thought.

"Yes, the Americans have never understood chess. But what can you expect from a country where emotion substitutes for thought?"

CHAPTER 54

Safehouse

Despite sitting next to a beautiful woman I dozed during most of the short, sixty kilometer drive north from Tel Aviv. I was exhausted, both emotionally and physically, but relieved to be free of the confines of the hospital. Sasha, as usual, was a maniac behind the wheel, but everyone in Israel seemed to switch to kamikaze mode as soon as they got behind a steering wheel. It was best to keep my eyes closed.

I was bumped awake when the car turned into the graveled drive of Ronan's "beach house" which turned out to be a superb villa a short five minute walk from the Mediterranean. The place was enormous, two stories of modern white concrete with vast expanses of glass. It was surrounded by gardens and a high wall that concealed a swimming pool with a pergola in its center. The iron gates opened electronically as we approached.

Once through the gates, Sasha steered the car into an underground garage.

"This isn't exactly the cozy cottage by the sea I was expecting."

"We have safehouses of all types. I hope you're not disappointed."

Waiting to greet us was a middle-aged couple who introduced themselves as Moshe and Marnie, the caretakers who lived in the place. Moshe took the small bag that contained my meager belongings and a larger suitcase belonging to Sasha.

Reverting to her role as personal shopper, Sasha said, "Tomorrow we'll buy a new wardrobe for you."

"You're staying?" I couldn't keep the pleasure out of my voice.

She smiled. "Of course."

"This is becoming a tradition." I had to smile. All I had were the clothes on my back that had been laid out for me at the hospital. "I get shot at, and you buy me new clothes."

Moshe led the way upstairs and through a gym room and sauna that faced the pool area. I spotted a wide pillared veranda facing the sea as we passed through a main suite with a mosaic wall depicting Caesarea as it had appeared in the time of the Romans. They ascended the central staircase, and Sasha directed me to a door on the top floor that led to a bedroom suite with adjoining Jacuzzi. Through the sliding glass doors was a large balcony facing the sea. I wondered whether the house also had a *mamad*, a safe room found in many Israeli homes.

"You'd better rest now," instructed Sasha. "I'll be down the hall if you need anything."

*****

Once in her own room, with over an hour to kill before dinner, Sasha decided there was time for a long, hot bath. Leaving her travelling clothes -- jeans, a cotton sweater, and sneakers -- in a pile on the marble floor beside the tub, she gratefully slipped into the soothing water. Completely submerged except for her face, she felt her muscles relax, and she sighed deeply, her eyes closed.

Unbidden, the image of Harry Connolly seeped into her thoughts. She had never known an American before, and this one intrigued her. He was handsome, tough, and certainly highly resourceful, completely at odds with her preconceived notions about Americans. She had seen his vulnerable side that night in her apartment in Vienna when he had told her something of his personal history. To be sure, he had been in at least a partial state of shock at the time, having just escaped death and in the process killing two of his assailants. Despite the popularity of shoot-em-ups in the American cinema, Sasha had gathered from her fellow Mossad operatives that CIA case officers talked a lot but were pussies when it came to a shoot-out. Connolly had given the lie to that, and she had seen him remain cool under pressure. She recalled that cold, wet night in Vienna when the American had stripped the clothing from Stankov's body in order to delay identification. Not even Ronan had thought of that!

She felt guilty about Marbella. Had she not laid down her weapon to search through Yudin's desk, she might have taken down the second assailant before Connolly was wounded. She also felt not a little anger towards Ronan for allowing the two Russian killers to penetrate the mansion. Her indefatigable superior had failed in his part of the mission.

She stepped out of the tub and began to towel herself dry in front of the full length mirror that made up an entire wall of the bathroom. Perhaps triggered by the sight of her own nude, well-toned body and the rough nub of the towel against her skin like the beard of a lover, she found herself unexpectedly imagining what the American would be like in bed.

Oops! This won't do! Don't go there!

She tried to suppress the libidinous images that sprang to mind. During her university days sex had been fun, a casual recreation, but she had not been in a long-term sexual relationship for a long time. Work had taken precedence. She had other goals, fired by the memory of her father and the loyal friendship and example of Eitan Ronan. By the time she reached thirty, relationships were a thing of the distant past and sentiment a luxury she left behind with no regrets. Now she felt forgotten warmth spreading through her abdomen as her thoughts returned unbidden to Connolly and his broad shoulders.

She closed her eyes and stamped her bare foot on the marble floor.

"This is completely irrational," she said aloud to her image in the mirror. "This is unprofessional."

*****

Even after the semi-somnolent drive from Tel-Aviv, I was still tired and spent the better part of an hour stretched on the bed preoccupied by Ronan's offer and its implications. Only a few weeks ago my world had been circumscribed by a long daily commute to a dead-end job, a small cabin, and a little black dog. It had not been much of a life. All the same, it had been my life, and as unsatisfying as it had become, the choices all along had been my own, the bad ones included – mostly bad ones.

These reflections were interrupted by a soft knock at the door, and Sasha poked her head in.

"Are you feeling better? Why don't we go down and have something to eat?"

She had changed into a blouse and skirt. It had been awhile since I had seen her wearing anything but jeans and sweaters.

"You look beautiful."

She smiled at the compliment. In fact, she smiled all the way downstairs as we went to join Moshe and Marnie around the kitchen table for a light supper of wine, cheese, bread and fruit.

CHAPTER 55

Caesarea

Afterwards, we walked onto the veranda to watch the Mediterranean swallow the sun. A cool breeze blew in from the sea, and carried the scent of Sasha's freshly shampooed hair – strawberries – and drew me closer to her like an insect drunk on pheromones.

She didn't move away. "It's beautiful here, isn't it?," she said, her eyes still on the sea. "I hope you appreciate what Eitan is doing for you."

We had not had a real conversation, just the two of us, since that night in her apartment in Vienna, and I didn't feel like talking about the Golem or his proposal now.

"I never got to ask you about that unarmed combat demonstration to put on in Marbella."

She looked up with a soft laugh. I couldn't remember hearing her laugh before.

"That was *Krav Maga.* It's a form of hand-to-hand combat developed a long time ago by a Hungarian Jew named Imi Lichtenfeld. It's really just dirty street fighting carried to the nth degree." There was pride in her voice when she added, "I was tops in my class."

"Why didn't Ronan intervene? It wasn't necessary for

you to take that kind of chance against an armed man."

She gave me a blank stare and stepped back a pace.

"Don't be foolish. That's what I'm trained to do. We did not want Eitan to be seen at all, no matter what. This was critical to the success of our plan. He would have stepped in if absolutely necessary, but then we would have had to kill them all, and there would have been no one to report to the Russians that it was Harry Connolly who had come to Marbella. Besides, after you shot the first one, it was only one man, and I never doubted the outcome. And as for Eitan, he was in another part of the house when they came through the front door and didn't realize they were there until the commotion in Yudin's office."

"He seems to make it a habit of letting people walk into dangerous situations so he can see what happens. That's what got Stankov killed and my neck nearly broken."

She had the grace to look regretful, although she did not hesitate to defend her mentor.

"By the time we saw what was happening, Stankov was already dead, and the Russian was on top of you."

"Stankov was killed because Ronan made a mistake, a fatal mistake. And he made another one in Marbella."

The memory of Stankov's death dragged my bitterness back to the surface. I didn't want it to happen, but there it was – a wound that refused to heal.

"He's good. I'll give him that, but even the best of us screws up sooner or later. You may worship him, but

Ronan is no god."

"I don't worship him," she retorted with some heat. She stepped farther away from me to the edge of the veranda and looked out at the sea, her back to me, hands on the balustrade.

"He is a *bachir*, my senior officer, and my mentor. He recruited me into Mossad from the IDF, and I owe him a lot more than you can imagine."

She turned back to face me, hugging herself against the chill that had descended over the conversation.

"You should trust him. He has your best interests at heart."

I took a step toward her. I didn't want to argue with her, but the words came nonetheless.

"He has only Mossad's best interests at heart."

"And you still don't understand about Yudin, do you?"

She regarded me solemnly with those unwavering hazel eyes.

"It was I who insisted that he must die."

I was taken aback, and when I didn't reply immediately, she turned away again, concealing her face. Her voice drained of emotion, she continued, "It was clear from what he told me that the Russians could still use him. In fact, he was key to their plans and complicit in their crimes. We could not leave him alive to help them, and we no longer needed him as a witness because the other Russian could play that role. It was the correct decision under difficult circumstances. Israel is engaged in a permanent war, and ..."

"I know, I know. It's the Mossad's excuse for everything." I was exasperated and struggling to control my rising gorge. "Ronan recited the whole permanent war thing to me yesterday. It's a popular justification that permits Mossad agents to do whatever they damn well please. But right now, I don't want to talk about Ronan's ideals or his ideas for me. I need time to think and put things into perspective. One thing is certain: he has the best interests of Israel and the Mossad in mind, and nothing more. That's just who he is, and maybe who you are, too."

Her eyes flared green fire. Our cozy moment evaporated in the heat.

"Yes, Harry. I'm sure that's what he was thinking as he held Jonathan Netanyahu's dead body in his arms as they flew out of Entebbe in '76, or when he was fighting the Egyptians with Sharon!"

Netanyahu had been the commander the *Sayeret Mat'kal*, the commandos who pulled off the legendary Entebbe rescue. Ronan was the product of his experiences. He had been fighting Israel's battles for a long time, perhaps too long.

"I think we should turn in for the night," she went to the door. "Tomorrow is another day."

The smack of the door against the frame was like a slap in the face, and I experienced a disconcerting sense of loss. We had had a few nice moments. Her scent still hung in the air.

Early next morning, I was already seated at the kitchen table when she came down back in her standard jeans uniform. I rose and pulled a chair out for her.

"I'm sorry about last night. I didn't mean to insult you or Ronan. I'm just trying to make sense of all that's happened."

"I forgive you," she said, but her voice was neutral. "We'll go out today and avoid serious talk.

We drove to the shopping district and spent an hour or so buying more clothes for me. Following a light lunch of fried fish and chips at one of the many upscale cafes, we finished the afternoon taking in the sights of the ancient city.

CHAPTER 56

Cause for Apology

Sasha's mood lightened as we saw the sights. Caesarea was dedicated to Caesar by Herod the Great over 2000 years ago and was replete with relics of the ancient civilization. Originally the site of a Phoenician port, it had been conquered and re-conquered many times. Herod made it the grandest city other than Jerusalem in Palestine, with a deep sea harbor, aqueduct, hippodrome and amphitheater. Eventually it became the home of the Roman governors of Judea and was the capital of Roman and Byzantine Palestine.

Archaeological digs begun in the 1950's uncovered the remains of these magnificent artifacts and structures. Over the years the city had become more cosmopolitan as the Israeli elite began to build their mansions there. It was an easy commute either to Tel-Aviv to the south or Haifa to the north. Herod the Great had had a good eye for real estate.

We returned to the house just as the sun was dipping into the olive colored Mediterranean spreading an orange glare over its surface, and by the time I showered and changed into fresh clothes Marnie had a fine meal spread on the dining room table. And again in egalitarian Israeli fashion she and her husband joined us to eat. Marnie had pulled out all the stops, apparently having spent the entire afternoon cooking, and by the time we finally pushed back from the table, we had consumed two bottles of excellent Bordeaux. While Marnie and Moshe cleared the detritus of the meal, Sasha and I retired to the living room where the ornate fireplace contained a blazing wood fire.

*****

I studied the contents of the well-stocked bar. "Do you prefer vodka or scotch?"

"I'll try some scotch with you."

I found a bottle of The Macallan 18-year-old single malt among the many offerings and poured us each a couple of fingers.

Sasha kicked off her shoes and nestled into a corner of the sofa, tucking her legs under. She still wore the habitual jeans, a white cotton pullover, and a green wool sweater wrapped around her shoulders. I studied her perfect profile.

I had known her for only a short, tumultuous period, but she was without doubt the most remarkable woman I had ever met. I had only just begun to plumb the depths of her character and abilities.

Kate and I had been high-school sweethearts and my familiarity with the intimate habits of single women in the

90's was negligible. I had been deeply in love with my wife and that loyalty now tugged at my conscience, but whether it was the stresses to which I had been subjected, the continuing uncertainty of my situation, the prospect of beginning an entirely new life, or just because she was so damned beautiful, I was developing feelings for Sasha and had no idea what to do about them.

All case officers are amateur psychologists, and I was no stranger to the way men and women related to one under extraordinary circumstances. It was possible, even probable that Sasha's only objectives were those of a Mossad operative trained to salute and give all for her country. Wily Ronan the Golem had thrown us together several times, and now he had done it again, this time in an unambiguously intimate setting. I should have kept my mouth shut, but the scotch loosened some inhibitions.

"So, why did Ronan send you along with me, Sasha? Does he think I'll try to escape?"

She sipped her scotch, gazing into the fire.

"Don't you enjoy my company?"

"Of course, I enjoy your company, but Ronan always has a reason for what he does. He is, as you said, your *bachir*, and you're following his orders."

I felt as awkward as a high school kid on his first date.

She frowned slightly as she tried to extract meaning from my words.

"Eitan wants very much for you to accept his offer.

It should be obvious to you that he hopes I can help convince you to do so."

This was what I expected but not what I wanted to hear. Despite a warning voice in my head that said to back off, I plunged recklessly on.

"What do YOU think, Sasha? What do you advise me to do?"

She turned to face me as she finally divined my meaning.

"You think he ordered me to sleep with you?"

She was angry, and rightfully so. Must all our conversations end like this? Was it real anger or case officer sham?

"I am a professional intelligence officer. I have a job to do, and I think I do it reasonably well. If I were a man, Eitan would still have sent me with you because you know me and you trust me - at least I thought you did. I would have thought you of all people would understand this."

She didn't wait for a response. "If our roles were reversed, would you handle the situation differently? I think not. My job is to guard and protect you. It's just a job."

She turned away. "Instead, all you apparently see is this exterior, and like all men your libido has taken control of your brain. There always comes a point where men think more with their cocks than their heads!"

The vulgarity shocked me, and I felt suddenly foolish.

"Sasha, what the hell is the matter with you? I never mentioned sex." Well, maybe I hadn't said the word, but my argument was as weak as a politician quibbling about the meaning of "is." Open mouth wide, insert foot. I was hoisted on my own petard. She knew it and I knew it.

She bolted to her feet.

"Once again you've spoiled what until now was a very nice day. I'm going to bed."

"Please sit back down."

I couldn't let her walk away like this. "I didn't mean to insult you. I'm sorry."

She halted her march out of the room and returned to stand, arms akimbo, facing me. I had never seen her so flustered. What did that mean?

I tried to explain myself.

"The past few weeks have completely and forever altered my life, and I'm trying to get my bearings. Believe me when I tell you that I respect your qualities and capabilities. And I do appreciate your being here with me. In fact, there is no one else I would want to be here."

She was a beautiful woman, and she could have no doubts about the effect she had on men. While she had not incorrectly inferred and then protested the implications of my questions, this only called more attention to her femininity.

But she was perfectly capable of calculating that her

outburst would push me further toward accepting Ronan's proposal. She was, after all, still an intelligence officer, and so was I. Our choreography was becoming confused, and I was stepping on her toes. We both knew the steps to the dance, but execution was becoming difficult.

"I accept your apology. I think I'll go up to bed now – alone."

After the door closed firmly behind her for the second night in a row, I poured another whiskey, a large one, and sat there for a long while staring into the flames.

Too much was happening too quickly. Perversely, our argument this evening made me even more certain that I wanted this exceptional, witty, and self-reliant human being in my life whether she was manipulating me or not.

She had become the only constant in the otherwise chaotic universe I had come to inhabit.

CHAPTER 57

Deal

After a week at the villa passed carefully tip-toeing around sensitive conversational topics, we returned to Tel-Aviv to meet the Golem in a room in a high-rise beachfront hotel. A table was covered with the standard Israeli luncheon fare: fresh bread, yogurt, the ubiquitous hummus, olives, fresh fruit, juices, a selection of cold meats, and a mound of sweet pastries.

At the appointed hour Ronan strode through the door and greeted us warmly, surprising me with a bear hug that did no good for still-mending ribs. Ronan zeroed in on the table groaning with Israeli goodies and roared enthusiastically, "Let's eat! I've been stuck in meetings all morning, and I'm hungry."

I was certain the meetings had concerned me.

Sasha and I had not returned to the subject of Ronan's proposal after our disastrous late evening set-to. By silent consent we likewise did not return to the subject that I suspected preoccupied both of us. We shared long walks along the beach, nice lunches in trendy Caesarea bistros, and always a hearty repast in the evening in the company of Moshe and Marnie, whom I came inevitably to think of as "Mickey and Minnie."

There had been plenty of time to think about choices. The past few weeks had altered my life forever, and there was no going back. I knew what I would say to Ronan. It was risky, but if successful the gambit would preserve my self-respect.

The big Israeli moved to the table and heaped food onto a plate. He waved a large serving spoon at us.

"Come on, you two. We need full stomachs today."

We worked our way through the meal while Ronan asked a string of innocuous questions about our stay in Caesarea.

"You like the way the Mossad lives, Harry? Did the house live up to your expectations?"

"Just about everything you've done since I met you has exceeded expectations. The house was no exception. Thanks for the hospitality."

At last, coffee cup in hand, Ronan became serious.

"OK, let's get down to business. Are you ready to talk about it?"

"I told you I needed time to think, and you granted it to me. I thank you for that. I've decided to accept your offer."

Ronan's face creased in his shark smile, and he extended his hand. "You won't regret this."

I waved the Israeli's hand away.

"With some conditions."

Ronan sat back with a thump, and the smile disappeared; his eyes narrowed as he anticipated a bargaining session. There is no one better at bargaining than Israelis, but I was gambling that I could win this match.

With a rueful expression Ronan said, "I already agreed that you would never be asked to work against the interests of the United States."

Across the room, Sasha folded her arms. She had no idea what I was going to say.

"When we talked at the hospital you said that Israel was grateful to me. You used the words 'incalculable value,' in fact. I'll work for you, but I need some guarantee of independence. I don't want to have to ask you every time I need a new pair of socks."

"What do you have in mind?"

"I want ten million dollars. That should about do it."

Ronan sucked in his breath, not pleased with this turn of conversation.

"That's a lot of money."

"Yep. But still a modest sum compared with the numbers you've been tossing about. Just think of me as a very inexpensive weapons system."

"I can't authorize such an amount on my own."

"There are probably only a few in your government who can. I'm not trying to make things difficult for you, but I need at least the illusion of independence. Accepting your proposal is a big step, and I don't want to feel like I'm stepping out of one box into another. I need some slack in the leash."

With a small personal fortune at my disposal I would have the power to say no to the Mossad. And this was precisely what I had decided would be most important in a relationship with them. I would not allow myself to become their creature.

"If you can't get this done, then have your people in Washington make some arrangements and put me on the first plane for the US I'd rather face the music there than spend the rest of my life as a Mossad house slave, even a comfortable one. I know what I'm asking, and I know the answer depends on just how valuable you think I can really be to you and how 'grateful' this country really is. Until a decision is made, I have nothing but time."

Without another word, his face like thunder, Ronan stood and walked out the door.

Sasha shook her head slowly as the door closed behind her boss.

"You're taking a big risk. The Mossad does not want the details of the *Voskreseniye* operation to become public or to become known even to the American authorities, which is almost the same thing. The way Washington leaks, the whole story would be out in no time at all, and we would have even more trouble with the Russians. It is vital that our participation remain concealed. You are the only link the Russians have, and Eitan will do what he has to do to preserve this fiction. The Mossad doesn't leave loose cannons dangling."

"Loose ends."

"What?"

"You said loose cannons. Cannons don't dangle; ends 'dangle.' You meant to say 'loose ends.'"

She was annoyed. "I'm serious. I'm trying to help you."

"Do you take me for an idiot? I know the risks, and I know that there's no way Ronan will send me to Washington. The other choices are no more palatable than an anonymous burial in the Negev. I will happily work heart and soul with you against the damned Russians. But I need a measure of self-respect in exchange for what this mess has forced me to give up. I'm a man without a country."

We had more coffee brought up, but there was little conversation while we waited. I was gratified by Sasha's evident concern for my well-being.

Finally, late in the afternoon, Ronan returned.

"It was not easy. I had to do a lot of talking. In the end the *memuneh* agreed to your terms, but he insists on a few 'conditions' of his own."

The Israelis agreed to establish a numbered account for me in the amount of ten million dollars. I alone would have access to the funds and decide how they were used. (I would, of course, immediately transfer the money to another account, just to guard against Mossad bean counters ever changing their minds.) In exchange, I would be available to them at any time and subject to their operational discipline.

Right now Harry Connolly was a wanted man, the subject of a widespread manhunt by a constellation of Western authorities and an illegal and much more lethal hunt by *Voskreseniye* and its allies. So Harry Connolly had to disappear.

And there was still a loose end – something I was determined to take care of, with or without Mossad permission.

CHAPTER 58

Entr'acte

Ronit Lotner stood across the street from the underwhelming façade of the local branch of the Cayman Banking and Trust Co., Ltd. It was a private bank, catering to individuals looking for what the bank coyly advertised as "a full range of private banking services with highly confidential investment management," in other words, "mum's the word where your money is concerned." It was counter-intuitive. Most people conceived of a financial institution that controlled millions, no, billions of dollars, housed in a steel and glass skyscraper. But this was not the way it was in the real world. In the real world, such institutions favored modest, unassuming quarters. Discretion was a concept they took seriously.

A week earlier she had been in London opening a business account for a fictitious company. Of British origin, Ronit was perfect for the role Tel-Aviv had assigned to her. In her late thirties, dressed in a dark blue linen Dior suit with Cesare Paciotte stilettos she was the epitome of the successful European businesswoman. Armed with an authentic British accent and impressive corporate documents supplied by Mossad technicians, she had opened the account in London and pre-arranged a large transfer of investment funds that her "firm" anticipated receiving shortly from a numbered private account.

Unlike the way it is depicted in movies, transferring large amounts of money is more complicated than simply punching the keys of a computer from a remote, anonymous location. Bank rules prohibit the acceptance of large funds transfers from anonymous accounts without prior authorization in writing from their own client. Ronit had performed the same act three times now, each time in a different country. Twice before she had engineered the transfer of funds from a secret Russian account to one she had set up for the Mossad. Sometimes she had only set up the receiving account, actually the more complicated of the two activities, and then when the funds had arrived had split them and immediately transferred them to other accounts set up by other Mossad agents for the purpose. It was labor intensive activity. Some banks permitted wire transfers to be initiated via the Internet, but this procedure was still relatively new in the early nineties, and in any event such "remote" transfers normally were limited by bank regulations to only a few million dollars and never more than ten million.

She was staggered by the amounts involved. This operation had been underway for two months and was by far the most extensive operation of its kind ever undertaken by Mossad with more than forty agents involved worldwide. Only three times had they been politely but firmly turned away by smiling bankers when they encountered several non-transparent strings of successive ownership, designed to conceal the true beneficiaries, and they were untouchable by the Israelis, at least for now. The Russians would not lose everything.

Ronit looked to her right down the block and made certain that Avram was there, sitting in the car with the engine idling. They worked in teams of two – one to deal with the banks and the other for security. Avram, she knew, would be prepared to extricate her from any potentially dangerous situation. Deadly force was permitted.

She took a deep breath to calm her nerves before crossing the narrow street and pushing the buzzer at the entrance. Once inside she encountered a well-dressed man seated behind a desk. The tiny lobby was devoid of any other furniture or decoration.

"Good morning," she said. "I'm Cynthia Morris. I called yesterday for an appointment."

After consulting his computer screen, the man asked to see her identity documents. She handed them over and waited while he matched their contents to the information on the computer. Finally he rose and indicated she should follow.

Beyond the reception area, the bank's quarters were small, but well appointed, with thick carpets, oak paneling and vintage oil paintings. Her escort showed her into an anteroom where she was greeted by another man, equally well-dressed, who exuded an air of quiet discretion.

He greeted her in French-accented English. "Ms. Morris, I'm very happy to meet you. We understand you wish to make a withdrawal?"

"I'll be transferring funds to our account in London. Our firm is planning a major investment in a telecommunications company."

"Of course. Would you care for some tea, or coffee? We are at your disposal."

"Thanks, but I'd rather get to business. We're on a tight schedule."

"Very well."

There was a lot of paper, but in reality the transaction at this end was uncomplicated. She possessed the account number and the pass code. A half-hour later, the transaction completed, Ronit bade the banker good-bye and walked back out into the street.

Avram gave the all clear signal, and she walked to the car. They drove directly to the airport where they boarded a flight for Paris.

By the end of April, the Israelis had recovered nearly fifteen billion dollars in illicit Russian funds. Eitan Ronan then called it quits. The operation had cost many hundreds of man hours in travel all across the globe, from Montevideo to Vaduz, and with each attempted transaction the job became more dangerous.

*****

It was six months since the meeting in Tel-Aviv. A portion of that time had been spent in a secret Mossad medical facility dedicated to making certain that your mother wouldn't know you if she looked you in the face in the noon day sun. They also had a method of altering fingerprints, or at least erasing them. One would not say the surgery was a pleasant process, and recovery was even more painful. They had not worked me over too extensively though; just enough to straighten my nose and thin my lips a bit. There was an unexpected benefit, however, once the bandages were off I observed with approbation that the surgeons' work had left me looking ten years younger.

The summer under the hot Israeli sun burnt my skin brown and daily jogs along the beach that became increasingly longer and more pleasurable dropped my weight back to 175 and hardened muscles I had been neglecting. All in all, the physical transformation was pleasing.

Mossad trainers put me through the mill, as well, mostly unarmed combat and weapons training. They had little to teach me about tradecraft, but new proficiencies with Israeli clandestine communications protocols were required.

I learned that the Mossad is a very informal service and highly compartmentalized, especially the Kidon unit. Lines of command were sometimes difficult to discern. Less than a handful of Mossad personnel were aware of my true identity, and they would keep it that way. Ronan would be my control, and Sasha was to provide operational support when required.

CHAPTER 59

Jake Triumphant

Jake Liebowitz sauntered into CIA Headquarters via the main entrance, the one with the statue of Nathan Hale outside and the statue of General "Wild" Bill Donovan inside - the lobby they always show in the movies. His Volvo occupied a coveted space in the small VIP parking lot just a few feet from the wide steps leading to the bank of heavy glass doors.

There was a spring in his stride this morning, and he wore one of his better suits, one that actually flattered his corpulent frame. His wife had insisted, and she also had splurged on the Hermes tie he wore. This was a special day.

He nodded a greeting to the uniformed guard as he passed through the security checkpoint and walked past the windows that gave out onto the well-manicured interior courtyard. He stood patiently at the elevators with other Agency employees until the doors opened. He exited on his floor and walked the short distance to the front offices of the Russia Section. It was early enough that only the faithful secretaries were in place at their desks.

Sadie Cochran, a Section stalwart who had served as

secretary for a string of Chiefs for over eleven years, had known Jake Liebowitz for a long time. She had followed the famously fidgety officer's progress and was proud that he had at last achieved such success. He was a gifted officer, one of many that had been eclipsed in recent years by clever bureaucrats like Barney Morley who didn't even speak Russian. This was a good day. Jake, she was certain, would return the Section to its former glory.

"Good morning," she beamed at her new boss. "My, but don't you look dapper! I'll bet Sophie picked out that tie for you."

Sadie knew Jake's wife, Sophie, and his daughter, Rebecca, now a sophomore at Georgetown, very well. She knew the Liebowitzes as a strong, closely knit family.

He smiled benignly. "Right as usual, Maggie. Have you picked up the morning traffic?" He referred to the daily collection of cables and reports from around the world.

"Of course," she replied with mock severity. "It's waiting for you on your desk. I'll fix a cup of coffee for you."

"Aww, Sadie, I don't expect you to do that for me. I'm still the same old Jake. I'll just grab a cup off the rack and fix it myself, as usual."

She stood and rushed past him to the coffee urn. "Jake Liebowitz, You're a big cheese now. Enjoy it. It'll be my pleasure."

Jake spread his arms wide, palms up, in a gesture of

surrender.

"If you insist, Maggie, only if you insist. And only if you'll let me take you to lunch today."

Sadie's cheeks glowed pink. "Jake, you're too nice, you know."

"Sadie, it's only the cafeteria. You'll be able to catch me up on all the gossip."

Jake entered his new office, recently vacated by Morley, while a pleased as punch Sadie started a fresh urn of coffee.

Pausing at the door he surveyed the corner office, now devoid of Morley's fatuous mementos, and began slowly to circle the oversized executive desk, running his fingers across its gleaming surface. Maggie had left the morning correspondence in a neat pile in the center. The stack of papers would include the PDB, the President's Daily Brief, State Department diplomatic correspondence, a précis of the morning news, as well as CIA operational "traffic" from around the world.

He removed his jacket and flung it carelessly into one of the chairs before taking his seat. He remained quiet for a moment, waiting for Maggie to bring the coffee, and reflected on recent events.

It had not taken long for the bureaucracy to deliver the hammer blow to Barney Morley. The misadventures of Harry Connolly in Vienna combined with the persistence of the Washington press corps created a scandal the Russia Section Chief could not escape. Gleeful politicians were standing in line to demand Congressional hearings on the "mole" debacle.

In typical Agency fashion a "retirement" ceremony in one of the conference rooms was quickly arranged for Barney. All of six people attended. Called upon to speak, Jake related a couple of amusing anecdotes from Barney's career and spoke warmly of his years of dedicated service. In the end, Barney Morley stumbled out clutching his service medal and a cheap watch but bereft of pride. The ceremony lasted only a half-hour, and the Seventh Floor could not wait for the door to slam on Morley's sorry ass. Jake had savored the moment.

Exit Barney Morley, enter Jake Liebowitz. As Barney's deputy Jake was immediately named Acting Chief of Russia Section. Discovering that he was perfectly willing to bear the burden of investigations and the inevitable internal turmoil engendered by the scandal, it did not take long for the Seventh Floor types to confirm him as Chief.

Even so, he was not entirely at ease. He mentally revisited the facts known about Harry Connolly, those known to Washington, as well as those known only to the SVR and himself. More than a month had passed and Harry Connolly was still at large, although it was possible he was dead. Every police and intelligence service in Europe had pursued the meager leads available to them, but the trail ended in that miserable hotel in Vienna. The CIA and the Europeans assumed that Connolly had long since made his way to Moscow and would turn up there sometime in the future whenever it suited the SVR. For the time being the Russians insisted they had had nothing to do with the fugitive.

But Jake knew that Connolly was not in Russia. He also knew that subsequent to the Vienna events he had left three corpses behind him in Spain. The unexpectedly resourceful Connolly had proven to be spectacularly resistant to dying. Liebowitz would never have imagined that the brooding, cynical, angry man he had known for so long could be capable of the actions ascribed to him. Allegedly Connolly had been wounded in the shoot-out in Spain, perhaps fatally. Jake hoped so. Russian resources were still casting about for signs of him and would continue to do so for some time.

He did have the grace to regret, ever so slightly, that his recent actions had been calculated to result in the death of one of his oldest "friends." But he no longer could afford the luxury of friends. Harry Connolly was expendable – and useful: Connolly was now mole suspect number one. And a dead man could not defend himself.

CHAPTER 60

A Loose End

The mystery of Harry Connolly's whereabouts haunted Jake Liebowitz. Months had elapsed since his disappearance and without official support of any kind, Connolly still eluded capture. If he were not dead, there was no way in hell that he could remain at large without help. What resources could Connolly have called upon? What sort of chits was he calling in? At one point in his career Harry had spent a long time on assignment in Paris. He had worked well with the French and was fluent in their language. Could the damned Frogs be harboring him for some perverse Gallic reason? And if this were so, what did they know about Jake? He had asked the Russians to check their sources in Paris, but it was another dry hole.

Even so, there was a French link between him and Connolly that could not be permitted to come to light: the cut-out communications link Connolly had established to stay in contact with Liebowitz while he was in Vienna. Although Jake had remained anonymous when he called the Parisian restaurant to provide the pay phone numbers Connolly was to use, nothing could be left to chance. The restaurant proprietors could well go to the authorities with what they knew, given the international notoriety of matter, and it could precipitate further investigation in Washington. This could not be permitted, and Jake insisted that the SVR tie up this loose end.

*****

In mid-May 1992, Igor Tsarov, walked through doors of the modest restaurant on Rue Roquepine in Paris's 8th Arrondissement. He had picked a Thursday evening when restaurant traffic was normally light. Arriving about forty minutes before closing time, Tsarov ordered a light dinner of charcouterie and a salad, finishing it off with a glass of house wine and a small bottle of Perrier.

The Russian was handsome with a thin moustache and blond hair worn stylishly long, and he cut a fine figure in his Carven suit. He easily established rapport with Maurice, the restaurant's proprietor, complimenting him on the quality of the food. Tsarov's French was impeccable with no trace of an accent. He had been assigned to France for many years as the Novosti correspondent, in reality a cover for his former KGB and now SVR job.

"This is quite a charming place you have," he commented as Maurice was clearing his table. He glanced around and confirmed that he was the only customer left in the dining room. "I know it's late, but would it be possible to have just a small dessert?" He placed a hundred franc note on the table.

Maurice was tired after a long day, but ever the good host, he replied, "Of course, Monsieur. But do you mind if I close up while you finish? You're our last customer."

"Of course not. Very gracious of you. I'll finish quickly."

Hélène brought the dessert to Tsarov as Maurice flipped the sign on the door from "open" to "closed" and began stacking the chairs on the tables.

"Do you and your husband manage this place all on your own?"

"Oui, Monsieur. We leased the space soon after the hotel opened upstairs, and we have run it all by ourselves for many years."

"Would you please call your husband over here?"

Tsarov's voice was casual, polite.

"Of course, Monsieur, but ..."

Her words were cut short when she saw that a small pistol had appeared as if by magic in the customer's hand and he was pointing it directly at her.

A short shriek escaped her.

Maurice rushed his wife's side, saw the pistol and immediately placed himself between his wife and the gun.

"Do you intend to rob us, Monsieur?"

Tsarov stood, holding the pistol steady on Maurice's mid-section and gestured with his free had toward the back of the restaurant.

"Just remain calm, and all will be well. I'll be gone in a few minutes. Let's go back to the kitchen."

He herded the frightened pair into a corner of the kitchen, out of sight of the front window. The Russian took careful aim now, his intention clear, and Maurice leapt toward him, intent on protecting his wife.

Tsarov pulled the trigger. There was no sound other than a click, but Maurice fell to the floor at the Russian's feet. Hélène did not understand what was happening. The gun had not been fired, but Maurice lay on the floor. She stared at him, mesmerized, as a pool of blood spread around her husband's head. She was still staring at his body when the second sub-sonic round penetrated her skull.

Tsarov replaced the PSS pistol in his pocket. The weapon was a special KGB covert operations weapon that used a unique cartridge with an internal piston to remain silent. When he fired, the gun's piston launched the bullet from the barrel and then sealed the neck before noise, smoke or blast could escape. The Russian calmly surveyed the carnage then stepped to the stove and turned on the gas on all the burners. He lit a cigarette and laid it on the counter before exiting the restaurant into a deserted Rue Roquepine and hurrying away in the direction of Boulevard Malsherbes.

The chocolate mousse had, indeed, been superb.

*****

The Vienna affair continued to reverberate, although

at a lower volume, as the investigations progressed. Occasionally a piece would appear on the Post's "Federal Page" describing the growing demoralization at CIA. Congress was again happily nipping at the Agency's heels.

Jake worked hard to overcome the malaise within the ranks. He held frequent meetings with staff and visited all the Section offices daily, reassuring "his" people that they were getting back on track, that the Section would regain its former luster.

People began to believe in him.

With his current access to a vast array of highly classified information and his position secure thanks to the deflection of suspicion onto Connolly, the SVR's risky investment in Jake Liebowitz was more than justified. If he could remain above suspicion he could look forward to a long and prosperous future at the CIA. He had the potential to rival even Philby as a Russian intelligence triumph over the West.

But as summer stretched towards autumn, Jake's concerns about Connolly did not recede. The official investigations into the disappearance all crashed and burned at the hotel in Vienna. The Russians' luck was no better. Simply hoping that the wounds Connolly had suffered in Marbella had been fatal was not enough for Liebowitz. Ever the perfectionist, he needed closure.

CHAPTER 61

Bad News

Sasha remained at my side throughout my recuperation and long stay in Israel. Though the circumstances of exhausting training left no room for romance, there was time to talk, and I gradually drew out of her the story of her childhood, her father, and the key to her relationship with Eitan Ronan.

The hot Israeli summer was waning by the time we returned to the Caesarea safehouse. The heat was still with us, but it was not so oppressive near the sea, and together we ran our daily five miles along the beach each morning before the sun rose too high.

The weeks and months had demolished personal barriers. Harry Connolly had ceased to exist, and this exotic Russian-Israeli creature was the only friend the ghost that remained now had. Her laugh, once so rare, came more easily now.

One morning we sat together on the villa's veranda after our run. We were still in our sweats and rested side by side on *chaises longues* sipping cool water from plastic bottles and watching the sea birds circle high in the lightening sky. Her hair was pulled back in a ponytail, and her skin still glowed with a thin sheen of perspiration.

After a moment I said, "You've become my best friend, you know, maybe my only friend. You must know that I'd like us to become more than that."

Her brow furrowed, but she said nothing.

*****

She had anticipated and feared this moment. She wasn't certain that she could call what she felt for this man 'love,' but it was close, perhaps as close as she could ever come to it. But her instincts were in the way. How could their professional relationship survive a love affair, or vice versa? She wanted the physical relationship. She yearned for it - this much she could admit to herself. But it would have a deeper dimension than the merely physical, and this was the problem. Would she be able to make the hard decisions? Would she be able to choose between her lover and the mission?

*****

"This time it's for all the right reasons, Sasha."

She stood and walked to veranda railing, her back to me.

"We were thrown together by circumstance, Harry."

I could almost hear the logic circuitry clicking in her

brain as she spoke.

"In fact, we've been together constantly for many months, and we shared those horrible experiences. It's only natural that you should develop," she paused for a breath, searching for the right words, still not daring to look at me, "certain feelings. This is what happens. It's human nature."

I stood crossed to her, and she took my hand, her eyes, like searchlights beamed into my core, belying her words.

"What you're feeling is natural." Her breath came now in short gasps. "You'll leave us soon, and things will look different when you regain your perspective."

"I think I know human nature as well as you. Don't you think I've considered all this myself? Can you truly say that you don't feel the same?"

She let go off my hand and hugged herself against the still cool sea breeze.

"You're right. But I don't think you fully understand what you're asking. There would be consequences, and I'm not sure I'm ready to accept them."

"You mean Mossad consequences."

"Mossad is a small closed universe that depends on a very delicate balance. There are no personal secrets. If an officer takes a lover or wishes to marry, the service must decide whether it's acceptable. Otherwise the internal equilibrium and the trust that guarantees it would be lost.

Everything must be cleared, and the service's decision is final. As for you and me, they are unlikely to agree. I would have to leave Mossad."

"Then come with me. I'll have the means to do anything we like."

I grasped her shoulder gently and turned her to face me before taking her in my arms.

She leaned into me, and her arms slid around my neck. She raised her face and we kissed gently, tentatively, and she trembled and wept softly as the final barrier between us fell and she buried her face in my neck. With unaccustomed tears in her eyes she raised her lips again, and our embrace became more passionate. I could feel the heat generated by her body and knew that she wanted me, needed me – badly -- now.

After a few moments, silent in mutual consent, we climbed the stairs to my room. Our clothing flung to the far corners of the room, our bodies came together almost violently as long repressed passion drove us to frantic, panting lovemaking.

We spent the rest of the morning in the room, the time divided between the bed and the Jacuzzi, the pure animal excitement of our first coupling giving way to tenderness as we explored one another's bodies. We spoke little, everything already having been said, but where I had hope for the future, I knew that she hoped she would not regret the irredeemable step she had taken.

*****

The next morning we returned to Tel Aviv for a final briefing before I left the country.

Sasha, her eyes straight ahead on the road, said, "There's something I must tell you. Ronan does not want you to know this, but I think you deserve to hear it."

There was a reticence in her voice that alerted me that she was about to say something she would rather not.

"There was an explosion in Paris last May."

My reaction was instantaneous. "Not Volodya!"

"No, he is safe. It was the restaurant you described to us on Rue Roquepine. It was destroyed, and the proprietors were killed."

"Maurice and Hélène?" My stomach knotted. "What happened?"

"There was a gas explosion, and the two bodies were found in what was left of the kitchen."

"An accident?" But I knew worse was to come.

"That's the official story. The explosion destroyed the restaurant and several other people were killed and injured in the small hotel in the same building. Autopsies on the bodies of your friends determined that they were dead before the explosion. Each had a bullet in the head. The French police investigated but could find no clues.

They concluded it was a robbery gone bad."

*****

Sasha had not intended to tell him about the Paris killings because Ronan wanted to keep the information from him as long as possible. He believed that with the passage of time the news would not wound him so deeply. But she knew better, and she found it impossible any longer to practice deception on this man, her friend and now her lover. She did not want to increase the burden of guilt she knew he carried, but he deserved to know the truth. She recognized in that moment that she had crossed a line, broken discipline, and she also knew that Harry Connolly would not allow these wanton murders to pass unanswered. Was she "changing sides," she wondered? Was her loyalty to Mossad and Ronan somehow diminished by this act of disobedience?

*****

I remained outwardly calm, but there was an icy hollowness in my gut. Two more lives, innocent lives - sweet people with a caring family - had been snuffed out because I had involved them in something they did not understand and should never have been a part of. Death followed wherever I passed.

"They were linked to me, and the Russians found out."

"I'm telling you this against orders because they were your friends and because you need to know that someone is still out there looking for you. I don't want you taking chances, especially now, so soon after Vienna and Marbella."

I closed my eyes, and there were Maurice and Hélène staring accusingly at me.

"Thanks for telling me, but I don't think those nice people were killed because someone was looking for me. I think they were killed to protect someone else."

Stankov still haunted me, as well. The sight of his face disintegrating that wet night in Vienna was an indelible memory. The hapless little Russian I had recruited those long years ago in Berlin had been murdered not only silence him, but also to protect the mole.

Someone had to pay for the destruction of my life and the consequent deaths of so many others. Only one other person had known of the involvement of Maurice and Hélène – Jake Liebowitz. Their deaths closed the circle.

His Russian masters might be out of reach, but Jake Liebowitz was not.

The Mossad had their rules, and they had their priorities and their secrets to protect. Going after Jake would not fit into their plans and risked blowing the seals off of one of their more successful operations. No amount of cajoling would convince Ronan that it was wise to move against Jake Liebowitz.

When I had previously raised the Liebowitz problem, Ronan had been adamant.

"What would you have us do? Should we advise the Agency that we suspect he's working for the Russians? What proof could we present? Even if we revealed the fact that you are still alive, and we WON'T do that, we would still have nothing concrete. Even if you are correct, Liebowitz would be warned, and then what would happen? The CIA doesn't like us very much anyway, and this would be like throwing a stink bomb into their living room.

"Why would Liebowitz have had to send you to Vienna in the first place if he already knew Stankov's communications plan and the meeting sites? All the Russians had to do was to wait there for Stankov to show up, kill him, grab the second disk, and go home."

"I think you already know the answer. The mole hunt in Washington was ratcheting up, and Jake was feeling the heat. The Russians needed a scapegoat to relieve the pressure on him. That's why they wanted me in Vienna and why they needed me dead. It was the perfect set-up, and they weren't expecting complications."

Ronan had merely shrugged. "As you would say, we don't have a dog in the fight." He smacked his fist in his palm for emphasis. "That's the way it is in our world. You know this as well as anyone. No one gets everything they want. It's not perfect, but our operation was a success. We can't risk blowing it."

The months in Israel had not diminished my determination to settle accounts with Jake Liebowitz, and the deaths of Maurice and Hélène now made the matter more pressing. How this might be accomplished I hadn't yet figured out.

The CIA was not perfect, but it was an organization populated for the most part with good people. It was not their fault that they were poorly led and poorly served by an inside-the-Beltway Washington class that valued scoring political points over having a viable intelligence service. In the end, everyone would get the intelligence service they deserved, one way or another. In the meantime, if I did nothing and a mole was permitted to gnaw away undetected and unchallenged, the Russians would have won yet another round. More lives would be at risk. And besides all that, I was sick to death of playing the unwilling pawn, sick to death of being used.

CHAPTER 62

Back to Paris

The Hotel Bristol near the shore of Lake Geneva boasted a fine bar that smelled of well-polished wood. It was dimly lit and the music from the hidden speakers was Chopin. My contact, a well-dressed man in his mid-30's, was seated at the end of the ornate bar, that day's pink copy of the ubiquitous "Financial Times" peeking out of his jacket pocket. I reflected that I should think of a different recognition signal.

I ordered a drink and surveyed the room before moving down the bar, drink in hand, to sit on the stool next to my contact.

"Would you mind sharing the 'Times' with me?"

The man twisted his head toward me. "Is there a particular article that interests you?"

"Yeah, I think someone called Ronan wrote it."

The man grinned. "Greetings, friend. Do you have your travel documents all together?"

I tapped the thick envelope in my inside jacket pocket.

"Excellent," the Mossad man continued, "Shall we exchange envelopes?"

Mine held the false documentation I had used for the flight from Tel Aviv. The one I received contained a new life. Today, Harry Connolly would become Ewan Ramsay, citizen of Ireland.

The Mossad had provided the complete package. They also had kept their word and established a numbered account at a Geneva bank with an initial deposit of ten million dollars. The first thing I did the next day was to move the funds to a new account at a different bank.

Another day, another flight, this time to Dublin where I culled a list of attorneys from the hotel phone book and started making calls. It proved astoundingly easy to set up a shell company in the economically supercharged Ireland of 1992. The Irish were intent on economic development, and the new, liberal tax laws attracted a lot of foreign business. I opened a bank account, set up credit cards, and engaged a real estate agent to find properties for sale in the west of the country.

These tasks accomplished, I was free to concentrate on a pressing objective – dealing with Jake Liebowitz. The plan was simple, but I would need help.

*****

The first cool gusts of October swept across the Boulevard St. Germain as I climbed the Metro stairs across the street from the familiar *Deux Magots* café. I had driven a rental car from London to Paris in order to avoid recording the cross-border travel in traceable airline records. I had left the car in an all-night lot in the 18th Arrondissement. A brisk ten minute walk from the Metro brought me to the familiar façade on Rue de Tournon.

Volodya's voice was delighted when I rang his apartment from the street and he heard the familiar voice.

"Come on up, my boy. Come up immediately!" He buzzed me in, and I creaked up the circular stairwell.

Upon opening the door, the old man squinted at the new face.

"It's me, old friend. I'm the same old Harry but in a new, improved model."

Volodya continued to stare as he ushered his friend to the living room.

"Yes, I see now. They made you look even more like that American actor. I can't believe it. Your new 'friends' said I would be seeing you, but I didn't think it would be so soon."

That surprised me. "Well, that was thoughtful of them. I wouldn't reveal to your Israeli contact that you've seen me, however. The Mossad might not like it if they knew I was here right now."

"Hmph!" Volodya sank heavily into a chair, waving me to sit opposite. "I wouldn't be so sure of that." He smiled. "Regardless, I'm happy and relieved to see you again, but I suspect it must be something more than your desire to see this old wreck of a Russian that brought you here."

"I need your help. There's no one else I can trust."

When I explained what was needed, Volodya regarded me unhappily.

"Are you sure of this? It will change your life forever." His eyes strayed to his dagger icon on the wall.

"It's a little late for that. My life is already changed forever."

"It will take several days to make the arrangements. Excuse me for a moment."

With a grunt, he stood and left the room, returning a moment later holding an envelope that he handed over. "In the meantime, you might want to see this."

Non-plussed, I tore it open. Inside was a three-by-five card with some handwriting: *Do what you must and return to us safely. If you fail, we never heard of you.* The signature was Ronan's.

So Sasha had been unable to conceal from her mentor that she had told me about Maurice and Hélène's deaths, and Ronan had guessed that I would turn to Volodya. The Mossad *bachir* was full of surprises.

Volodya's arrangements consumed an entire week. All the while I lodged with him to avoid registering in a hotel. There would be no trail anyone could follow.

I left the Irish documents with Volodya for safekeeping and boarded a non-stop flight from Charles DeGaulle to Chicago, armed with a French passport that identified me as Thierry Reynard, a matching driver's license, and a sheaf of American Express traveler's checks. In Chicago, after completing passport control and Customs, I used a key that had been couriered to Paris to retrieve a package from a locker in the main terminal at O'Hare. The package contained a Glock-17, a full clip of ammunition, and a silencer. In a few days, if all went well, I would return the items to a locker in the same airport before boarding a flight back to Paris. I would mail the locker key to a local address provided by Volodya.

Using the French alias driver's license and a wad of travelers' checks I rented a car from Hertz and began the long drive eastward across the Midwest – towards Washington.

CHAPTER 63

Full Circle

There had been an early frost that year, and the blazing colors of autumn accompanied me across the flat American heartland and over the mountains into Maryland. The long drive down Interstate 270 left behind, I crossed the Potomac into Virginia via the American Legion Bridge, only a few miles away from the sprawling campus of CIA Headquarters around which my life for so long had revolved. Its long, antiseptic corridors had led to a dead end. Had it all been illusion? The man I had been had ceased to exist as surely as any chimera of the imagination.

I spent the night at a chic boutique hotel within easy walking distance of the charming Old Towne Alexandria shops and restaurants. I had refined the plan over and over during the long drive, but the anticipation of carrying it out permitted only fitful sleep. Morning and afternoon were spent walking the familiar streets.

*****

Through the deepening dusk I navigated the tree-lined residential streets of Annandale, Virginia. Leaving the car several blocks away from my first stop, I took a path through a heavily wooded park familiar from past jogs, arriving finally at a well-maintained backyard that bordered the park where I settled down to wait, hidden in the gloom under the trees.

An outside light flashed on illuminating the yard, and the figure of a woman I recognized as my former neighbor, the same neighbor who had discovered Kate after her aneurysm, appeared briefly as a door was opened. The tiny, black figure of a Scottie coursed into the yard for his evening outing as the door closed behind him.

I waited a few moments before softly calling, "Angus!"

Ears erect, the dog skidded to a halt and cocked his head.

"Here, boy. Come here."

With a yelp of recognition Angus raced toward the trees and propelled himself into his master's arms. The normally reserved dog whimpered softly as he licked my face. Ten minutes later we were in the rental car heading out of the neighborhood. It was an irrationally sentimental act, but I needed to salvage something positive from the past.

The next stop would not be so pleasant.

*****

Jake Liebowitz had been at home for less than a half-hour when the phone rang. His house, modest by suburban Washington standards, still was quite nice and in an upscale neighborhood in Potomac, Maryland. He still drove the same old Volvo he had had for years. He and his wife, Sophie, had raised their daughter in this neighborhood, between tours abroad, and with her husband now such a senior position, Sophie did not expect to be uprooted again. Their daughter, Rebecca, had just begun her sophomore year at Georgetown. As far as Sophie was concerned, their life was idyllic. She had no idea that her husband was a monster.

The phone rang just as she was mixing their pre-dinner cocktails. Jake answered. "Yes?" He did not try to conceal his annoyance.

"Jake, we need to talk."

Liebowitz froze. "Who is this?"

"You know who it is, Jake."

Liebowitz shot a quick glance at his wife. He didn't want to alarm her. A call from the long missing Harry Connolly was the last thing he had expected.

"Where are you?" The ice that had so suddenly formed in his gut seemed to have melted and flowed to his bladder, and he felt an urgent need to pee.

"I'm right here, Jake, in Virginia. You need to come see me right now."

"I don't think I can do that."

He needed more time to think, to get help, to find a way to control the situation. He would call the Russians.

"My people have your house under surveillance. If you aren't in your car and on your way within five minutes, I'll send them in to drag you out. Is that what you want?"

Liebowitz was shaken, but he said, "I don't believe you."

Connolly's voice was diamond hard. "You know what happened in Vienna, don't you? If you want this to be violent, I can oblige. But you don't want your family involved in this, do you? Rebecca is still at Georgetown, isn't she?"

The implied threat smothered Liebowitz as he struggled to control his fear. Loyalty was a relative value for Jake, but family mattered to him.

Sophie, drinks in hand, came out of the kitchen. "What's wrong? Who's calling?"

He made up his mind.

"Something's come up at the office, honey. I'm afraid I have to go back in."

*****

I was more than entitled to lie to Jake, and the bluff was working. Success depended on his believing every word I said. In the end, Jake had to believe there was a chance he would live through the night or the plan I had conceived would not work.

"That's good, Jake. There's no need to alarm Sophie. Remember, my people are watching, and I have your phone line covered, as well. Listen carefully, and don't deviate from my instructions."

The instructions were precise. Liebowitz would not be sure he could believe me and would consider calling for help, but he also knew I had survived the best the Russians could throw at me and left such a trail of mayhem in my wake that it was impossible to believe I had acted alone.

He would reason that I could not have entered the United States without professional help because my name figured prominently on every watchlist. Jake couldn't ignore the possibility that everything I said on the phone was true.

The CIA's new Russia Section Chief would come, albeit reluctantly, to the designated spot at the far edge of the huge shopping center parking lot at Tyson's Corner in Northern Virginia.

He would wonder how much I only suspected and how much I really knew. We had been friends for a long time. I had trusted Jake, and he would know that he was the only person who could exculpate me. What else could possibly have tempted me out of hiding?

I watched as his car entered the parking lot and rolled to a stop. He killed the engine and lights as I had instructed. Jake did not see me as I swiftly approached the passenger side of the car, and he was startled when I rapped on the window. He made a visible effort to remain calm and leant over to unlock the door. The unfamiliar face startled him further.

"Hello, Jake. How've you been?"

In the dim light of the car's interior he finally recognized me through the slight facial modifications. I had been his friend, the man he had so effortlessly manipulated just seven months ago because he knew me so very well, knew precisely which buttons to push.

"Jake, old buddy. I'm sure you thought you'd never lay eyes on me again."

"I'm glad to see you, Harry, really glad. Now we can get all this silliness straightened out, clear your name."

"How long have you worked for the Russians?"

The verbal jab was brutal, and his face crumpled with the realization that I had figured it out.

"What are you talking about? That's crazy!"

"You sent me to Vienna to die. Did you really believe I wouldn't put it together? It could only have been you who set me up. The visit by that death squad to my hotel was a pretty strong clue. You told them where to find me, didn't you? No one else knew where I was."

"How can you say that? I did everything I could to bring you in. Someone must have leaked it when I tried to set up your exfiltration! We've known each other too long for his, Harry."

He sat very still with both hands on the steering wheel, struggling to remain calm. There was sweat on his face now.

"Do you know how many bodies I've left bleeding because of you? Have you counted all the deaths, beginning with Thackery?"

Jake tried to make himself smaller in the cramped space of the car. His protestations of innocence weren't working. This was a war of wills, and he might think he could still best Harry Connolly. He tried another tack.

"I thought you had just gone berserk in Vienna. You can't blame me for wanting to distance myself from you. Now that you're back, I can help you. I can fix everything."

"I don't need any help from you or anyone else at the CIA. I can never come back. You made certain of that. And now you're Chief of Russia Section. Life never looked so good, did it? Well, I'm doing OK too. I only have one problem – you."

I slid into the car beside him and closed the door. I could almost smell his fear.

"I never meant it to go this far." He let his voice crack and managed to fake a sob. "I never wanted to see you hurt. It was the Russians who did all the wet work."

"Don't bullshit a bullshitter. You knew exactly what you were doing. I was the perfect fall-guy: a disgruntled officer who had been shunted to the sidelines. You set things up so everybody would think I was the mole, an accusation that my death in Vienna would make impossible to refute."

His eyes told me I was right. It was time to open act two.

"But maybe there IS something in what you say."

He was ready to grasp any straw, and now I had given him hope.

"Just tell me, Harry. Anything you want."

He would be thinking that if he could get away, the Russians would give him asylum. He might still be valuable to them, even as a defector.

Anger grabbed my throat, turning my voice into a harsh rasp.

"I know what you're thinking, Jake. But consider this: here I am, in spite of all your efforts, in spite of being hunted all over the world and labeled a murderer and a spy. No matter where you go, no matter what you do, you should know that I can get to you."

Jake nodded and refused to meet my eyes. "What do you want?"

"I want you to go on working for the Russians just like you are now. Only you'll really be working for me. You'll enjoy it; you'll be working for the CIA, the Russians, AND for me – a triple agent. What do you think?"

Now he would be thinking he could play along, and on his next trip to Moscow he would ask for asylum. He would be safe. At the end of the day there was no way that I would be able control him. Jake Liebowitz, master manipulator, would wriggle out of this and triumph. They would write books about him.

I watched him closely, calibrating his reactions.

"I've done a terrible thing, I admit it." He hung his head and continued to avert his eyes in mock contrition. It was all I could do not to slap him. "I've got to make it up to you somehow. This will be a big risk, but I'm willing to take it. But I don't see what good the information would be to you. Who are you working for now?"

"First, tell me everything about your collaboration with the Russians - from the beginning." I withdrew a small recorder from my jacket pocket and placed it on the dashboard.

He spilled it all: that first trip to Moscow and his unsolicited proposition to the Russians, how he had revealed the identities of the few remaining assets the CIA was running in Russia, how he had manipulated the entire Russia Section at Langley, and finally the actions he had taken in the Stankov affair. He confessed to informing the Russians of Thackery's meeting with Stankov, an act that ultimately led to that young man's death, as well as how he had set me up.

The longer he talked the more relaxed he became, as though it were cathartic to share his story with someone who could appreciate its beauty and complexity, revealing how brilliantly he had played the role, how he had set everything up and achieved his goals. By the end of his recitation he had regained a measure of composure and some braggadocio crept into his voice.

"That's it, Harry. I think you and I will work very well together, don't you? Just like the old days, sort of."

I pocketed the recorder and opened the car door. It was almost over now.

Jake's relief was palpable but short-lived.

I leaned back through the open door. It was time for act three -- the final act.

"In the end, Jake, it all boils down to trust and loyalty."

He looked up to find the business end of my silenced pistol pointed directly at him. Mesmerized, he could not tear his eyes from the pistol that loomed huge and black and deadly less than three feet from his face. He cringed against the driver's side door, putting as much space between his body and the gun as possible.

I had played this out so many times in my mind that I felt detached, like a theater-goer watching a familiar scene. I heard myself say, "I'm going to shoot you now."

Jake's eyes widened. He raised his arm instinctively as I fired, and it was shattered by the impact of the bullet. Before he could scream, the second shot struck his forehead, and a crimson spray washed over the inside of the windshield as his body slumped against the driver's side door. A look of disbelief lingered on the dead face.

More than hot, expanding gases from the explosion of gunpowder propelled those bullets. Betrayal by a trusted friend gives birth to powerful emotions. It is a loss that can never be recovered. Jake's perfidy had cost me an innocence of spirit that somehow had survived baptism into the world of espionage -- a faith that there still was some goodness in the world.

This was not self-defense. It was murder pure and simple -- an execution. There could be no legal justification for the crime, and by its commission I had placed myself beyond the pale.

I contemplated the corpse of my erstwhile friend. Blood is viscous and emits a hot, coppery odor. It stains everything it touches, including men's souls. As Lady Macbeth discovered, the stain is indelible. Some can accept the burden; others cannot.

Harry Connolly had become a ghost, erased as thoroughly now as the dead man in the car. The man who had taken his place was still a stranger.

As I turned away and walked back to my car a venerable Bolshevik expression came unbidden to mind: "*Smert' shpionam*," Death to spies.

CHAPTER 64

Aftermath

The unsolved murder of senior CIA officer Jacob "Jake" Liebowitz still cropped up in the Washington press from time to time, and at least two books were being written by well-plugged-in members of the press corps. The CIA itself was reeling from the published revelation that Liebowitz had been living a double life as a spy for Russian Intelligence. This information had come to light as the result of a tape recording sent anonymously to the "Washington Post." Technical analysis revealed that the recording had been edited to remove some of the information, leaving only Liebowitz' voice detailing his crimes. While there was considerable speculation regarding the source of the recording, there was no doubt that the voice was his.

The American authorities still sought traces of Harry Connolly. There was strong suspicion that he had somehow been involved in Liebowitz' death, although concrete evidence was lacking. Regardless of the contents of the tape, Connolly was still wanted for questioning concerning the deaths in Vienna, Austria.

Two Congressional and one Senate committee would resume their investigations following the Christmas recess. In Moscow, the American Ambassador delivered a strongly worded protest to the Ministry of Foreign Affairs, and the SVR *Rezident* in Washington was expelled. The Russians steadfastly denied any knowledge of the matter.

*****

In Moscow, Stefan Sergeyevich Stankov and his mother received notification that $500,000 had been deposited anonymously into a numbered Swiss bank account in their name. In Paris, Maurice and Hélène's daughter was informed that the future of her children was secure.

EPILOGUE

December 1992, Republic of Ireland

In the coastal village of Cleggan, several kilometers from Clifden, Connemara, waves broke against the bleak winter shore of Ireland's rocky west coast. The wind was picking up, and the radio warned of a coming gale. Gray clouds scudded low across the sky nearly touching the sea, and rain was already borne horizontally on the wind, pelting against the windows.

I stood at the large porcelain kitchen sink shucking fresh oysters that had been delivered earlier in the afternoon by a fisherman friend from Ballyconneely Bay at the south side of the peninsula. A pair of five pound lobsters moved sluggishly in a crate lined with damp seaweed. Dinner would be a treat this evening.

The half-shells arranged carefully on two plates, I covered them carefully with waxed paper and placed them in the fridge next to a couple of bottles of Puligny Montrachet before moving into the living room.

Several bricks of peat glowed warmly in the native stone fireplace, their sweet scent expanding to fill the room.

As soon as I alit on the leather sofa before the fire, a black Scottie hurtled from his bed on the hearth and flung himself onto my lap to press his silky head against me hoping for a scratch behind the ears.

The crunch of gravel sounded from the drive, and the dog perked his ears and barked. I rushed to the window. A small car pulled through the gate and parked beside the stone house.

I smiled as Sasha stepped out.

THE END OF THE BEGINNING

The Author

Michael Davidson was raised in the Mid-West. Heeding President Kennedy's call for more young Americans to learn Russian he studied the language, and military service took him to the White House where he served as translator for the Moscow-Washington "Hotline." His language abilities attracted the attention of the Central Intelligence Agency, and following his military service Mr. Davidson spent the next 28 years as a Clandestine Services officer. Seventeen of those years were spent abroad in a variety of sensitive posts working against the Soviet Union and the Warsaw Pact.

Made in the USA
Lexington, KY
02 November 2012